Under the Dead Lady's Corset

KILLING TIME Book Two

Under the **Dead Lady's Corset**

A Dr. Jude Avery Thriller

ROBERT W. WALKER

PROSPECTIVE PRESS

Winston-Salem

P ROSPECTIVE P RESS LLC
1959 Peace Haven Rd, #246, Winston-Salem, NC 27106 U.S.A.
www.prospectivepress.com

Published in the United States of America by PROSPECTIVE PRESS LLC

TRADEMARK

UNDER THE DEAD LADY'S CORSET

Text copyright © Robert W. Walker, 2021
All rights reserved.
The author's moral rights have been asserted.

Cover by Stephen Walker
All rights reserved.
The copyright holder's moral rights have been asserted.

ISBN 978-1-943419-65-4

First PROSPECTIVE PRESS trade paperback edition

Printed in the United States of America
First printing, October 2021

The text of this book is typeset in Minion Pro
Accent text is typeset in DCC Ash

PUBLISHER'S NOTE

1

She awoke to the odd sensation of hearing voices. like a radio talk show turned too low to catch only mumblings, nothing coherent. The voices did not rise above that level until, it seemed to her ear that one of the voices had melded with the others to repeat one word over and over—her name: Judith, Judith, Judith…until she bolted from bed, sat up and found the voice gone like some specter had been in the room, but whatever it had been was gone—poof—the voice no longer eerily calling her name.

All in my head, she told herself, shaking it off, shrugging, internally laughing at whatever leftover dream she was having, a dream as with most on wakefulness, without substance, lost in the fog of the inner life, the unconscious world. Not even the slightest remnants given over to the conscious mind. Who was calling her name—gone? What was the message to be relayed—gone? Where might it be now—gone? Why now—gone? How was it, pleasant or unpleasant during the dream, no way to know—gone for good?

The overhead fan answered in the silence of Jude's bedroom with a *wump, wump, wump*. Her alarm had gone off without any memory of a dream of someone calling her name. She'd shut it off, dozed for another fifteen minutes, and had awakened to the sound of her name being repeated in her ear, like some intruder from another time and place, a stranger or a friend, a foe or a helpful warning.

It'd felt like a compensatory thing—a warning to wake now or be late for work perhaps; perhaps as harmless as that.

Of course, she was under a great deal of stress on the job, still being looked upon as the newly hired medical examiner for the county, despite her having been an integral member of the team that had uncovered a horrid horde of murderers a year ago—a ring of snuff-film killers who spanned the continent from Chicago to Miami to LA and back.

Something about the sound of a voice calling her name lingered, made her shiver. She wanted to get that voice out of her head now, and the shower beckoned. A hot spray was soon releasing tension from her neck, and she thought perhaps she needed to get a decent set of pillows and toss out her old ones. The shower head might need replacing as well. She wondered if her landlord would pay for a new one or not, and she decided no way. As this thought passed, after a mere millisecond, again came a voice that said, "Juuu-dithhh." It came so suddenly that it startled her, and she tore back the shower curtain in a foolish, if brave, attempt to confront whomever it was, but there was no one there.

The shower finished, she quickly put on coffee with her Keurig for a single cup and rushed to dress while the coffee brewed. Once ready for the drive to work, Jude Avery turned off and unplugged all electrical devices in the flat. She'd rented this place long enough, and now she was tiring of it and looking for something with more space, but up until now she'd never considered the flat haunted.

She closed and locked her door, thinking she'd lock the 'voice' inside there as well and not give it another thought today, and tell no one! People will think me mad, she told herself.

◆　◆　◆

Dr. Judith 'Jude' Avery, Cook County Medical Examiner, incautiously and in a rather business-as-usual fashion, peeled away the sheet that Ralph Doan, her dutiful assistant, had placed over the victim's desiccated and decayed body. An unusual specimen that'd been found by sewer workers working not far from downtown Chicago's Magnificent Mile—from Tribune Tower at its south end to the old Water Tower at the north end of the mile, ending at the old Drake Hotel. Both the hotel and the water tower were part of Chicago legends and ghost stories. The old water tower was the only building in downtown Chicago to survive the Great Chicago Fire of 1871, a catastrophe that had, in its aftermath, changed the city from a prairie town, begun as Fort Dearborn, into a thriving, world-renowned metropolis.

Jude had only moved to the city for the job she'd landed here, a prestigious one she feared would go to another candidate, but she learned after being hired that Dr. Dean Grant wanted a single person, male or female, and still with the qualifications required to do top-drawer forensic autopsy work. Since she was now a citizen of the sprawling city, residing alone in an area that had a long history behind it, she had taken up studying the history of her new home.

Chicago had been a huge railroad hub before air travel, and cattle drives from as far west as Missouri and Montana had entered the city with enormous herds, It had become known as the Hog Butcher for the World, although it butchered more cows than hogs. All manner of commerce flooded tsunami-like into the city in the aftermath of the great fire, which had only quadrupled Chicago's growth while improving the fire codes. Other than Hog Butcher, some preferred to call the former fort Sin City, given its number of taverns, bars, pubs and brothels.

But after the concerted rebuilding of Chicago, and well after the great fire, came the Chicago World's Fair in 1893. On the verge of a new century, Chicago showcased the advancements of science and industry, medicine and agriculture, and mankind in general. The Chicago World's Fair had become what Daniel H. Burnham, the architect of the World's Fair Pavilions, had envisioned when he'd created the buildings of the great fair, situating the entire affair within sight of the ocean-like Lake Michigan. "Make no small plans," was Burnham's motto, and he and the city had since then lived up to that aphorism. Jude liked that dictum, and she'd adopted it in her work at the Medical Examiner's Office.

She had also adopted many of the habits of her neighbors, taking weekends to mingle with the tourists on Michigan Avenue's Miracle Mile. It certainly drew tourists from across the globe; after all, it was the area where Oprah Winfrey did her shopping, having an apartment right off the Mile, and not far from the Water Tower—both the original and the Water Tower Mall—a Mall that one shopped by going up and up, as the stores went straight up, level after level. Quite the attraction in and of itself, a mall that did not sprawl outward, as there was no acreage and only asphalt and concrete and steel skyscrapers on all sides. Only one way to build now in downtown Chicago—and that was up. Tragic

Jude had taken in The Miracle Mile with great excitement, after getting her most recent paycheck. Now that she was making a decent wage, she enjoyed mingling where tourists shopped in droves and spent big bucks on places like the Hyatt Regency. A great place for a whiskey sour at any hour, as it featured an all-night bar. Most medical people working anywhere near the area showed up at the Regency, and from what Jude had seen, many a romantic interlude, trysts, and adult games were played out there as well. Jude, always a great judge of character through her reading of micro-ticks in a person's face, believed she knew when the lady or the man, or both, were married and in the throes of trying to decide if they should go through with adultery.

These had been Jude's thoughts during a routine, rather slow day until Ralph told her that a 'weirdly discovered' corpse, one found below City Hall that'd been jammed behind a brick wall, "Is on its way to us." This news floored her. It sounded like something out of a gothic novel or an Edgar Allan Poe horror tale.

An unusual but decidedly female corpse, a woman whose body had wasted to near dust and bone for unaccountable years, undetected. She amounted to a skull and loose bag of bones, or so it appeared. That'd been the description that had slowly trickled back to the ME's Office. Unofficial armchair detectives like the crime scene unit, as well as Chicago detectives who'd had a look at the bones encased and held together by an old-world corset, had decided on the spot that the victim must have been at one time a missing person's case.

After Ralph had enumerated the strange details and the conclusion that the detectives had reached—a woman bricked up in the tunnel system might be a missing person, Jude said, "Quite the deduction, Watson." She often called Ralph her Watson.

"Ya think," he'd joked back at the time.

This Jane Doe had obviously died in a horrible state. Possibly asphyxiation but also possibly starvation, dehydration, as a brief look at photos of the scene showed a relatively large room for her cell. A cursory examination of the skull and bones showed no tell-tale marks, abrasions, or knife scrapes, so trauma likely wasn't the cause of death. After all, she'd been bricked up behind a wall in a tunnel that ran near the train stop below the State Building.

Avery felt a tingle of shock run through her, precisely now—at the moment—as she stared anew at the pitiable remains on her autopsy slab. She did so with mixed feelings of excitement, fearful unguardedness at the notoriety and sheer interest this case would most assuredly generate. There climbed up from her gut a healthy dose of disgust, and nausea as well. Excited at the sight of a badly preserved loose bag of bones, seemingly held by a tattered corset as the dress had completely deteriorated. At least one pregnant fly had to've been encased with the dead woman to have spawned maggot debris embedded in what little remained of the dress.

The discolored and worn material would go to the separate forensic division of the FBI experts in Quantico, Virginia for minutia and possibly a recreation of the dress. The corset, too, once removed would go to the same team at the FBI for any possible clues. The skull would go to a lab at Quantico wherein re-creation sculpture of the features would be done. A process that, like the dress and corset, would take weeks if not months, given the heavy case load on Jude's counterparts at the FBI. Part of the skeletal remains would go to yet another lab for testing of the bone marrow and more. Hopefully, out of all the various labs and tests, a picture of the victim would come into focus.

Victimology, it was called. You study the victim and get to know her as a fully-realized individual and sometimes you get lucky just by ferreting around in her circle or web of friends and associates, and given the new technologies with respect to Link DNA, a great deal more could be done today than in this poor woman's world. The end goal of victimology was to identify the victim—even after all these years. After so long, it would be a miracle of sorts, certainly it was a longshot; a bank shot, actually. Just figuring out her timespan, to begin to get an idea of just how long she'd been in that wall.

The maggots might help determine that. Jude had no idea if there'd been any living flies found coming out of the wall where Jane Doe #2080 was found. So far, that was her designation: 2080—meaning the eightieth Jane found since 2020 began. Sad state of affairs on top of all else that'd happened this screwed up year.

Perhaps the bug people on staff at Quantico might discover some useful information from the insect leavings. That kind of science had come a long way. They might get a round number fix on how long she'd been in the wall. At the same time, Jude would go to work on the organs, determine if she was a heavy smoker or drinker. There appeared just enough tissue left to make such determinations. The bone marrow, it would tell its own story. Questions such as was she young, middle-aged, decrepit, and if she was healthy or combating some illness.

◆ ◆ ◆

Ralph had told her that there'd been no insect activity that he could see on the body, adding, "No meat 'pon dem bones, not to speak of either, Doc."

Most organic tissue was attached to and encased in and dangling from below the bones. Still, the concealment had preserved the torn and tattered dress, and the corset below it. It was a flowing dress, almost a bridal gown—almost. As for the undergarment, the corset was an item from a time when women were depicted in the Wards catalog and the Sears and Roebuck bible of commerce as squeezed into hourglass shapes. A terrible constriction nearly as bad as the constriction of the feet of privileged women in China for so many years. In both cases, unwise, but by the same token every woman wanted that hourglass figure. Sign of the times. What the culture bears and gives birth to—fashion. Which was not always comfortable. Certainly not by this biting corset that Jane Doe had gone into eternity with. The thought literally hurt Jude as she mulled it over, But then, she was, this Jane Doe, surely a creature of her day.

Jude imagined her as the belle of the Chicago World's Fair, circa 1893. Unfortunately, the walled coffin had preserved cloth a great deal more than it had flesh. Her features in particular had decayed to the point of no return, eye sockets a pair of black abysses. There'd been a big difference between cloth time and flesh time in the ominous space behind the wall. It'd been reported that she'd been shackled to the back wall. Something haunting and pathetic about her agony, like something out of the gaslight era, out of an early Gothic novel, and this image, as fogbound as it was, seemed imprinted on the skull and gaping mouth.

"Just telling ya what Luther and the others said," Ralph told her. "No flies, no larvae. Nothing alive."

Jude frowned. "Sealed airtight, and eventually, lack of air would've become a problem even for flies."

"Reckon so. Never gave it much thought. Little critters breathing in air."

"Going to be damned hard to determine who she is, and once I cut away the dress and corset, holding her together. Likely, she's gonna… you know…"

"Separation."

"She falls apart."

"Sad, I know," Ralph said. He was a big bear of a medical assistant, from head and jowls to feet and toes, everything overlarge, but he was a gentle man. Despite his bullish appearance, Jude would trust him in a china shop. He was also efficient and dependable. A stickler for being both on time and having his mind on the job at hand.

"So many bodies pass through here," Jude said, "bodies with and without names, but nothing like this."

"Nope. Right about that."

"On this same slab with nothing of relative difference except for the cruel manner of death—well murder, actually."

"Relative difference, Doc?" From the scrunched brow, she could see that Ralph was confused by the phrase relative difference that she'd used. He'd been distracted lately, and she had chalked it up to his studies. He had settled on becoming a nurse practitioner, said he wanted to work with some live patients some future day. He always spoke more about what was to come than what was going on in the here and now, and yet he maintained a steady vigilance on what was called for on the job. "As to murder, yeah, that much appears certain. Who'd question that. But was she dead when put behind the wall?"

"Damn, who bricks up a living woman, even in the Gothic era?"

"Relative, Doc, as most cases," Ralph returned to the word relative, looking as if he'd figured out what Jude was earlier talking about, adding, "As in maybe eighty percent, anyway; turns out to be the husband or a boyfriend, right? Relative…all things being equal back then."

"But who bricks up a live victim?" Jude continued cutting away the clothing from Jane Doe.

"Edgar Allan Poe."

"I mean all we get are the usual suspects in here on a daily basis."

"Usual suspects? Great crime film, kept me and Sheryl guessing."

"Usual in that is—death by natural causes, death by cancer, death by renal shutdown, pancreatic cancer, liver damage of the drunkard, and/or how many we crack open to find Covid-19 lung damage, and/or just the general shutting down of organs, not to mention the tedious number of deaths by suicide."

Ralph shrugged and almost said nothing, screwing up his features instead, when he said, "Yeah, but sometimes the suicide case might have an interesting—ahhh—edge. That is a twist or angle to it—like in the method of dis-dispatch."

"Aha, yes, as in that case of the weather forecaster, Nick Noel, WBEZ."

"Who'd'a thunk it?"

"Offs himself accidentally, auto-erotic play that became deadly—hardly intentional suicide, but difficult to explain to an unknowing wife or family member like mom."

"Then there's the suicide-by-cop end of lifers."

Jude nodded knowingly. "Actually, I do love uncovering a truth, when in fact it wasn't suicide by cop but murder by cop."

Jude did find most suicide victims' stories and histories, their breakdown and breakaway from reality, from family and friends, their utter depth of a depression, a monster loaded on their brains. No one could ever hope to even begin to fathom the nature of this evil imp. Yet the incubus of the mind's dark side, the succubus of the flesh, Jude determined far more interesting than the method of killing oneself. Far more interesting than cataloging the shape and size of self-inflicted wounds documented in an autopsy. She, like Ralph, found the various 'escape' attempts, and the final resolute escape chosen by the victim of tenacious desperation clinically fascinating. The old phrase 'man's inhumanity to man' too often was eclipsed by man's inhumanity to himself, if not to herself.

Jude would never forget the backstory of a veteran named Samuel 'Sammy' Dewalt, who some believed on the verge of recovering from suicidal ideation. Others said Sammy might well've been on his way to committing suicide, that is from all accounts, but the former Vietnam vet never got the chance to take his own life or to recover from his suicidal thoughts. Some monsters impersonating human beings made that decision for Sammy. The veteran came in on a gurney, murdered, and brutally so; after they'd removed his hat, it was found that the poor soul had been beaten to death by a pair of vicious, thrill-seeking murderers.

Murderers that Jude had put out of commission with a great deal of help from her senior medical examiner colleague, Dr. Sybil Shanley. The two of them had worked the Dewalt case with the forbearance of their boss. They also had had the assistance of members of the FBI in various states. The end result of the Dewalt case had brought positive notoriety to Dr. Grant's office. Since then, Jude had been given almost as much respect and latitude as Sybil enjoyed under Grant.

Jude felt a coursing excitement at the prospect of an interesting and peculiar case that might or might not interest editors as a worthy write up in Transformations, the prestigious medical journal of WAME, the Worldwide Association of Medical Examiners. And as far as incautiousness, yes, that too was swimming through her thoughts as she worked in a mental state of unguardedness over Jane Doe #2080. Yes, she also felt a tinge of gullibility as well, as in what if? What if this thing on her slab was a hoax, a bad joke? Something cast in a mannequin maker's shop, or in the back rooms of the Field Museum in an attempt to create a Neanderthal look-alike, the project a bust gone wrong and left out in the elements until a guy like Luther Noble should stumble upon it, toss it into a body bag, and sneak it into her lab? That's how vile the remains looked. A relatively young ME, she'd never seen the likes of such desiccation and decay. Crazy or not, the possibility still flit through Jude's head like a startled bird that some lowlifes in the employ of Cook County Medical, like Luther Noble, could fashion a mummified body like this human-sized piece of beef jerky just to make a mockery of her skills and standing in the ME's Office—and in Grant's eyes, of course.

But the thought of this all being a joke fell away almost as quickly as it'd taken shape in Jude's mind. It fell away with the realization that the tattered remains of the clothes amounted primarily to a corset— obviously not a recent vintage, one from Frederick's of Hollywood or Victoria's Secret. No, this was an antique with a thousand ties, no sign of Velcro or modern manufacture. A real original.

No, surely that cretin, Noble, wouldn't dare. Or would he? The nagging idea of a complex conspiracy to get her clung to her mind. Damn me, she thought.

As best as anyone might, Ralph had prepared the shriveled corpse, a creature blackened by the lack of elements, as in zero oxygen. He'd handled the corpse, quite literally, and he'd warned her of Jane Doe's fragility. "Like old parchment and loose bone, Doctor." He'd not told her that it was unreal, a fake case put together by that prankster, Luther, and if it was anything but real, Ralph surely would've warned her before she had gotten this far. This fact alone set her mind at ease about the ugly prank she was all too ready to believe was underway.

Finally, certain of what lay before her, Jude began her autopsy of the unknown corpse. Her gloved touch assured her anew that, regardless of the parchment-like skin, worn black and thin, despite the appearance of a Halloween costume store dummy, despite the splayed limbs of brittle bone, that this thing before her was real. Once, no doubt, a handsome, well-formed, petite, feminine human being. One who deserved her care and attention as any other, and not simply due to the sheer uniqueness of her surprise visit from the past, her unusually discovered self. The lady in the eaten-away-by-time corset lay before Jude like an artifact of old, a story untold. One that might forever remain untold. In point of fact, Jude feared she'd never be able to tell this one's story, but at the same time, she must try.

In the time it'd taken her to cross the cramped autopsy room, Jude Avery had determined that the Jane Doe before her, the woman's remains were real, and that Jane'd been discovered, or rather uncovered, only after many years—possibly over untold years—of being concealed below the building considered the beating heart of old Chicago: City Hall. A famously haunted building, or so urban tales informed tourists and ghost hunters.

Here was evidence of haunting in one sense. Already, she could imagine word getting around, and Jane here being given an appropriate apparition name like the Ghost of City Hall or the Wailing Banshee of Chicago the Revenant of the Rails, as the underground portion of the El train ride whizzed by, commingling her voice with that awful crying.

Jude could see the headlines at the grocery check-out line now. City Hall haunted for over a Century. Certainly, City Hall and the mayor would be wanting this case buried anew, before it should wind up as top of the crease, front-page news at the Tribune. The Enquirer was one thing, the Tribune quite another.

"You know, you're right," she said to Ralph. "This case is strange, and it does have the ringing bite of something out of an Edgar Allan Poe horror tale. Certainly, a crypt-like story attached to it, the fashioning of secreting away a woman, maybe a wife, behind a wall. But to what purpose? And who was behind it?"

"Behind the wall?"

"Behind the murder. Behind constructing the wall, not to mention the sheer age of this mystery."

"Yeah, poor woman, she was intentionally put away below the city by someone who might've been a stone mason."

"No one noticed it was a fake wall in a hundred years, right—stone mason as killer?"

"Or a mason hired by the killer." Ralph had come closer and stood now at the opposite side of the slab, facing Jude.

"Bastard placed her in a coffin, shackled to a wall," Jude said. "Dry place to be sure, apparently there was no evidence any water ever seeped in, but yet damp enough, due to water pipes overhead, to actually help in the preservation this long. But how long?"

Ralph shrugged. "Tough egg to crack, Doc."

Even as she guessed at how long this woman had gone missing, Jude hadn't a solid clue. Other than perhaps doing some concerted research on when the tunnel was built below City Hall, what had she to work with? Jude had to wait and hope for the forensic answers to come. Until tests on what few tissues from the shrunken organs she'd harvested might say.

Long years out of sight to be sure, but to be precise? Jude feared that she'd never know what exact day or hour the dead lady had expired, why she was bricked away, or who was behind this horror. However, she might determine if the poor soul had been walled up alive or after she'd expired. Jude was hopeful it was the latter case. A close examination of the lungs, more precisely what was in the lungs might tell the tale. Another of Poe's short stories popped into her mind—the Tell-Tale Heart. Regardless of who'd done this brutality, he'd be dead and long gone himself, and he would likely have escaped any punishment for this crime. But if he were capable of this, perhaps the killer had been discovered for other crimes and locked away or even executed, as execution was more of a possibility a hundred years before.

Luther Noble and his team had indeed brought the body in with a great deal of clamor and talk of how shocked workmen were to discover a corpse below City Hall. Lisa, who worked closely with Luther, was turning into his gopher. When asked, she'd said, "All I know's the workmen said they were there at the underground tunnel to replace corroding pipes that fed into City Hall when they'd discovered the remains inside a wall!"

Jude had sat Lisa down to lay out every detail of what she saw at the scene. Lisa was known to embellish, so Jude had pleaded with her for just the facts. The young employee was adamant that the body was not shackled to the wall but lying in a heap at the bottom of the enclosure. "Had any of the workmen touched the body after discovering it? Had they released it from the shackles?"

"No, they insisted. She was not shackled." Luther had made the same point before he'd left.

Perhaps that much had been exaggerated or embellished—shackled to a wall? But there were shackles in the wall. "Full on, back wall." That's what she was told, but could she trust the story the deniers—the transport staff—who'd brought this pile of rubble in, could she trust them to be telling the truth? Frankly, she still imagined the lot of them down the hall in the breakroom having a grand laugh at her expense. If not for being gullible, then simply assuring that she and not Sybil Shanley, or another ME, got this case, targeting this head-scratcher to Dr. Avery.

Fear of being gullible and taken for a ride as the still new kid on the block, wanted to take hold. It wasn't as if that bunch hadn't targeted her before. She was not like the others, not a born and bred Chicagoan, not a Cubs or White Sox fan, not a Bears or Bulls fan, and she didn't frequent their tailgate parties.

To make matters worse, it'd gotten around the building, thanks to a so-called friend, that despite all her ability as a medical examiner and a surgeon of the dead, that she could not watch horror movies or read scary stories like those of Poe, King, Matheson, Bloch, or god forbid Blatty's The Exorcist. She much preferred the forensic case files of the FBI, preferably those of Dr. Jessica Coran, whose Instinct Series had run to sixteen books now.

She shook it off, these trivial matters, as she must concentrate on the here and now, but then again came the sheer enormity of disgust at the sight before her—this godawful permutation of the flesh, and in combating the disgust, to overcome it, to do her job, she must also tussle with a bout of old-fashioned nausea, as she'd been feeling rather stomach sick all morning due to an undercooked, poached egg that the cafeteria lady had promised to deliver perfectly—Not!

Regardless of her growling stomach and misgivings about starting in on the mysterious case, part of her wanting to shove the 'discovery' away in a storage bed in the wall behind her and come at it another day, she pushed through it. Earlier, she'd asked Luther Noble and then Lisa, privately, if there'd been any valuables or items found on or around the body at the point of discovery, and Noble had shrugged and grunted, "Nah, nothing. Just some chains in the wall that might make for a bundle at auction or on eBay." Lisa had corroborated this statement. That they'd found no necklace, bracelet, broach, watch, or even a ring. It didn't jive with a woman of Jane's day to have no jewelry on her person. Jude didn't want to believe that Lisa and Luther divvied up the goods, but it had been known to happen with unscrupulous first responders. Still, she had no proof whatsoever of bad conduct.

Jude recalled having asked Luther a second time about how the body was found. "She was chained inside a wall?"

"Looks that way." He smiled then grimaced at these words.

"You found her chained to the wall like in a dungeon?"

"Doc, she was prone as her wrists turned to bone and she slid right down outta the chains and down the wall, you see? You got the picture?"

"Thanks, Luther, but how much of that is bullshit and how much is true?"

"You're the one with all the degrees, Doc. Cipher it out. But those workmen didn't go near her. Superstitious bunch to begin with, and it was an unholy find."

Noble left with a twittering laugh, ushering his partners with him, two other men and the lone woman, Lisa. Jude had made formal complaints against Luther Noble, and another called Smitty, but they were union members, and it was a powerful union. So, it appeared she was stuck with them, unless she provoked one of them to strike her or, as Noble would like to do, jump her and dominate her. Nothing was about to happen unless one of the good old boys did something outrageous like attempt to harm or rape another person.

Their Human Resources Department proved useless. Her boss, Dr. Dean Grant, head of the ME Department had talked to Noble, lectured him, and for a time, things had gotten better, but a guy like Noble needed a lesson, not a lecture, to make things stick, Jude believed. Her only true friend in the building was Dr. Sybil Shanley, and she had given Jude several tips in dealing with Luther. And with Grant for that matter.

"Luther hates being embarrassed," Shanley had told Jude, "and he doesn't do well being referred to as a child or a baby. It infuriates him. He has a complex about his intelligence, fearful he has none in comparison to anyone who wears a stethoscope and knows how to write."

Jude had put this information to use on more than one occasion, drawing attention to Noble's showing off and his hand size, intimating that his privates were nothing to write home about, and that any pulse down there would not register on her stethoscope. Such remarks would send Luther packing out of a room—including the cafeteria or the break room. Useful too in getting him out of her lab when she wished it to be so.

"So where do I start with you, dearie?" she asked the corpse with no features, her skull without eyes, sunken caverns staring back. Jude flicked on her recorder to take down all her words as she worked. At the same instant, Sybil Shanley, all suited up like Jude, stepped into Autopsy East 2, saying, "I heard you got an interesting case this morning—that I was bypassed." Dr. Shanley said a warm hello to Ralph, who returned the greeting, and relieved, gave Shanley his spot at the slab, muttering something about a phone call he must make, and left the ladies to their work.

"Word travels fast around these parts!" Jude said, happy for the intrusion and good company.

"Thought I'd have a look-see, curious." Shanley was as tall as Jude and ten years her senior, and she had made a great role model for the younger ME, and Jude now valued her friendship above all others.

◆　◆　◆

It'd been a proving ground case for the newly hired Dr. Jude Avery. It had also made her attractive for hire by other big city departments, and she was not so sure it wouldn't be wise of her to take that offer from Atlanta or LA, either one was a boost in income and could have other benefits—like no Luther Noble. But then, she realized that there were

Luthers everywhere, so for now she'd decided Chicago was home base. After all, the food was terrific and Second City was great fun, and there were so many theaters and great plays to see.

Jude again pushed back on trivialities flooding her mind like purposeful flags waving her off this case, but again she marveled at the condition of the body, saying, "I have to tell you, Sybil, when Jane here was first wheeled in, I thought it was a trick."

"Really, a joke you mean?"

"She looks like something an archeologist dug from a glacier—Cro-Magnon woman or maybe an unwrapped mummy."

"Trust me, I've had the same thoughts, now seeing her, but it appears she was sealed off behind some sort of wall in the old subway tunnel that runs beneath City Hall, exactly where now?"

Jude shrugged. I dunno—somewhere down there, they're saying below City Hall and the State Building?"

"You mean you haven't gone to have a look at where she was found?"

"No, no one called. The Noble team just dumped her here—a few straggly tatters of sash and clothing, that period piece corset, and nothing more. No one called me to the scene. Not sure if—"

"If they called anyone on such a scene, it'd be Dean." Sybil knowingly said, interrupting Jude. "I suspect Dean's been to the scene—likely got the call direct from Luther, who's been trained to contact him on any highly unusual and sure-to-be high profile cases."

"Which this certainly is, and—"

"Jude, you've been warned regarding red ball cases going to Dr. Grant."

Jude joked, "Yes, I've heard that rumor, but—"

"Dr. Dean Grant loves a photo op more than…more than the mayor and his insufferable PR bitch."

"And Dean and Mayor Rollins have no love lost between them, I get it."

"So, of course, this corpse dug up right below Rollins's office—City Hall—of course, Dean's gonna be all over this case."

"Well, it is his department. But begs the question of why Noble brought it to me, specifically, rather than—"

"Maybe, and likely, Noble was following Dean's orders? Telling the mayor and the city aldermen that he's put his best people on it."

"That bad, huh?" Jude said and laughed. "Hide the whole of it in my care?"

"Dean's always being squeezed by the politicos."

"Aren't we supposed to be an independent arm of city government? Apolitical?"

"Ha! No such animal, no matter how people want to believe in unicorns and mermaids. Except for Disney, ain't gonna happen. Especially not in Chicago!" Sybil said and laughed at her own remarks, then shook her head and frowned. "Can't have it all."

Jude began singing the Rolling Stones tune, "You cannnn't always getttt what-chu wannnnt".

Sybil, her hands gloved. high-fived her. "Still wanna go down there?"

"Where?"

"To the subway, to City Hall catacombs, for a look-see?"

"Whataya mean? I never said I'd… Okay, sure I'm curious, sure, but who's got the time?"

"We'll charge down, have a look, grab lunch, and be back before anyone notices."

"All right, but my beater is in need of gas."

"Forget that! We'll do this by the book, sign out one of the department vehicles. Go official-like as Dean assigned the case to you, and you politely asked me in on it, of course, for my experience and know how."

Sybil got on her phone to arrange for a car, and then she called to warn her first assistant, Lionel Snow that she'd not be around for a couple of hours. Taking this cue, Jude did the same, texting a similar message to Ralph Doan after getting a busy signal on her call. She noted that she'd be back by two PM, and until then to place Jane Doe #2080 in a wall compartment, wincing at texting the last two words, thinking how cruel that the woman was finally free of her wall-coffin only to be put on hold in another cold wall-coffin here in the lab.

As she dressed down, removing mask, gloves, and gown alongside Sybil, who got out ahead of her, Jude, stripping away the final glove heard a voice that seemed to be inside her head and yet over her shoulder as well say, "Juu-dithhh." She listened for it a second time when her phone blipped with the message from Ralph that said he'd take care of everything in the lab. When she finished reading the message, the voice that had somehow followed her from her flat to her job was gone; nowhere to be heard.

"Let's get down to City Hall, shall we?" Sybil jammed her head back in the changing room and then stepped in and took Jude by the arm. Together, they found the elevator for the underground parking garage. There an attendant with a key pointed them in the direction of the car, and Sybil clicked the button that made the car in question burp and beep. Jude tried to keep up with Sybil's buoyant step. A part of her mind wondered if the voice calling her name, definitely feminine, had anything to do with the dead lady in the corset.

2.

When the two ME ladies arrived at City Hall, they might have been taken for a pair of tourists, but one of the security guards checking them in for anything more dangerous than a penknife, recognized Sybil Shanley. "Here for that creepy business below the building, Dr. Shanley?"

"Yuri, how are you, and how'd you know?"

"I figure fast. Either you come for that mystery, or here to rub shoulder with Mr. Mayor."

This elicited a laugh from Sybil, "Elbow not shoulder, Yuri." Jude at the same time gave Yuri, a dark-haired Russian-American with a Cubs ball cap setting off his security uniform, a quick brushstroke with her eyes, even as Sybil introduced Jude as Dr. Avery.

"Ahhh, they got you help. Good thing, yes?" Yuri nodded, smiling.

"How do we get down to the old tunnel, Yuri?"

"Where they found the body, yes?"

"No, where the dragons live—where else?"

By now, Jude was smiling at the friendly banter going between Yuri and Sybil. Jude stared about the enormous hallway, filled with passing people, most looking quite businesslike and lawyerly with their three-piece suits and briefcases. The hallway itself was awash with mahogany wood, Italian slate tile and golden walls, and gleaming chandelier-styled lights. The entire effect said this was the seat of government, and Jude was but a speck of sand in the flow of humanity. The corridor here had entryways and exits at both ends, each spilling out on a separate street and the hubbub of the downtown Loop area.

The building would certainly make a Mississippi lawyer like John Grisham and writer William Faulkner feel at home, Jude imagined. The vaulted ceiling gave the pedestrian causeway a cathedral-like appearance and feel. She could only guess at what the interior offices and the Mayor's Office must look like.

"Pete, I'm going to escort the doctors," said Yuri to his partner, who'd been on his cell phone the entire time. A hefty, balding fellow with jaundiced skin, Pete grunted his okay and went back to his screen time, but he was stopped when Shanley said to him, "Hey, Pete, I wasn't kidding last time I saw you, and you still look like a candidate for the morgue. Get to a doctor after your shift today—go to the ER if you don't have a family doc."

"I'mmmm fine," Pete said with a wave of the hand.

"You are walking death. Tell him, Jude." Jude gave the man a closer look. "She's right. You have two options, die or get help. You're turning yellow from liver damage, and you may also be juggling a few blood clots as well."

The gravity of his situation, given that he'd gotten an immediate second opinion, had Pete going a grim gray now in his complexion. Yuri said, "Hey, Pete, I think I'd listen to the doctors."

"Ahhh, all right, after my shift, I'll walk over to Northwestern."

"Take a cab or Uber," Shanley advised.

Yuri led them to a service elevator. "Gas odor was causing a problem last month, and that was fixed, and this month it's the toilets. All at once, overflowing, backing up, causing another kind of stink."

"Other than the stench of politicians?" asked Sybil.

"How could you tell the difference?" added Jude, as they boarded the elevator.

After Yuri laughed at this, Sybil said, "Good one, Jude. Glad to see you loosening up."

They rode the elevator down to the sub-basement, where the doors opened on a wide vista of an underground cavern lined with sleek, slate walls that put a modern patina on a place dug out by men of another era. "I gotta get back. Pete, he ain't so bright like me, and you guys're right about his health."

"Talk to him, Yuri. It might save his life," Sybil said.

Yuri never got off the elevator. His last words as the doors closed were simple. "Creepy down here, knowing that some lady was in the walls."

Sybil half-smiled at Yuri's summation. "Yuri's good at hiding his superstitious side."

"Hell, he's right. Knowing someone over maybe as long as these tunnels were built; walled up down here. It's creepy as hell." Jude felt it too. Some places, old mansions, weathered farmhouses, abandoned churches or simply ruins, brick walls left after a bombing, or even the vast panorama of a battlefield held spectral vibes. Vibrations from the ghosts of all deceased people, from the skin-walkers to the banshees, the scryers, the revenants, all rising from their graves if not off the last remains of the dead. Vibes not everyone was clued into, but Jude, even more so as a child, caught the stir of echoes while visiting Civil War battlefields.

Maybe the corset lady has been reaching out, calling my name, she thought again.

Visiting battlefields with her father, a man who loved touring through mass graveyards and places like Gettysburg and Shiloh, one who stopped to read the plaques and the gravestones, one who explained it as "An opening of the heart to walk grassy fields where thousands of soldiers had lost their lives in a matter of a few hours." Jude, as early as four, could sense the loss and hear the roar of the battle, the whisper of ancient cannons going off, and the cries of bloodied men. While it all played out inside her head in a place where others only heard the ring of silence and witnessed only the silent markers and displays of cannon and ammo dumps amid a beautiful park of greenery and trees—there, for Jude, came the shadow soldiers, even ghosts horses, a thunderous number of them, all pulling arsenals and wagons.

Now in this strange place that Jude did not know existed when she climbed out of bed this morning, here far below the bustling city above, here, where the Blue Line elevated trains dove below the city, sending up a deafening roar on a schedule of one after another, as passengers entered and exited, arriving to what was now called The Loop, and leaving from here for their homes, yes, Jude imagined the cacophony like some foreign orchestra tuning up their strings and brass. She distinctly heard a particular train screaming on rails with its sudden stop now, and the racing on by a non-stop, and on the other side of the platform whizzed by a soaring ghost train that left a strong wind in its wake.

Then a real noise, a loud noise came to Jude's ear. A noise so frequently heard in Chicago that most people tuned it out—a jackhammer. Sybil yanked Jude as if from a trance to follow her lead, as they moved through the shimmering, surprisingly well-lit tube-like tunnel toward the sound of cursing workmen whose four-letter words were softened by the jackhammer. Sybil hurried now ahead of Jude. The circular track and tunnel had the men out of sight, but their voices were undeniably close.

With the jackhammer paused and silent, suddenly Jude heard a male voice saying, "What would you know about the workings of a woman's mind, Jack?"

"A sight more than you!" This one guffawed but stopped short, frozen on seeing Sybil and then Jude materialize, as if from nowhere, their approach having been hidden. "Well now, speak of ladies!"

Three workmen stared at the two ladies, eyes wide, tongues slipping about, when Sybil held up her City Health Badge that reflected the light.

"More cops, eh?" asked the starrer.

"City Health Department," Sybil lied, and Jude wondered why but imagined that the term health department would carry more weight these days, or with these men, than if she told the truth. Besides, it was not awfully far from the truth.

"How can we help you ladies?" This one's shirt pocket read Frank in cursive red thread.

"We're here to take air and insect leavings and other ahhh…samples in and around the body discovered here earlier today," Sybil again lied but only partially. "Make sure there's no health questions to ask and answer. Just a precaution."

"It's by order of the mayor," Jude suddenly lied now, deciding to up the ante.

"Well, I'm foreman on this job, so I'll take you where we had our ahhh…fright." The man who'd been guffawing moments before had taken on a serious tone.

Another of the three workers put in with, "Frank, okay if we take a break then?"

Frank glanced at his watch. "Sure, back in fifteen."

"Let's go topside for some air," said the third workman.

Sybil and Jude followed the foreman, Frank. Talkative, Frank, sounding a bit nervous in returning to the discovery point, was saying, "You guys oughta coordinate better. First the cops show up, then the ME, then the paramedics with the stretcher, and now the Health Department. Thought we was done here. Got no hankering to mull over what we uncovered, not in my head, and that's for damned sure."

"Yeah, hard to deal with, I'm sure." Sybil was close behind the man.

Jude followed in single file along the narrow passageway that swept around the bend. "Not an easy sight to ponder."

"Hold on—you ladies have seen the body?"

"Stopped in at the ME's for a quick glance, yes." Sybil stared him in the eyes, as Frank had stopped, turned, and had asked the question.

"Then you were sent here by Dr. Grant, eh?"

"Yes, that's right."

"To be thorough, I see. Grant struck me as a thorough man."

"Aye, that he is."

"And so are we, ahh thorough women," Jude said. "Can we get on with it, then?"

"Yeah, yeah, sure, of course. It's right here."

They'd arrived at the shattered wall, the opening a mere four by five feet, festooned with a crisscross of yellow crime scene tape. "Grant insisted we leave it untouched for a time."

Sybil and Jude, side-by-side, studied what the back wall, so recently uncovered displayed, two wrists chains meant to hold a person's arms up overhead. The rusted over metal might well have DNA from blood as the victim, if walled up alive, might well have fought against her chains. "I guess Luther wasn't lying about the one detail." Jude shrugged as she could hardly believe hearing her confirmation of Luther Noble's description. "But he said she was on the ground—the floor, as if gravity had finally freed her body from the wall."

Frank was nodding. "Yeah, sure, the thing—she, you say? She was on the floor inside and not in the shackles."

"He have a photographer with him, Dr. Grant?"

"Blitz, I think he called the old fellow, yes."

Sybil exchanged a knowing look with Jude. "The old German, Fritz…Dean calls him Blitz."

"Does good work."

"The best. So, what're we looking at here, Jude?" Sybil put a hand on a loose brick, pride it away and tossed it aside. "You fellas didn't take the wall down to the bottom." Her full attention had gone back to Frank, whose meaty features were blank and inscrutable.

"Well-hell, we saw the body, and that thing, like you said, damn fright it was, so we stopped with the drill and the pickax. It was young

Eddie doing the hard labor, and he was first to see the shackles and to lay eyes on the bones."

"Eddie, one of your guys on break?"

"No, hell no. Eddie's my sister's kid, and I got him the work, and he just got so bummed out, said he ain't coming back. First day on the fucking job, too."

"Poor kid," muttered Sybil.

Jude imagined the boy's fright, when Frank laughed and said, "The poor kid is twenty-damn-four and still on his mommy's couch! He's a grown man, and he oughtn't to've walked off the job no matter! My boss is going to chew me out over this."

"Can we get the rest of the wall taken down, Frank, so we can get in there without having to crawl in and get cut on jagged brick?" Sybil asked him in a tone that might melt butter, sounding like a woman propositioning a man in a bar.

"You know, I'd be happy to oblige, but—"

"Great!" She cut him short.

"—except I promised Dr. Grant that'd we'd leave everything untouched, you see. I mean, I'd like to help you lovelies, but I've read stories and seen Dean Grant on the tube, and I do not want to tangle with that man."

"You don't understand. We're here in Dr. Grant's stead."

"Stead? You mean like instead or—"

"He sent us," Jude put in.

"We're to take care of this matter for him as best we can, you see?" Sybil finished.

"Well now, I see…in that case, sure. We'll bring that little patch-a-wall down in no time. You can step into like a walk-in bathtub, harrr!"

"How long will that take?" Jude asked, glancing at her watch, sure that she was never going to make it back to the lab as promised, and sure that Dr. Dean Grant was definitely going to learn that two of his chief staff members were AWOL.

"I'll just call my guys back, and we'll get started on it, but cellphone's no good down here, so may take a while, cause I gotta round 'em up."

"I can handle a pick and I presume you can operate the jackhammer."

"Been awhile. As foreman, I leave the heavy lifting to the others. Hell, I give the orders!"

Sybil gave him a sexually charged grin. "I'll bet that pint-sized jackhammer's like a thunderbolt in your hands, Frank."

Frank's grim look became a warm smile and a shake of the head. "All right, I'll do it. I wanna see you swing that pickax."

Jude caught Frank's wink for Sybil.

3

Jude had pretty much known to back off while the jackhammer sent up a huge plume of dust from the old-fashioned brick and mortar that the drill, a relatively small handheld jackhammer, tore away at. The noise was deafening, and it traveled down the cavernous tunnel like a racing away screeching banshee. Frank loosened up what remained of the wall, and Sybil tore into it like a pioneer woman in a mineshaft,. With each blow, bricks came away in a red cascade of clinking stone. Huge pellets of mortar flew about, and Jude had thought Frank chivalrous when he'd handed Sybil and Jude goggles left by the other workmen. In fact, the foreman was just being practical and safe.

It was less than five minutes when Jude and Sybil, standing under a fog of mortar dust, their clothes dusted in it, were on hands and knees clearing away all the bricks and mortar that had fallen inward and had covered the floor. Now, like a pair of archeologists, using their state-issued ballpoint pens and gloved fingers, they searched for anything that might be worthwhile—anything that they might take back to the lab for analysis, any missing clues that even the imminent and intelligent Dean Grant had possibly overlooked.

"Looked to me like some of the dust was disturbed." Jude shouted over the latest train passing at Frank, asking, "Did anyone climb in here and come out with anything other than the body? Like a watch or a bracelet or anything?"

"Not that I could see, no. Of course, we were told to push off, so we did…"

"Something's rotten in Denmark." Jude kept moving broken brick and mortar chunks, searching the area where Jane Doe's remains had lain.

"What're you getting at, Jude?" Sybil continued her own search about the rubble, bumping against Jude here inside the cramped interior of the death wall, where the odor of decay persisted still.

"Just doesn't make sense the CSI team—Luther's guys—found nothing of her jewelry; not so much as a ring?"

"Whoever walled her up may've stripped away any jewelry."

"You know how much a working watch that old or a diamond ring could bring at a Chicago pawn shop?"

"You do have a suspicious mind, kiddo. I rather doubt that Luther's gang would risk their jobs over a few baubles."

"Once word gets out about this lady in the wall thing, headlines and all, anything purportedly connected with the case, well it could sell at a hefty price."

"Do ye have no confidence in your fellow man, child?" Sybil joked. She then took on a serious tone. "You do know if we do find anything worthwhile at this point, it will reflect badly on Luther Noble and his buds, and if we were to turn up something actually crucial to learning this Jane Doe's identity, and anything else about her—you do know that Dean's going to be pissed at us for upstaging him, even if no one else ever knows the truth."

"Recalls the old adage."

"What's that?"

"When the truth is too dull to tell, fall back on the legend."

"I recall it as if the truth is unfit to print, print the myth. Or maybe it was legend."

"Yeah, that's it, like in the movie, The Man Who Shot Liberty Valance."

"Tom, John Wayne's character did it, but Jimmy Stewart's became the legend, right."

There were more bricks to move and toss aside, and chunks of mortar, and the mortar dust had made a blanket of itself over everything within the small space that they now occupied. "Anything?"

"Naw, nothing."

"Waste of time, it appears."

"You'd think the killer would've thrown in something, anything to, you know, identify her." Jude's voice reeked of frustration.

"It's not like the guy was planting a time capsule. I mean we shouldn't expect any help from the killer, even if he did preserve the crime scene for us. How often does a killer do that for law enforcement, ha!"

"Guess he was thinking maybe Lake Michigan? You know, for all the jewelry and identifying stuff, like her purse."

"That damn lake hides a lot of secrets, for sure-for sure? Gangs and vermin, they use the terrain they crawl in."

"Understood. In Miami, it's the ocean and the tides."

"Or the swamp."

"In Vegas, it's the desert."

"And here it's the big lake, normally, but suppose this guy—this one vermin—he uses these tunnels?"

"Convenient, I suppose at the time of their being built, maybe?"

"Damn straight. Do it right, and the big lake will never give it up—a gun, a knife, a purse, a wedding ring."

"An unwanted boyfriend, or someone else you're done with!" Sybil said and laughed.

"An abusive step-father."

"Mother-in-law."

"A comedy act that pisses you off."

Jude began to laugh too, when her fingers hit something hard and metallic. She instantly cleared away dust and debris and stabbed away with her pen. The sound reported to both their ears that she'd stricken something. Jude began swiping away at the mortar blanket at this spot to reveal a tintype circa mid-1800s, maybe pre-Civil War? It came up out of the layers of dust and plaster wretchedly filthy, but Jude snatched her blouse from her pants. Using the shirt tail, she wiped at the old smeared photo on the tin plate.

After a moment's cleaning, the ancient photo depicted a beautiful young woman in a large bonnet beside a handsome young man, his dashing features marred by a too-large mustache, a bowler hat in hand, a wolf's head cane in the other. The two were stiffly posed as if by the hand of the photographer, but their smiles and faces appeared the pinnacle of happiness. They might be a newly wedded couple, if one were to guess.

"I've read about this type of picture processing,," Jude said. "It dates back to turn of the century, if not further still, as this kind of processing fell out of use around 1860—before the Civil War."

"Pre-Civil War, is it really?" Sybil seemed unable to look away from the photo.

"God, she's been sleeping here since before the end of slavery. No that can't be true. The picture can't be of her and her man."

Sybil was not hearing Jude, as her imagination was running wild. "Someone wanted her silent. That's for sure. You think she had anything to do with the war? A spy for sure! I've read that women were very adept at the profession even then, before they had the vote!"

"I don't want to burst you romantic bubble, Sybil but the brickwork and tunnel only date back to the forties, so no to all your spy stuff. I've been reading up on the history of the tunnels and underground Chicago."

"Killjoy!" Sybil continued studying the sturdy faces of the couple in the tintype.

"Really do hope we find poison in her system."

Jude understood why Sybil would hold onto such a hope. "Yeah, can you imagine being walled up down here, and you're fully conscious the whole time?"

"Maybe she wasn't… conscious, I mean. I mean…I hope."

"Gotcha, understood."

"Horrible way to go and to be buried alive is what it amounts to. That is, if she wasn't killed first and then put behind the wall to conceal the murder."

"Problem is then why the shackles?"

"Yeah…sonofabtich."

"Whoever did this, yeah, a real son of a bitch."

They continued clearing the floor of the little dungeon meant for one. There was nothing more to find. They had to be happy with what little they had found for now.

"You need any more wall taken down?" asked Frank from behind, revving the jackhammer for emphasis.

"No, no! Think we're done here."

"Ahhh, there is one more thing, Frank," Jude said, pointing to the shackles. "You think you could pry those out for us?"

"Really? You want those things?"

"Could have some useful DNA on them," explained Sybil.

"You two, you're not Health Department, are ya?"

"Wondered how long he'd take to figure that one out," Sybil said to Jude.

"Hey, Frank, we work alongside Dr. Grant—both medical examiners ourselves, and you, sir, are an unsung hero, and should we demystify this case, we won't forget you."

"Is there a reward?"

"'Fraid not, as the reward is knowing you did a good thing."

Frank frowned at this, grumbled, and started the drill biting into the stone around the right-side shackle. Again, the noise was deafening, driving the ladies to grab the protective ear muffs left by the now errant other workers. Jude was just wondering about them, when they suddenly appeared from around the bend.

Once Frank, now with a little help from his men, finally extracted the shackles with Jude pleading for him to only handle them by the chain portion pulled from the wall. Dr. Shanley then whipped out a small device that she flipped open like a Star Trek Shatner communicator. She then asked Frank for his fingerprints and as he agreed, she took them electronically. She then followed suit with the other workers, saying, "In case we locate any unusual prints, we can rule you guys out."

"Later, we'll need to get this Eddie fella's statement as well," added Jude.

"Separate the chaff from the wheat, eh?" asked Frank.

The adage caught Jude and Sybil a bit off guard, as it was unexpected, coming from Frank, who, seeing their reaction, added, "I watch a lotta Forensic Files on TV."

The other workmen returned to the area they'd been working on before the interruption, but Frank stayed close by Sybil as she and Jude were finishing up, bagging what evidence they had and tucking it into a valise that Jude had carried from the lab. She had bagged the tintype and the shackles in brown paper bags before placing everything in the coroner's valise, but the chains were too large to entirely fit into the valise, the end of one hanging over and needing to be wrapped about the leather valise in a snake-like fashion.

As she completed the wrap, Jude realized that Sybil was in the process of exchanging information with Frank. "Should you come across anything else down here that strikes you as peculiar, call me."

"Peculiar, down here everything's peculiar." Frank smiled wide for Sybil, showing off a row of healthy teeth in a Burt Lancaster grimace of a smile.

"Unusual or peculiar, yes."

"Ahhh, sure, like a chance encounter with a pretty lady down here,"

Frank said, continuing to flirt. Then he threw down the gauntlet. "Hey, I'm in the book, Agostini, Frank Agostini."

Jude took note of both the man's wedding band and the lust in his eyes. He was definitely taken with Sybil. "Well now, we'd best get back, Dr. Shanley. Dean'll be waiting at the lab by now."

"Thanks, Frank," Sybil said, giving the foreman a firm and well-placed elbow-to-elbow 'shake' in lieu of the handshake.

Frank said, "In earlier days, I'd've kissed your hand, me-lady."

This felt like the verbal equivalent of holding a woman's handshake a smidge too long. When Shanley pulled her gaze free, Jude could not see Sybil's facial expression from her vantage point, but she had watched this entire time as Sybil used flirtation as a bargaining chip. But Jude had once seen Sybil use it as a weapon, so Jude could imagine those big eyelashes flashing.

Frank didn't want her to leave, and Jude was a third wheel. "I'll be at the elevator, Dr. Shanley." Jude calculated that if Frank heard the word doctor enough to describe Sybil, that he'd snap out of it and realize there was no future that would ever put the two of them together, not even for a one-night stand, as Sybil didn't do one-nighters.

All the same, like a medieval knight in work boots, Frank escorted his damsel in distress, his damsel in awkward surroundings, to the elevator, where Jude smiled wide, the doors opened, and the two medical ladies boarded. Then, suddenly, Frank leapt on as well. Still unable to 'let go', he said, "My turn for a break from this hell down here; get some fresh air, maybe a smoke."

With the elevator rising, Jude muttered," You know, Frank, fresh air and cigarette smoke abrogate one'nother."

"Abro-what?"

"Nullify, she means," put in Sybil.

Frank still looked confused. "Didn't get through seventh grade. Words ain't my thing."

"They cancel each other out, smoke kills fresh air."

"Gotcha, got it now, Dr. Aviary," Frank slaughtered her name.

In that brief ride to the surface, Jude had managed to embarrass the older man, and she'd done so without trying, and worse yet, she'd managed it in front of Sybil. When the doors opened on the City Hall corridor, Frank rushed ahead of them, his face hidden, his shoulders forward in bad posture, a sad-looking figure. "You hurt his feelings, Jude. Why'd you do that?"

"Smoking is bad for you is all I said."

"Abrogate?"

"All right, it's a highfaluting word. So, shoot me."

"I didn't need you saving me from Frank. He's a good guy."

"One you used, so don't get all highfalutin' either."

"Hell, I flattered him and got what we needed from the man. You, on the other hand, judge him, and you dashed his small fantasy."

"Is that what you are? Some guy's small fantasy?"

Sybil laughed at this. "Come on. We best get back. No time for lunch."

"This bag's heavy as hell." Jude decided that Sybil wished to change the subject.

"The bag's contents, you mean."

"Yeah, that too."

Yuri waved as the two came down the corridor from the service elevator, readying to exit City Hall at the exit where they'd entered. Their car was parked in a lot around the corner. Yuri added words to his wave, "Hey, Sybil, when're we going out? You and me?"

"Next week—call me!"

Jude ushered her through the revolving door. "Yuri, too?"

"Men are men."

"I suspect that our Jane Doe was buried alive by one."

"Can you be so sure it wasn't a woman? No greater evil than a woman scorned."

"Too early to tell, I'd say at this point, but odds have it as a man."

"Odds have it as a white man."

"Given the times, yeah."

"Given the statistics on the male gender, and the color of the victim."

"If she's the same woman in the picture."

4

When the ladies of the Chicago Medical Examiner's Office had returned to their Cook County digs, they had to sign in the 'evidentiary' items found at the unusual crime scene below City Hall. They had no idea if said evidence would or wouldn't reveal any useful clues or direction for the most interesting investigation of the year so far: Jane 'City Hall' Doe. They had the shackles placed into a box and the tintype placed in a protective container, which was placed atop the chains. They then immediately signed the evidence out for forensic investigation, so now Jude was responsible for its whereabouts.

"Protect it with your life," Sybil only half-jested.

Beepers for both lady doctors went off simultaneously. "It's Dr. Grant."

"Me too."

"On the warpath, no doubt."

"How're your nerves?" Jude asked.

"Readying them; suggest you do the same."

"I've no nerve when it comes to Dean, have you?"

"I say we confront him together with the chains and the tintype at hand."

"You know best. Let's do it."

When Jude thought of the famous Dr. Dean Grant, she thought of the array of unusual and classic cases he had cracked to be elevated to Chicago's top medical examiner. One in particular, he'd solved was a case involving two brothers who serially murdered together and scalped their victims, and oddly, one of these bad boys was a little person, a dwarf. Another case involved a killer magician—a kind of reality show wannabe killer.

After replying to Grant that they were on their way to his office, Jude and Sybil freshened up a bit, touching up makeup and pinching cheeks. And soon enough, they were standing before Dean's desk, Jude dropping the box of clanking shackles onto the boss' divan. From the box, she lifted the tintype photo and passed it to Sybil, who passed it to Grant.

Grant's eyes went wide with the photo. "Are you saying this is her—the victim?"

"We might assume so, given where it was found."

"Which is where exactly?"

"We saw Blitz's photos of where the bones were at on the floor of that walled-in coffin, and my guess from the shots, it was on her person at some time. She was lying over it, so kinda under her corset at her back."

"How it got there's anyone's guess."

"If under her…" Grant held up an index finger, indicating he was thinking and needed silence for the moment. "Could have fallen atop it, I assume, after it was dropped into the wall?"

"By the killer?" asked Sybil.

"You think he placed the photo in with her?" asked Jude.

"Possibly. We may never know."

"Inside the wall and on the floor between the rubble and her body," added Sybil.

Jude put in, "It was covered in mortar dust. Yet from the photo Mr. Fritz, ahh Blitz took, she was lying over the tintype."

Grant again raised a single finger for silence. "One, photo drops, two, mortar dust covers it in the rubble, then three, her corseted body atop that? Does not make a whole lot of sense, doctors."

"Luther's people somehow missed it."

"Missed the damn chains as well; left them back!" Grant shouted anger from the gut.

"Damn…I was so upset with Luther, I sent them back for the chains, but by time he got around to it, I hear that you two had gone down there and you took the chains."

"In the box," said Jude, pointing to the heavy box she'd carried in with her, while Sybil had carried the tintype. "We had all of the evidence signed in, sir, officially."

"What's the idea of you two going down there, Sybil?"

"My idea, not Jude's."

"After seeing the condition of the corpse, sir," Jude said, shrugging, "Sybil and I thought it best that we see the scene firsthand, and given the fact that nothing was recovered from the scene in the way of identifying items—no jewelry for instance…well, I for one, just wanted to get a-a feel for what the victim had endured."

"Commendable of you, Dr. Avery, and you, Sybil? What's your excuse for butting in like you did?"

"Same like Jude, I thought it odd not a thing was found on her person, except for her corset." Sybil's tone dripped with an odd sarcasm.

"You did, eh? I recall a dress."

"Not much left of the dress, doctor. Falls apart at the touch." Jude took a deep breath and slipped into the chair beside Sybil and across from Dean.

"We may never solve this one, you two, and as far as City Hall is concerned, it is ready-made for the back burner."

"Why is—"

"What the hell?" Sybil leapt from her seat, meandered about the large office, placed a hand across her mouth to keep from saying what she was thinking.

Jude, confusion crinkling her features, said, "This could be a groundbreaking case, sir. I was thinking link DNA might turn up descendants, and-and who knows what that could lead to?"

"That's like drawing for an inside straight, Jude, and you know it."

"No, it's like failing to win the lottery because you didn't buy a ticket," Sybil corrected Dean.

"Are you two conspiring to explode my ulcer? What possible good will uncovering the identity of this woman and her killer do anyone today in this city or state? We get paid on the taxpayer's dime. Can you imagine what a guy like Dick Hackensack at the Tribune could do with a story like this?"

"Dick Hacklesby, financial page manager, sure, but that's really not our worry, boss," countered Sybil. "You know very well it is our job to bring any justice and truth we can to this victim as much as anyone wheeled into our labs."

"It's not like it was in the pre-pandemic days, Sybil, and you know that as well as I…man, it's not going to sit well with anyone that we spend time, energy, and money chasing ghosts from the past like this City Hall Jane Doe."

"Dr. Grant, Dean, you're turning into one of them."

"What them?"

"A bureaucrat!"

Jude gasped, expecting Sybil to be canned on the spot. But Grant took her verbal blow calmly. He stood and walked around the desk and leaned on the desk as close to Sybil as he could and near whispered, "Besides all else, Sybil, the governor and our mayor's going to want this to disappear. After all, we've got both the continuing struggle with the pandemic and now a rash of suicides and shootings? So…"

"I'll work on my own time," Jude calmly said.

Grant glared at her, his keen eyes like darts. "You're on twenty-four hour call as it is, Jude," he said, looking frustrated. He stepped to the windows overlooking downtown Chicago, the bustling streets below. "From that old timey picture, I admit, got goosebumps knowing where it surfaced from. I imagine it was stuffed between her bosom and the corset. Handsome couple in the tintype," he muttered, still facing outward. "How long do you estimate she was in that wall?"

"The tunnels—first of them—were built in the early 1900s," Jude replied, "but the Red Line underground portion not till maybe the mid-forties. As for the tintype, it would've come from sometime prior to the Civil War She appears a young woman in the photo, maybe just out of her teens if not younger. I'd say anywhere from 1855 to 1871, possibly around the time of the Chicago fire or rather a few years after. Sir, I don't think—"

"Why then?" he asked.

"The aftermath of the fire is when Chicago got a helluva boost in building and reclaiming and growing. Hell, by 1893, the city was host to the World's Fair! By then, a mere twenty years since the fire that threatened to end the city, you can bet the early coal and supply trains were running through the first tunnels built."

"How do you know all this…this history?"

"She reads. And she's gone nuts for Chicago's history."

"I've exhausted the Chicago Historical Society. Like to know all I can about a place where I live."

"Hell, you know more about this place than most folks born here." Grant smiled at Jude, putting her at ease.

Jude wished to get back to the question at hand and get the focus off herself. "Like I said, the tunnels would've been under construction in those years, and I have to guess the killer had access to the work area, knew it well enough to plan how he meant to wall her up without any witnesses or interference."

"Unless it was a spur of the moment crime of passion incident or accident," countered Grant, "and it was just a matter of how to hide her body, hide the crime."

"Still, he had to have had access to the location and feel damned safe," said Jude.

"Sounds like he may've read Poe's stories," Sybil said.

"And time…" added Jude. "The tunnels must at the time been safe. Maybe during a worker strike, a holiday weekend, who knows, but whatever, the killer, knowing he had time to complete so complicated a scheme of murder would have felt it his safe place—ha! As safe as The Cask of Amontillado."

Sybil built onto this line of questioning and brainstorming. "Well, yes, there is that, but he'd've had to have access to brick and mortar, and do the job when no one was around, so he'd have to also know where the tools were kept."

"Wonder if he was a grunt worker or a foreman, or even a well-connected architect or builder," Jude said. "Wonder how far up it goes, and what relationship she had to this lady and gent here." She tapped the picture of the young couple."

"No matter how you slice it, even if you two could answer all the questions, who does it benefit when we are inundated with corpses out there? Some littering the hallways!"

"All right already, you want us to drop it, and maybe we will, Dean, and maybe we won't."

"What's that supposed to mean?"

"Let us pursue any leads for a week, and we revisit the question after it's time's up."

Jude could not help seeing that Sybil held great sway over the boss man. Rumors had it that they'd ended an affair some years back. True or not, they appeared to have a fondness and mutual respect for one another. Shanley, like Grant, had had her own share of successes in the field as well as in the clinical lab.

Grant paced the room a bit before returning to his desk chair and dropping his weight into it. A Marlon Brando smile with creased lips—like moving parts of an animated character danced across his features. "All right, but I reserve the right to pull the plug on it at any given moment if it is reasonable to do so."

"Reasonable, fine word meaning what? What do you mean by reasonable?'

"Rational. I allow your rations of enjoyment working on a case to nowhere, up to the point where it becomes irrational to do so. Clear enough?"

"Clear, aye-aye, my captain," Sybil teasingly said.

"And you, Jude? After seven days, no results, close it down, understood?"

Jude hesitated, thinking, what the hell can be accomplished in seven damn days?

Going to the windows that Grant had vacated, Jude studied the tall buildings that filled the view, taking a moment to study the movement of people in windows opposite them; people doing common, ordinary day-to-day jobs, and this gave her pause, even as Sybil was urging her to take the deal. Seven days, one week, hardly enough time to uncover the story behind the lady in the Sears and Roebuck corset inside the tunnel wall. She knew Sybil's take, 'do the week' and come back for another and another as she worked Dean again and again. But rather than answer Sybil, Jude instead fell into thinking about Chicago's famous skyline and historic buildings of the city, and the famous Chicago architecture, and her first thought-image morphed from the soaring skyscrapers into the architecture of underground Chicago, which she'd read about in the Chicago Tribune, in what had proven to be a fascinating if hefty account that'd called the underground here essential in the workaday world of downtown Chicago.

The story of the long history of the building of underground paths and tracks for trains eventually gave way to the more modern, all the way up to the Elon Musk financial debacle called Block 37 CTA—Chicago Transit Authority—Superstation. Rendered in architectural drawings, it appeared a space age underground train station. The idea was to take commuters from the high rise business offices of the Chicago Loop to O'Hare Airport in under twenty minutes and avoid the always tangled Chicago traffic. But not long after the excavation had begun, Chicagoans had another word for it: boondoggle, a godawful waste of money totaling in today's market some 431 million bucks.

The City of Chicago was accused of literally burying piles of taxpayers cash after it plowed the money into the superstation in the heart of downtown. Incredibly, the city pressed ahead and constructed the station, despite having no guarantee that the service the enormous station was intended for, a futuristic airport link proposed by billionaire Elon Musk's The Boring Company, was feasible.

Work began on the superstation back in 2005, but it soon became apparent that the express service would never come to pass, and the city halted building work in 2011. The superstation remained unfinished still. In total the disastrous megaproject had indeed cost taxpayers $400 million in 2015 dollars, the equivalent of $431 million in 2021.

Virtually unknown layers of tunnels, passages, sewers, pipes, and other infrastructure crisscrossed below the city. On any given day, thousands if not millions of pedestrians passed over what few gave a grain of consideration to—a network of forgotten, largely silent and sealed, hollowed out tunnels below their feet. Only one of these underground tunnels was well-worn and heavily trafficked by pedestrians, and it was called the Pedway.

Folks who worked in the Loop area and most long-time Chicagoans knew that the fastest way to get back from lunch, so as to be on time, was to use the tunnel below the Daley Center. The most user-friendly layer of Chicago's underground, the Pedway System, which, on her rare day off, Jude had explored by joining a group called the Loop Interior Architecture Tour.

The term Pedway, she learned, proved a conjunction word, one formed from pedestrian and way. Functionally speaking, the Pedway acted as a collection of basement-like hallways which connected buildings, train stations, and underground parking structures in the Loop— so called since the El or elevated train made a loop around this area of downtown Chicago. Small parts of the Pedway consisted of "skybridges" or links to the upper floors of adjacent buildings and passages that remained at street level by cutting through lobbies. Jude still had her copy of the handy Pedway Map to take off and explore this essential layer of underground Chicago on her own anytime, as it proved a great walking exercise as well.

Even though the Pedway was used by many a Chicagoan, the most well-known portion of underground Chicago had to be its underground streets, such as Lower Wacker or Lower Michigan. Hollywood films like The Dark Knight and The Blues Brothers had immortalized these dark and atmospheric, if dirtier, concrete spaces below Michigan avenue, for example.

Jude had become somewhat fascinated with these lower level streets, but when she asked Sybil and other locals, especially the lifers, she learned that few Chicagoans had any interest in these streets, and many acted as if they didn't even know of their existence, and yet below level at the Tribune Tower, just across the street at this level, stood the original Billy Goat's Tavern. Ironically, a place that everyone seemed to either know of, or had heard of.

Sybil had one day tired of hearing about Jude's explorations about the city, and she'd suddenly taken her in hand and entered a building, called The Realtors Building, a mere ten floors high, that stood across from the Tribune Tower. Once inside, they'd taken the elevator to the bottom floor, where the door actually opened on a rather cramped little restaurant at sub-level, and it was the infamous Billy Goat's Tavern that Jude had read about in one of her collected brochures.

A hangout for journalist mostly, Jude saw nothing spectacular at all, and she soon found that the food proved the same, nothing spectacular. Not even goat burgers on the menu—only goat cheese. On one wall hung a stuffed goat's head, one with enormous horns.

Over a quick lunch, Sybil had said, "Our multi-layered city has lower level streets, yes, in some parts of the Loop, and River North, because these streets, well, they allow easy access for freight transport and trash disposal."

"Ahhh, that's clever!"

"You know how crowded it gets down here on a weekday!"

"Oh, yes, makes sense."

"Having the down here, well, it in turn, makes the street-level above a tad less crowded. Some sections, like East Randolph near Maggie Daley Park, are even triple-decked."

"I hadn't heard of that. Triple, you say?"

Sybil continued on, adding, "A great thing about the multiple layers is how it keeps the trash away from where most people work, live, and commute. Which is fine with me, 'cause that then keeps the rats away from pedestrian level—and me!"

"Surely, being a medical examiner, you can't be afraid of rats."

"You've not seen a Chicago River rat, have you, my girl?"

Their waiter, a thick-armed, Italian in a greasy apron, overhearing this said through clenched teeth, "We got no rats in here!"

"We're talking about the boat wharfs, Tony." Sybil pointed with a knife, obviously familiar with the waiter. "Rats the size of cats."

Tony grimaced, dropped their orders on the table—house salads—and rushed back to the safety of his counter. At the same time, Jude had gulped at the image of a rat as large as a grown cat, and she fell silent, striking her salad with her fork,

After a few bites of the so-so salad, she said, "I thought you had no interest in my newly found hobby of scouting out Underground Chicago."

"I don't, not really. I prefer the Art Institute on my days off. Relaxing. Then the Field Museum to visit with Bushman."

"Bushman?"

"Stuffed 450-pound silverback gorilla. Died at Lincoln Park Zoo when I was a kid. Always held a soft spot in my heart and still does."

"But being a lifer here, you know stuff like that, and I don't. Forgive me for wanting to get to know my new home."

"We Chicagoans like our iconic animals—the Bulls, Bears, Cubs, Goats, Gorillas."

Jude laughed at this. Sybil then said with a shrug, "But we have enough to contend with aboveground in this gun-crazy place."

Jude's turn to shrug then. "I got a thing for reading gravestones in old cemeteries."

"Anything as long as it's below decks, eh?"

"But you see, when I lived for a time in Atlanta, I kinda fell in love with underground Atlanta. Now there's a lively underground—jazz clubs!"

Sybil mulled this over for a moment, stabbing at her salad. "You have only scratched the surface here, my dear, when it comes to cemeteries and interesting permanent residents. This city is chockful of huge cemeteries. Not so much underground jazz, though."

"Ohh, I intend to visit some more famous Chicago cemeteries!"

"You've already begun on your first love? Ha!"

"Meaning?"

"Cemeteries!"

"Oh, yeah, that I have."

"But you're missing some real fun."

"Meaning?"

"Meaning, you've walked the Pedway, but did you go below the Pedway?"

"Below it?"

"Below the Pedway and below the underground streets, you will find the sewers."

"Not interested."

"Well now we agree. While no human should actually-really want to explore the sewer tunnels, it is where our population of 2.3 million rats live."

"Back to rats. Sybil, you have an odd fascination, and it's damn gross to imagine that many rodents below us, especially when I am trying to eat here!"

Tony, overhearing the single word rat again coming from their table, glared from the counter. He next spoke in his boss' ear while pointing at their table. Jude was amazed at the man's hearing as a juke box was playing the Roy Orbison's Pretty Woman, and it was at the long guitar riff.

"Some speculate their numbers," continued Sybil about the rats, "are down from three mill."

"Down! Three million is down?"

"Hey, it's a reasonable number for a city our size."

"Really?"

"Trust me, you don't want to know how many are in New York." Sybil laughed and forked her salad bite to her mouth.

"Frankly, I read somewhere that most cities have as many rats as the human population, if not more."

"I can well guess where you got that fact from." Sybil somehow spoke around chewing.

"I guess there was a reason why we med students had all that rat study in our training."

"An ME's gotta know a rat-torn body from a torture victim."

"Creighton's Manual for the Functional Lab."

"Me too—had to read that damn thing and take tests on every damn chapter."

"The Grey's Anatomy of forensic medicine."

Sybil's hand on Jude's shoulder brought her back to the here and now, staring out Dean Grant's office window; she was no longer in Billy Goat's Tavern on lower Wacker Drive, but in the office suite, a room that was populated with books sharing shelves with skulls and bones, and the bric-a-brac of a lifetime of collected items of value only to Grant—like a real New Guinea shrunken head he'd picked up on a vacation the year before.

"All right, you've got two weeks then!" Grant was saying, leaving Jude to wonder how Sybil had talked the boss into an extra seven days. "Now get on with it and take those shackles with you!"

Jude lifted the evidence box filled with the chains, and Sybil retrieved the tintype from Grant, who barked a final order, saying, "And hey, both of you are to keep it low key, and keep me posted every step of the way."

The ladies were quickly out the door and in the outer office, saying goodbye to Marge, Grant's secretary, who whispered, "He's in a mood today. You ladies had him pacing."

"Well now, we've calmed him considerably now, Marge," Sybil assured the elderly secretary. On the elevator that would deposit them on their floor, Jude asked, "How'd you talk him into another week? Two weeks."

"I didn't."

"His idea?"

"No, I mean sorta, yes, but it was your long pause, staring out the window. You played the bluff perfectly. He folded."

"You mean by saying nothing, I convinced him. I'll have to try that more often with people."

Sybil laughed and the doors opened. "Where do we start with City Hall Jane?"

"The shackles—see if we can get some useable DNA, enough to send for a genealogical link and get that underway."

"Good move. Then we continue with the autopsy you began this morning."

"Thanks, Sybil."

"For what?"

"Talking me into all this!"

"What? You're the one who talked me into all this!"

"Hold on!"

Other people up and down the hallway, seeing the two MEs cama-
raderie looked a good bit jealous of their relationship.

5

After hours, the weary Jude Avery thought of home and a hot shower, a good meal and to read a little and curl up with her pillows and get a decent, full night's sleep, but something in her had her sensing an approaching doom, a sensation like a premonition, a thing shrinks called 'awfulizing'—fear of one's future, but in her case it felt like fear of going home and being alone again with the sound of that strange female voice calling her name as if warning her of this pressing, suffocating moment in days ahead, almost as if—she hated to think it but was unable to avoid the image of herself being bricked up and left to suffocate and die behind a wall. While the bus came to a stop, she felt as if she were in a coffin, and she rushed to get off at the last minute, angering the bus driver.

She'd gone down to her car at work only to learn it would not turn over. The battery most likely, but it was late, and calling for help, she imagined would take hours for a replacement on the used Mazda.

Now she was afoot in the neighborhood, alone on a darkening street a few blocks from her flat. Ahead of her, she saw a group of young men, high school or above age, raucous and shoving one another, and she simply felt a fear rising. She assumed the boys would roust her and tease her. Alone as she was. Detouring on Kedzie off Addison, she must pass by the neighborhood branch of the Chicago Public Library. Once at the library entrance, seeing a light still burning inside, she entered on a whim.

Once inside, Jude began investigating the history of the tunnels below the city. A reference librarian worth her weight in gold, Meriam Oglala, a mildly dark-skinned original American of the Oglala Sioux, guided Jude to a very helpful segment of the nonfiction shelves, a treasure trove of information on the building of the infrastructure in Chicago over the years, and specifically, the underground.

Jude was fast learning why this city was called The Melting Pot within The Melting Pot, after Meriam left her with a book laid open on the table before her, open to a fascinating photo of men employed in the building of the Blue Line, the one that ran so close to City Hall. Jude began studying the old photo, a type of picture that was the precursor to modern photography which came into being during the Civil War. She also read the caption below the picture to realize Meriam was wrong. This was not the Blue Line, City Hall station.

The caption read: Abandoned freight tunnels pepper underground Chicago. Constructed in the early 20th-century." Photo in the Public Domain.

Jude studied the image more carefully than before. She realized immediately that she had been wrong about when the tunnel under City Hall was built, as that Red Line was installed in 1947, but the coal-bearing underground tracks dated to the early 1900s. Why then the tintype rather than a photograph? Photography had become the norm from Civil War days, mid-1860s to present. Perhaps the tintype then was an heirloom that the lady in the corset had held close—perhaps it was a picture of her parents rather than herself and a suitor.

In the photo in the book that Jude examined, there were several men of the period depicted along with a long coal train. She half-imagined the more well-dressed man, whose clothes marked him as wealthy by the then standards. He looked to be in charge, a real Simon Lagree appearance with that waxed mustache and fashionable watch fob. Ha, she thought, maybe he's my long dead killer, enamored of walls and bricking up people he disliked. But of course that was beyond a stretch.

As she read the article accompanying the photo, she learned that these tunnels transported more than coal, water, and other supplies throughout the city, as they provided underground space for telephone wires. Not long into the nineteenth century, newer and cheaper infrastructure passed these tunnels by, and between 1947 the 1950s people began to forget they existed.

"Which was good fortune for the rats, I imagine," Jude said to herself.

Meriam, the Native librarian, had returned just in time to hear Jude's muttered remark, and she answered with, "It took people being found imprisoned in walls to remind everyone that they are still here."

Jude didn't miss a beat, replying, "The rats or the tunnels, you mean?"

"Both. Some construction crew accidentally broke a hole in one of the tunnels back in the early '90s. That hole happened to be below the Chicago River, near the Kinzie Street Bridge. You see?"

"Not sure I see, no."

"Water—Chicago River water came spewing into the tunnel! Caused massive flooding in basements throughout downtown. The water ultimately caused more than a billion dollars of damage. Afterwards, the city installed watertight bulkheads to seal off the underground freight and cable car tunnels." Meriam then pulled up an artist rendering of the Water Works and Water Tower on Michigan Avenue, which today acted as a marker for Water Tower Mall.

Meriam, getting rather close in on Jude, then read aloud the caption below the panoramic drawing. "The iconic Water Tower drew fresh water to the city via a hidden ten-thousand-foot tunnel."

"All very interesting," Jude replied, studying the beautiful etching.

"Says here that the pumping station at the historic Water Tower drew water from Lake Michigan via a five-foot tall brick-lined tunnel that ran underground and out to a water intake crib."

"Crib?"

"That's what they call these intake valves built out on the lake. Not sure of this tunnel's exact location or current use—if at all."

Meriam smells of fresh cut flowers and mint, Jude thought, as the other woman leaned in over her. "So mysterious!"

"What's that?" Meriam said these two words in the most sensuous voice that Jude had ever heard.

"All these underground tracks and tunnels, just kinda creepy knowing about them and thinking about the once teeming life of workmen and travelers through this underground world."

"Oh, please, we haven't even gotten to the deep underground."

"Deep underground? You mean there's more and deeper tunnels yet?"

"Afraid so, yeah."

"And they're called—"

"The Deep Tunnel System."

Jude took a deep breath. "Wowsa, I guess."

"They're the least-known or understood feature of the Chicago underground. Actually, officially known as the TARP system."

"TARP?"

"Tunnel and Reservoir Plan, locally called the Deep Tunnel. It's a system of large diameter tunnels and vast reservoirs designed to reduce flooding, improve water quality in our fair city, and protect Lake Michigan from pollution caused by sewer overflows."

"Large diameter, like big enough for a grizzly bear to wade through?"

"In the city that lives by the mantra of 'make no little plans', the city has undergone one of the largest and longest civil engineering projects in American history. It has cost billions and taken decades to construct the Deep Tunnel."

"Sounds expensive."

"Worth it, I think. Now that it's functioning. You see, it keeps stormwater runoff from contaminating the lake and prevents catastrophic flood conditions."

"Really? Makes sense. You certainly know a lot about it."

"Well, to be honest, a couple of friends in my activist group—Red Lives Matter—studied the system at great length with a crazy scheme to lay a bomb down there."

"Oh my god! Tell me you weren't seriously considering that."

"We were all a lot younger then. Young and foolish." Meriam took in a deep breath of Jude from the back of her neck and her hair. "The tunnels are often underneath existing waterways, like the Chicago River. They work to funnel excess water to reservoirs and run-off canals on the edges of the city. We coulda made one hell of a splash back then."

"I guess you never quite know what's afoot or underfoot in Chicago."

"Or what you can find at the library, for that matter."

"An untamed Indian princess."

"Feral, like a wild animal."

Jude felt her insides churning at the turn of the conversation. "I was on my way home when I decided to stop to do a little research."

"I've seen you in here before. Most people nowadays use Google and to hell with us."

"Google can only take a girl so far," Jude replied, and looking around the room, finding them alone, she turned in her seat and met Meriam's kiss, shocked, even startled, but that only added to the excited danger of the moment, and so Jude returned this stranger's kiss, thinking, From her perspective, I am the stranger. Perspective's everything.

"How late are you here?" Jude asked.

"Closing time, eight since Covid, was ten before."

"BC and AC, eh?"

"Before Covid and After Covid, yes."

"Any battle with it?"

"Got it, beat it."

"Me too."

"Think it has a lot to do with our blood type and DNA."

"I'm O, how about you?" Jude asked.

"We're Sympatico—O."

"That and T-cells, immune system is all good."

"You some kinda doctor?" Meriam asked, throwing back her long, flowing black mane.

Jude didn't want to frighten her off, and she didn't want to be alone tonight. "Something like that, yeah." A doctor for the dead, she thought but did not say.

"Nurse practitioner, I'm guessing. That's my goal…to become a nurse practitioner. Working toward it."

"But you're a reference librarian, and we need good librarians—people like me, anyway."

"Got bored after the health crisis started, and I wanna help. Books, records, iTunes and audiobooks and directing people digitally on this stuff, where to go, what to sort through doesn't feel like really helping, contributing, not really."

"Nonsense, people need books to escape into nowadays more than ever. You do a great service, all of you librarians."

"Well that's kind of you to say. I get a kind vibe from you. Did from first day I noticed you rummaging around in the stacks."

Jude looked at her watch. "Ten till eight. You wanna get coffee after your shift?"

"I'd love to, sure. So said the Indian Librarian."

Jude smiled at this until Meriam said, "You have the greatest smile," before leaning in again for a second kiss. Then Meriam moved off to begin the routine of shutting down the library. She got on the PA and announced that it was closing time as she played a Leonard Cohen rendition of his famous song, Closing Time.

Jude felt an instant positive vibe coming off Meriam, and she felt a great attraction. Talk about a fantastic smile and figure. Jude had had boyfriends, and she had had girlfriends. She was bisexual in nature, and even as a kid growing up, she'd never labored through any angst over it. In her estimation, sex was sex and love was love, and should ever the twain meet, male or female, boy or girl, she'd feed the child within, and so, she felt prepared her entire life for a loving sexual relationship, but so far failure. For a long time now, she'd had neither sex nor love. She had been losing out on finding a binding, strong, healthy partnership despite a number of attempts. Nowadays, Jude found herself living alone with her cat, Squeakums.

The nearby coffee house, like the branch library here in their Humboldt Park area was closed early as well, due to the lack of customers. There was outside seating, but the lights were dimmed and then completely shut off as the Closed sign went up. "My place is half a block up, and I've got plenty of coffee and maybe even a roll and cookies. Living off junk food lately."

Meriam accepted with a nod, and she took Jude's arm in hers, suddenly aware of the gun in Jude's coat, a shoulder holster. "Don't tell me you're a cop or something," Meriam said, as they walked to their destination.

"No, medicolegal business."

"Oh, I think I get it. Can't be too careful in the health department."

"No, you can't."

"Kinda makes me feel safe, being with you."

"I want you to feel safe…being with me."

Once in the door of the duplex apartment she was renting, Jude hit the lights, and showed off her recent purchases and decorations. "Haven't been at this address long, but I had a couple days off, so I got some things done around here."

She then let Meriam kick off her shoes and get comfortable on the newly installed couch while she brewed coffee in the kitchen. From the living room, Meriam called out several times complimenting her on this and that. Soon, Meriam had wandered to the kitchen, where Jude had set out a cookie jar and cups and saucers, creamer and sugar. With the coffee ready, they sat beside one another at the cramped-in table in the kitchen area.

"You must be a first-year resident, I guess," said Meriam.

"Oh no, not! I am a full-fledged doctor."

"You forgive me, but on a doctor's salary, you could buy this building, but you're renting the apartment."

"Noticed the bill on the coffee table, eh? I am somewhat new to Chicago—moved up from Atlanta—gosh been two years now. Didn't have a decent chance to really look for a place, so I got kind of dug into this area, but only moved to this flat a few months ago."

"You seem happy with it."

"For now I'm relatively comfortable here."

"I see, well, it is a warm and cozy place. I would've killed for a place like this when me and my sisters and brothers were growing up on the res."

What if she's after my money? Jude's flitting thought threatened to ruin both the moment and the evening. But she pushed the thought back down. "I'm just learning where everything is in the city," she confessed.

"Well, you found a friend, and I've been here for years. Did all my studies at Northwestern, in Evanston, visited in the city as often as I could. Never went back to the res. Got a scholarship designated for Native Americans. They almost flunked me out, but I learned I'm a fighter."

Talking with Meriam Oglala was easy, and soon they were on their second cup of coffee and scarfing down a store-bought cake along with the cookies. Jude caught sight of the clock and realized how time had flown by. "I'm trying to become a good Chicagoan. I signed up with this group, company actually, called Chicago Detours that offers guided walking and bus tours of architecture, history and culture to public and private groups. They're damned serious about preserving Chicago history."

"Passionate, are they?"

"You know how passionate you say you are about wanting to become a nurse practitioner?"

"Yeah, I get it."

"These guys are over the moon about history. They see it in every cornerstone and old building, down to the door frames."

"So, I imagine these guys calling themselves Chicago Tours are history buffs."

"And history educators, artists, writers, and storytellers, and this particular group, well they are fiercely proud to be one of the very few tour companies in Chicago that has earned a five star rating on both Yelp and TripAdvisor."

Jude realized it was well into the wee hours of the night, and Meriam was blinking, looking sleepy, her big dark and mysterious eyes closing even as she was speaking. "Will you stay the night. Meriam?"

"I thought you'd never ask."

"Do you need to call anyone?"

"No, live alone."

"Except for Mr. Squeakums here, so do I." Jude petted the mewing cat, took Meriam in hand and led her to the bedroom, and using exaggerated hand gestures, treated her to the sight of her bed. "I could sleep on the couch, if you prefer," Jude added.

"No, no! I want you with me. We can cuddle if that's all right with you, Jude."

"I thought you'd never ask."

With a single nightlight at bedside, the couple began to undress one another in the semi-darkened room. Ignoring the cat at their feet, going in and out of their legs to rub himself, the two women embraced and shared a lingering, passionate kiss. Each explored the other with her tongue. Jude wondered if this was too good to be true, as it felt so right.

She took a moment to lock the cat in the bathroom, and when she returned, she found Meriam on her bed, nude, arms wide, fingers curled, inviting her in. As Jude crawled catlike into Meriam's arms, she thought, I have a right to this; I have a right to peace and pleasure in another's arms.

She also thought that she wouldn't be hearing any banshee calling her name, as long as she had Meriam with her. It just couldn't, it just wouldn't happen. Nor would she again feel that heavy sense of impending disaster.

6

"Are you awake?" It was Sybil Shanley's voice on the other end, but Jude was so not half awake that she couldn't recall answering the phone.

"What do you think?" Jude managed to put four words together. She'd shaken off her grogginess, wondering when the phone had rung, and how long had she'd been holding it in hand, saying nothing till now.

"Who's calling at such an ungodly hour?" Meriam said, rolling over.

Being awakened by her phone at odd hours was not an unusual occurrence in Jude's line of work—but typically it was Grant's secretary looking for her to accept an additional case, that she was needed at a crime scene. But this time the call was from Sybil Shanley.

"Errr you sitting down?" asked Sybil.

"I'm lying down. What is it, Sybil?" Jude put a hand on Meriam's backside, patting her to assure her that she could and should go back to sleep.

"Hard to believe but Frank and his pals uncovered another body in the tunnel, not far from Our Lady of the Corset."

Jude knew she wanted to immediately distance herself from Meriam. She got up, naked, threw on a robe, and went into the hallway and for the bathroom. "Another extended portico rounding a corner, another fake wall? Another victim, killed in the same manner?"

Meriam, however, had heard some of Sybil's words, and was quite aware that Jude was moving off so that she could not hear her reply. What she did hear had her sitting upright, turning her eyes on Jude, shrugging as in confusion, as Jude disappeared from the bedroom. "What kind of doctor are you?" she called after Jude.

"You alone?" asked Sybil on hearing Meriam's voice.

"News—TV," lied Jude, not interested in explaining Meriam to Sybil, and certainly not as Jude fought the robe on with one hand while continuing with Sybil. "Really, a second corpse in the same condition? Shackles and all?"

"This one's still in its—ahh—his shackles. Some indication this one's what's left of a man."

"Got to get down there, have a firsthand look before anyone contaminates the scene—this time!"

"I'm with you."

"You sure this isn't just a ploy for Frank to get another shot at you?"

"Very funny. No, afraid this is legit."

"Meet you there—I assume same general location, right."

"Under the State Building, yes."

"This is getting damn mysterious, all quite…quite interesting in a professional sense."

"I'm finding it rather Edgar-Allan-Poe mysterious."

"Poe, yeah, weird. You think the killer could've been inspired by Poe's writings?"

"I dunno, but two bodies below the city, shackled and walled up, makes me wonder."

"The horrid thought of it all."

"You thinking they were placed in their stone coffins alive?"

"I am, yes. Why use shackles otherwise?"

"This thing blew my mind yesterday, now this. Okay, meet you at the scene."

◆　◆　◆

"It was odd, how the wall looked, similar to the other one, and we started tapping, and it sounded hollow to my old ear."

"Experienced ear," Sybil replied to Frank.

"Yeah, like that," he snapped his finger, a salacious grin on his face, "and I didn't want to believe it, but we removed one brick at eye-level, and I got this military-grade flashlight, and damn almost shit my pants when I saw that skull staring back at me! Bigger one than the other one."

Jude asked if Frank had contacted Dr. Grant, and he nodded. "He's the one told us to bring down the wall for you two—that is, before you got here."

"Dean called me, and I called you," Sybil explained to Jude. She then turned to Frank the foreman. "How many shifts are you working, Frank?"

"This is a City Hall job—as many shifts as it takes to fix the pipes! Good overtime pay, though."

Jude thought it surreal that they stood on the wide platform here as trains came and went even at this bloody early hour, and all night, she imagined while the skeletal remains of not another woman, but some decayed male from the past, listened to the passing trains for an eternity. What remained of his clothing was wretchedly worn by time, despite the 'time capsule' he had remained in all these years, chained against the backdrop of brick and mortar. The shackles identical to those found in the first grave.

"You think he has any connection to the first one we found?" asked Frank, for even Frank could see that the skeletal remains and the skull was much larger and more likely that of a man than that of a woman's skull.

"If I were a betting girl," began Sybil, "I'd say so."

The fact appeared as obvious as the sound now of Dean Grant's voice. "Made it! We're here!"

Ralph was with Grant as they approached the new find and the ladies of the lab. "How in the world does this happen?"

"A rerun, obviously," quipped Grant, going straight for the sight of the deceased prisoner of the wall. "Like the goddamn Man in the Iron Mask without the mask."

"Count of Monte Christo, maybe?" replied Jude, which got her a glare from Grant.

Ralph had given Sybil and Jude a salutary and quick salute, while Grant had been quipping about the curiosity of find, while examining the carcass. Ralph Doan gave Jude a quick gesture, index finger-to-lips, the universal sign for silence. He did so behind Dean's back while Grant was talking.

"Tall fellow for his day, about as tall as the fellow in the tintype you two found at the first location. You think it could be the groom?"

"While it may look like a bride and groom picture, sir," replied Jude, "we can't be sure. In fact, after a bit of digging the other night, the couple in the photo might be other people—like maybe her parents."

"Whose parents?"

"Jane City Hall Doe, sir."

Grant scratched behind his ear, his hair disheveled from rushing from his own bed to here. He had a palatial McMansion home is Prospect Heights. Jude could tell that he'd already made up his mind as she had at one time: that the tintype would prove a depiction of the deceased. "Get an expert on the tintype then and see what he or she says of it. This fellow here—" Grant paused to lift the chin bones and thus the skull upward, the bones holding it to the neck popping like rusted tie rod ends—"this fellow, we need to get this fellow's skull to Audrey Stroud. Reconstruct the features, see if he comes into focus for anyone in the public, maybe. Not likely, but he might even look something like the man in the picture."

"Stroud is the best," began Sybil. "But that'll take some time. She can't be rushed."

Jude agreed, adding, "You rush her, she will take more time! But as tintypes went away around 1855 and the freight tunnels dug in first years of 1900, while ours was begun in '47, well it would jive that the tintype is more likely our vic's parents, maybe even grandparents—given the timing and disparities of—"

"No one wants to hear about disparities, Dr. Avery. We want the polar opposite: similarities, pieces of the puzzle, consistencies, a pattern here. I don't suppose there're any photos, a wallet, anything identifying about big foot here?" Grant, jabbing an index finger at the new find without actually touching it, added. "And how many damn more bodies are we gonna uncover down here, people?"

"Ring and pocket watch on a fob all intact," said Jude, "unlike the woman of no jewelry—which I still find rather—"

Grant again cut her off. This time with a question to the foreman. "Frank, when your men first unearthed the lady yesterday, did you see any jewelry or anything taken off the corpse's hands, fingers, pockets?"

"None, no, and I disallowed my men from going near it, called 911, and kept my crew back, so no."

"But had you seen anything on the corpse like a necklace, a ring, a broach—anything?"

"A roach but no broach," Frank said jokingly, and then his face went flat on seeing how flat the joke went over. "You know, I can't be sure. It was a shock to the system, so to speak—and I hadda calm my sister's kid down. He was more disturbed than the rest of us combined. Kid hadn't ever seen a dead person ever, you see, and getting it that way—right in his face, well, you can imagine."

"First to see it, right?"

"Right."

Grant gave Frank another of his business cards. "I want you to have your nephew come in for a talk."

"But his mom's going to put a stop to that, I can tell you."

"I can have him arrested on suspicion of robbing a body, the ghoul law, Frank. I'd rather have him come in voluntarily—just for a talk."

"I'll do what I can, sir."

"The address is on the card. At his earliest convenience."

"Sure, sure, Dr. Grant."

Grant then turned to Sybil and Jude, Ralph like a bodyguard at his side. "This expands this case exponentially, ladies."

"You mean City Hall's going to really be on our backs now?"

"I mean the press is going to have a field day, and this kind of publicity, shit, our city fathers hate. They're already dealing with the damn virus and crazy gang violence, but now we pile on a pair of ugly murders dug up from the past, and how that just feeds into Chicago urban legend as the home of Al Capone."

"Ahhh, Dr. Grant," began Jude, ignoring Ralph's motioning, again-with-finger-to-lips gesture, "I doubt Capone was a sperm cell when these two were walled up."

"Well hell, Jude, I fucking know that, but cute…Capone wasn't even a sperm cell yet—nor was he born in Chicago."

"This case is more about Poe than Capone," Sybil said, then yawned wide and snatched out a cloth and coughed as a result of breathing in the particle-saturated air in the tunnel.

"Poe, sure—an obvious observation, but there's no way to know if his writings really inspired this-this whatever it is? A hate crime, long before anyone ever used the term?" Grant paced the platform. He then asked Frank to leave them in peace as they had to talk among themselves. "But call your nephew, let him know we wanna talk to him today, okay, Frank?"

"Sure, sure, but the kid's in no trouble, right?"

"None, none at all, as long as he cooperates. Just want his first impressions on seeing the corpse."

"Yo, and hey, Dr. Grant, when we first saw the woman, she was upright."

"Upright?"

"Same as this one, in those shackles."

"But the unit team and Dr. Shanley and Dr. Avery said she was prone on the ground."

"She wasn't on the ground when we opened up that wall, sir. That's all I know. She was all in one piece."

Jude recalled how in the body bag the lady's torso was complete under that breath-thieving tight corset, but one arm and both lower legs were separated, as had been the skull. Jude and Ralph had had to reassemble the parts on her slab, like an archeologist reassembling an ancient find. The corset had held the torso intact.

"So she was dropped maybe by Luther Noble's unit?" asked Jude.

"Never saw that, no," replied Frank.

"Hell, the noise it'd've made," Grant, his anger in tone building, continued to pace, but he stopped at Frank for an answer just as another train rushed into their sphere, drowning out all other sound.

"There's your answer, sir!" shouted Frank.

Grant, as if pacing helped him think more calmly, went off and returned, but this time to Jude. "You still wondering about nothing having been found on Jane Doe, no jewelry that might help in identifying her? 'Cause I am."

Jude nodded, agreeing. "This fellow, he's got a gold band on—a wedding-style ring for a man. Has an antique watch, which, if we were to wind up might still keep time."

"Hell, yes, and an expert in antiques might even tell us what time it was when the watch had ticked down from, giving us the time or thereabouts—time of day—he went into the wall. We'd at least know an approximation, working backwards."

Ralph put in, "Nice gold-plated watch fob too."

"I think we can assume the workmen didn't go ghoul on the lady in the corset, but as to Luther Noble and his unit?" Grant was clearly disappointed in verbalizing his suspicions.

"We'd assumed the killer had taken all identifying items off her, but if that were the case," began Sybil.

"Then why not do likewise with the tintype?" asked Grant.

"If the killer took all her jewels, then why not do the same with the male victim?" asked Jude.

"You have your equipment with you, Sybil?" Grant asked, and she hefted her valise.

"Good. Everyone's a witness." He lifted both the watch fob and watch from the dangling corpse with great care. Sybil held out a brown paper bag to drop it in, but Grant hesitated and instead of dropping it into the bag, he opened it and began a sad, melodic tune akin to a child's rocking horse lullaby. "The thing works after all this time,"

Ralph added, "Doesn't mean it will keep time."

A low tick-tock sound occurred when the tune wound down. Then the tick-tock died off as well. Grant started to wind the watch, but he knew better. It wanted to be wound, begged it of the hands holding it, but he didn't want to change another thing about it. "Gotta get this into the hands of an expert." He carefully placed fob and watch into the brown bag, then Sybil tucked it away into her valise for proper chain of evidence.

"Terrible thing a watch like that becomes in the wrong time and place," muttered Ralph. Jude, then Sybil, followed by Grant stared at Ralph Doan for further explanation. "It was maybe left on him purposefully, same as the tintype for her, maybe. For further suffering. I mean, just imagine how loud that clock ticked inside the wall."

Jude instantly understood. "Imagine if you will, picture being walled up inside here with your watch ticking away like a soundtrack to your death."

"Tick-tock, tick-tock," answered Grant, contemplating the horror of it all, the silence now once again shattered by the sudden arrival of yet another train entering the station. People going about their lives and business, knowing the ramp up to the street level they wished to find themselves on, oblivious to the drama going on nearby. And while the Chicago Coroner and his MEs considered this devious detail of the pocket watch in silence once more, but silence again killed by the now departing train.

"The sound of the watch counting out the man's life would have been killed by the sound of the trains, some respite," Jude said.

"That watch might bring a small fortune at a Sotheby's Auction," Grant said. Then in all seriousness, he continued, "I will be seeing Luther Noble about the lies he appears to have perpetuated regarding how the Jane Doe was handled, along with any trinkets that disappeared."

Jude exchanged a look from Ralph to Sybil and back again to Grant. "I needn't remind you all about the dead veteran's hat, and how Luther played games with it."

For a moment, no one said a word, until Dean Grant added, "I wanted you two to process this one and Ralph is to oversee and assist, and only when you are satisfied, call in Marshal Lawrence's unit to transport the remains. Whatever happens with the mishandling of materials in the first case, we'll keep Luther away from this one."

"Will you have a serious talk with him about antique watches and jewelry?" asked Jude, point blank, and she saw Ralph wince in response.

Under his breath, Grant said, "Best to leave such matters to me, Jude."

"I will be happy to, but happier if something is done about that man."

"You have my complaints to back you as well, Dean," Sybil put in.

"His union rep is a real piece of work too, but if he has taken, or has condoned theft in any of his crew, well…taking material belongings off the dead, that's a nail in the proverbial coffin."

7

The entire way back to the labs, the two ladies conversed over a plethora of issues and matters surrounding these strange findings. Two names they kept coming back to, however, were Luther Noble and Edgar Allan Poe. Luther regarding the possibility he and his crew had divvied up items found on the female corpse, Poe regarding the possibility that the man's stories could have had anything to do with these two murders.

But they knew to keep all their shoptalk to themselves. As for Noble and his unit, Grant was looking into that, doing his job. As to Poe, the pair of lady scientists realized, except for cursorily reading required stories in high school and college—Poe stories—that, combined, they knew very little of the man and his history on the planet. To learn more on Poe and to explore the idea that his tales of frightful ways to die had been influential in these killings, Jude decided to do some digging on Poe. "In all my spare time!" she half-joked as they entered their floor from the garage elevator.

"I'll see what I can find as well," Sybil said.

Another day and night passed with no call from Meriam. Jude wondered if she'd been frightened off, hearing what she surely heard while in her bed the morning Sybil had called about John City Hall Doe. One, the nature of her work was enough to frighten off anyone, and two, Meriam could have taken the other female voice on the phone as someone that Jude was involved with. Either way, Meriam was being silent and rude.

Jude was in no mood when on her way home tonight, she detoured to visit the library to confront Meriam, but she did have the excuse of doing research on Poe, an excuse that would give her cover for dropping back in, and thus getting a chance to engage and challenge Meriam about her long silence.

Once inside the branch library, a half hour before closing time, Jude found no sign of Meriam. Had she left the job? Another librarian roamed about, putting up fresh posters with a stapler snapping mildly as she tacked up materials.

Since she was here, she sought out and found a section on Edgar Allan Poe. She had found the mother lode and was skimming titles to determine which might be of use when she came across one that read: Who Killed Poe? with a sub-title that read: 13 Theories of How Poe Died. "Books, damn sure are wonderful vessels," she whispered in the silence of the stacks, as she fingered several other titles with the word Poe in them. In fact, there were too many tomes to choose from, so she began grabbing the thinnest of them.

With an armful of books in the crook of her arm, Jude went for the reference desk to sign them out, and just as she got there, she heard a familiar voice on the PA system—Meriam's voice. Was it a recording? As she had each book checked out, the young lady behind the counter asked if she would like a bag to carry her books in? "Only two dollars and it goes to support the library."

"Sure, sure. That'd be fine." Jude looked past the girl at the desk, and she finally asked, "Where's Meriam tonight?"

"Oh, she's in the office." A slight drop of one shoulder indicated the office back of the barricade-like countertop.

"Can you, that is, would you mind calling her out? I'd like to say hello."

"Absolutely. One moment."

Jude, her compilation of Poe books in hand, waited to see Meriam materialize. She feared the newfound friend would slip out a back door as the lights dropped away, leaving a semi-darkened room in which the buzz of electricity had become a murmur, a faint heartbeat, when finally, Meriam, looking stunning with her long-flowing hair in two braids, stepped into view and stood in the light flowing from the open office door.

"There you are," said Jude. "I was looking for you."

She shrugged. "Paperwork. I'm in charge these days. My boss has fallen ill and is hospitalized. That's why I've not been ahhh in touch."

"Oh, dear, am sorry to hear about your boss. Sounds like she's a good one."

"She's the best, but she's diabetic with lupus, so she goes through these periods. I suppose I shouldn't've told you all that, but you're so easy to talk to."

"I've been thinking a lot about, well, about you, yes, but really about us." Jude bit her lower lip.

Meriam gave her a closed mouth smile and a nod. "Me too."

"I'd like us to get to know one another more ahhh better, better more…however one says it."

Meriam's smile opened like a blossoming flower at this. "I was worried. You didn't call, Jude. I thought maybe it was over already."

"I didn't call only because-well, my job. It's kinda being on-call twenty-four-seven. You saw that, right?"

"I did. Doctor's life these days."

"I am a doctor to the dead. A medical examiner."

"Ahh, aha, so, yes, I see. And you chose to keep that from me."

"I work under—er—for Dr. Dean Grant, Chief Coroner for Cook County."

"Not literally under, I hope," she tried to hide her concern with humor, but Meriam swallowed as if digesting this new information. "Then you do important work."

"Often just routine, day-to-day stuff, really, but occasionally we, I, I get something seriously important on my plate."

"Well now, perhaps you can tell me all about it over dinner. This time, my place."

"Oh, but I have to think about Squeakums. Been alone all day. Needs feeding."

"Understood, we'll do my place another time."

"I've got some frozen dinners in my fridge."

"Ice box it's called on the res." Meriam, curious, asked as she pointed to the bag of books, "More on underground Chicago?"

"Poe, she's boning up on Edgar," said the other librarian who'd turned out the office light and had alighted. "Good night, girls," she said and waved at the door.

Meriam produced a set of keys, and they left the empty library in its semi-dark slumber. After walking the few blocks to Jude's apartment, they quickly settled in, and while Jude fed the cat and mewed over Squeakums for a short while, Meriam, invited to do so, was picking through the freezer for what she felt like among the stack of Stouffers frozen delights. When she called out that she was going to have the Chicken Alfredo, Jude called back that this sounded good. "Put on another!"

Soon Jude had laid out the Poe books, and she instantly became enthralled with the first one that'd caught her eye, *13 Theories on Poe's Death* being the sub-title. Even as Meriam was acting as cook, Jude began scanning the opening page, which read:

In June 1849, Edgar Allan Poe embarked on a speaking tour to raise funds for a literary magazine he'd hoped to publish. On September 27, 1849, Poe was supposed to board a ferry from Richmond, Virginia bound for Baltimore, Maryland, and then on to New York. A mysterious illness ensued, one that had him doubling over. As a result, the night before the ferry trip, Poe visited a doctor in Richmond for a fever and stomach cramps.

Little is known for certain about the next few days, except to this day they remain a mystery. Poe did arrive in Baltimore the day after his visit to the Richmond doctor, a man named Nels; this on September 28, but EA Poe failed to go on to New York.

It was a number of days later that Poe turned up inside a tavern in Baltimore on October 3. He was in bad shape, nearly unresponsive in what onlookers assumed was an alcoholic stupor. A note was sent to a local doctor, and Poe was soon admitted to a hospital. One odd detail is that the clothes Poe had on did not appear to be his own. Instead of his usual black wool suit, he was wearing a cheap, ill-fitting suit and a mans bawdy straw hat, as one might see on stage in a comedy.

In the hospital, Poe continued, like a drunkard, to drift in-and-out of consciousness, hallucinating demons, and speaking nonsense when he was awake. One remark, recalled by his doctor, was that "Snodgrass had the facts." In another rant, Poe said that Ludwig had killed to make it look as if Poe had murdered a woman. "Used my story. Duplicated my story but in real life, man!"

Poe was given sedatives and was bled out by leeches in the hope that any poisons in his system would be removed with the 'bad blood' sucked up by the leeches. But alas, on October 7, he died.

A Baltimore newspaper reported enigmatically that the cause had been "congestion of the brain." Jude let that phrase sink in, a euphemism for drug use and alcohol poisoning perhaps? Or for what she was had interpreted it as—a tumor? She made a cup of hot tea, and came back to the marked page in the book and read on:

Several theories about Poe's cause of death have emerged. The most prominent is that he died from complications of alcoholism. J.E.

Snodgrass, the doctor who saw Poe in the tavern, believed that Poe had been drinking heavily and that he ultimately succumbed to the tremors and delirium that can accompany alcohol withdrawal. A number of secondhand accounts seem to support Snodgrass, saying that Poe had encountered acquaintances in Baltimore and had simply, easily, given his penchant for alcohol, gone on a drinking binge, which was hardly out of character or practice. Poe had engaged in bouts of heavy drinking throughout his life.

At the time of his death, however, he had recently joined a temperance society. Moreover, John Moran, the attending physician at the hospital, was convinced that Poe was not drunk and hadn't been drinking in the days leading up to his death. The duration of his final illness, and the fact that he seemed to recover slightly in the hospital before worsening and dying also seemed inconsistent with alcohol withdrawal.

Jude was interrupted in her reading, as Meriam brought both their meals into the living room where Jude was working. By now Squeakums was curled about Jude's lap, and shooed off, the cat found a favored spot on the ridge-like top of the sofa that Jude sat on. Meriam took the spot beside Jude, and between bites, she asked, "Why Poe, why now?"

"Has to do with my job."

"The dead woman found in the wall under City Hall?"

"You know about that?"

"It's all over the news."

"Ahhh, had hoped it'd stay quiet a bit longer for the sake of everyone involved."

"Public's right to know, transparency, all that."

"Yeah, understood but, well, hard to work with reporters dogging your every move."

"Since you're coming clean with me, Jude, I should tell you that I am involved in every street protest I can get to. Some having to do with Red Lives Matter and Black Lives Matter, but some having to do with Police Transparency and the lack of it."

"I see, and I agree most often that the protesters have a right to—"

"We have more than a right. We have a moral imperative, and we have a necessity to change the systematic racism found in policy after policy in both the laws and how they are enforced."

"I don't disagree."

"Nor do you understand."

"I think I do."

"No. You are one of them."

"One of them? One of whom?"

"Law enforcement. We know that even when an autopsy is done on a George Floyd or a Travon Martin, that we cannot take it at face value, that the findings are, lamentably, often crooked double-speak."

"That's not the case in Cook County, not with Dean in charge."

"Maybe not since he's been in charge. But even he can be gotten to; I have no doubt."

Jude gave this a moment's thought, knowing that the governor and the mayor could and had influenced Dean in some cases, but all she said was, "You don't know Grant. I do."

"I know he likes the camera on him more than the victim."

"You don't know that; you don't know Dean." Jude found herself feeling oddly out of body, defending Dr. Grant from Meriam Ogalala. "Is that your birth name—Ogalala, same as your tribal name?"

"It is my name and the name of my people."

"Isn't it time your people became Americans in the sense of, well, what's the word. Adaption, acclimation?"

"You disappoint me, Doctor Avery."

"I don't mean to. I'm not prejudiced or biased toward any group."

"Really?"

"Really. Except maybe against the filthy rich—those who did not earn their riches, but got it through a trust fund and use their wealth for all the wrong reasons." Jude laughed on saying this, a short nervous confession laugh.

"I just want you to know that when there is a just cause, and the people in charge are lying to us all, whatever the core cause, or the negative man's reaction, I am on the front lines, representing the Oglala. It is why I had my name legally changed to show who I am."

"I see, and I respect that—admire you for it."

"Do you, really?"

"Yes, really." Jude, her dinner only half-eaten, scooched closer to Meriam and began tenderly touching her and kissing her. The couple had to lay aside their dinner plates as they stretched out on the sofa, sharing one another's caresses, while Squeakums, ears back, watched the dance of lovemaking. His now annoying mewing and crying increased with the passion of the lovers, until suddenly, Jude stopped and said, "I'm sorry, but I can't do this in front of my baby."

Meriam laughed at this, while Jude lifted the cat and returned her to the confines of the bathroom. When she turned to go back to Meriam, she was startled as Meriam had followed her here and had dropped her clothes down to her bra and panties.

"Get those clothes off, doctor," Meriam said in a commanding, deep voice.

"Yes, yes, whatever you say, master." Jude began stripping away her own clothes. "Shower?"

"Only if you're in it with me."

8

With Meriam in a deep slumber on her bed now, Jude returned to the living room where the cat had polished off what'd remained of the frozen gourmet meals—had done work on both hers and Meriam's; reward for all that time spent locked away in the bathroom. Jude was anxious to continue where she'd left off in the book, upset with herself for not having marked her place when so distracted by Meriam earlier. But then who could fault me with Meriam in the room and looking so gorgeous?

Jude lifted the book and made for the kitchen, where she laid the tome on the table and went about putting a snack together for herself. "No, nothing for you!" she told the cat, who despite having a distended stomach from the Stouffer's leftovers, begged for scraps. "I should never ever have started feeding you scraps! Beggar!"

Once settled into her kitchenette chair, munching away, Jude again began to read from the book she'd earlier started in on. The page read:

A number of diseases have been proposed as possible causes of Poe's death, including diabetes, heart disease, epilepsy, and tuberculosis. One of the most intriguing possibilities, suggested by a Dr. Oswald T. Griswald, PhD, a medical historian and American Literature professor associated with the University of Chicago, is that Poe may have died from a case of rabies. Baltimore was, after all, teeming with rats and rabies was not uncommon even in the city. Besides, Poe's delirium seemed to get better and then worsen again over the last days of his life, a pattern observed in patients with late-stage rabies.

Furthermore, Poe's hospital records indicated that Poe had difficulty drinking water. This may have been a manifestation of one of rabies' characteristic symptoms, a fear of water. Swollen throat and difficulty swallowing as well. Griswald's theory appeared in an article dated as early as 1979 in a long defunct and popular magazine devoted to Poe called Your Daily Poe Transfusion. Before the article ended, this Professor Griswald added that there was also a question of whether or not Poe's death had come as a result of a brain tumor. In essence, it appeared to Jude that the man did not want to believe Poe's demise was a tragic result of alcohol and drug poisoning. A belief that had endured over generations.

Another theory discussed in another article by Griswald, who appeared the local expert on Poe, was that Poe may have been a victim of a violent crime. Because the tavern where Poe was found was being used as a polling place—it was common practice in the 19th century for voting to take place in drinking establishments—it has been proposed that Poe may have been caught up in what may seem by today's standard an unusual form of electoral fraud known as cooping.

In a cooping scheme, gangs working for corrupt politicians would grab unwilling bystanders off the street and force them to vote repeatedly for a certain candidate. Victims were often beaten or forced to drink alcohol to make them pliant and compliant. Disguises were used to allow the victims to vote multiple times. This could explain the bizarre outfit that Poe was wearing when he was discovered.

With the fragmentary and sometimes contradictory evidence that exists regarding Poe's last days, it truly is hard to imagine that there would ever be a completely satisfactory answer as to what killed him. For the many armchair detectives who enjoyed exercising their powers of ratiocination on his death, that might be good news.

Jude stopped reading at this point, and instead, she began thinking about a what if, suggested by that last paragraph. To never, throughout time, know precisely the cause of death of a man so renowned as Edgar Allan Poe should not be tolerated. A flash of thought had him walled up in that brick coffin below the city while some look-a-like was bled to death by leeches. It's certainly makes for a fuller story, but highly unlikely that they had Poe's remains in her autopsy freezer. Regardless, had anyone thought to have Poe's remains exhumed and put through a rigorous examination? With modern forensics, if he had been poisoned, for instance, or if he died of liver failure, it might be discovered exactly and scientifically and unequivocally what killed the dark genius.

At this juncture, Jude realized she'd need more than books, that she'd need to interview a living expert, someone who'd forgotten more about Poe than she would ever know. She put it all aside for now, and she, with Squeakums following, returned to the bedroom and crawled in beside Meriam and went off to the land of nod.

The following morning at Jude's Cook County lab

By ten AM, Jude and Sybil had continued their autopsy work on the skeletal remains from the second find. They had by now fed all the data that they could, this early in the autopsy, into the ARC—Analysis Recon & Composite application, a computer program that actually read the data and from the information, including the DNA analysis, bone marrow analysis, and what little remained of the tissue below the corset for Jane Doe, and the fabric for John Doe to develop a composite of characteristics and a likely likeness of the victims. It was a remarkable program, but it had its limitations. Still, it gave the team a loose idea of what the victims looked like in life, despite the blowup doll appearance of each.

"Don't worry," Sybil began at the appearance of the first victim, the Jane Doe, now being called City Hall Jane. "When Audrey Stroud gets through with the skull sculpting, we'll have a clearer image."

By this time, the skulls of both victims had gone to the sculptors at Quantico. Sybil was on a first-name basis with the head of that department in the FBI, as she'd worked with her on several previous cases.

"I sigh because our man is not looking anything like the guy in the tintype."

"We may never know who these people were. A mystery wrapped within a wall of mystery. Just the way they were done away with—so Poe."

"I get it."

I thought the victims would speak louder to us by now."

"You're rushing what cannot be rushed, Jude."

After a bit of silence, as the two MEs went about their work, Sybil asked, "Said you did some reading last night on how Poe died?"

"I did. Found it a fascinating mystery."

"The original man of mystery. Predated Spiritualism and Houdini, of course."

Jude, staring at the image of the male created by the computer, a three-dimensional representation that turned to demonstrate all sides, all features down to the ears, color of eyes and the skin tone, as well as the size of fingers, toes, and penis. "He kinda fits what Dean said, the general look of the guy in the tintype. Generally speaking, of course."

"I don't see it," Sybil said.

"About the jaw—rather plump, pudgy even. And older than the woman. Could be related…maybe."

"Just imagine it, Jude, you're a romantic at heart."

"Why do you say that?"

"You so wanted the victim—first her with the tintype to be the same person on her wedding night with her groom. 'You get your wedding photo taken with your man, happiest night of your life, and it ends with your being walled up—alive'! That's what I mean—gothic romanticism like those bodice rippers we love to read."

From the remaining collapsed and dehydrated lungs of both victims, Jude and Sybil had determined that the victims had inhaled flying particles that under tests turned out to be a mixture of carbon monoxide and concrete dust. They were both breathing while shackled to the back wall.

"One of Poe's stories is an exact match for this kind of sick revenge. It's actually an ancient method of corporeal punishment. Doled out to convicted murderers in some ancient cultures."

"Really, and you must know it went out with the dark ages. Casketing people in confined spaces to starve and dehydrate to death—cruel and unusual punishment."

"Yes, but in the early 1900s, the turn of the century, there was a new fascination for this movement called Spiritualism,"

"I've read about that. Curiosity of the great beyond."

"The undiscovered country."

"Seances, and all that, yes. Levitating tables, smashing lamps, shaking chandeliers, and all a hoax as proved by Houdini himself."

"There was also growing fear of being buried alive, and Poe played on that fear in his readers."

"Yes, published stories about it, I know, so what?"

"Not one but two stories specifically use this form of tortuous punishment, Sybil. It's called immurement. And it was central to the stories."

"Im-mure-ment? Meaning?"

"Punishment, eye-for-eye stuff using bricking up someone in a damn wall."

"Coincidence maybe?" Sybil's tone left no doubt of skepticism. "What stories?"

"*The Cask of Amontillado* and *The Black Cat*. Twice he returns to the punishment of another human being by this most awful means."

"I remember The Pit and the Pendulum more. Swoosh, swoosh, that damnable thing taking its time to slice the victim in two. But hey, Poe could've been another Jack-the-Ripper if he hadn't taken life's miseries out on his pen."

"Just so many nuances to this case and his works."

"Like the wise man often says, life is full of oddities and coincidence."

"In our line of work, and all we see, Sybil, and you can still believe in coincidence? You really are an optimist after all, aren't you?"

"How dare you call me an optimist!"

"How dare you call me a romantic!"

They laughed at one another now, until Sybil asked, "Poe would've been long dead by the time tintypes came into use, right?"

"Poe died October 7, 1849. Tintypes went out of use in or around 1855. That's a window."

"There may be a Poe connection, but that's a stretch, Jude."

"I'm going to see an expert on Poe at the University of Chicago, a Dr. Oswald T. Griswald—"

"Sounds rather grizzly or worse, grizzled, unless he's a young handsome devil?"

"No, looked him up. Old professor of American Literature, and strangely Medical History. Teaches a course in medical history as well, specializing in Poe!"

"How poetic. Not!"

"I've an appointment at four. Care to join me?" Jude asked.

"Sorry, got plans."

"Oh, really?"

"Nothing juicy. Just have to get Moe to the vet."

Moe was Sybil's Schnauzer. "Understood. Nothing serious, I hope."

"He's off his food, never a good sign."

"Well now, do take care of him."

"I need him; he is my de-stressor."

"Ready?" Jude indicated the on-button at the overhead recorder and camera.

"On with the work at hand, yes."

As they continued the final processing of the male victim of immurement, taking the dew-sized remains of fluid from the decayed lungs, and remnants of bone marrow, Jude began thinking anew of this thing called immurement of corpses, a rare find indeed and yet they had two within a day of one another in Cook County, Chicago.

She again thought how this case, however it shook out, could be one for the books—the journals—the annals. The recurring drumbeat of drama, tombs below City Hall, the image of catacombs and mausoleums, not to mention refrigerated drawers in a coroner's office. And atop all this, the specter of Edgar Allan Poe and his morbid fascination with brick walls closing in on prisoners of torture, imprisoning living people in walls. All during a time of intense interest in the beyond, in seances, and the Spiritualism Movement. And on close examination of the corpses that'd been walled off from the world, they'd died not of asphyxiation but starvation and dehydration.

Jude heard her name being called out with the screeching of the rails, as trains came and went. She imagined the numbers of people boarding and deboarding trains below the city, Chicagoans and visitors, who may have heard strange, muffled cries coming from somewhere in the subway. Echoes racing to this point and away from it, spiraling down the tunnel. All the while the ghosts of two murder victims so near, close enough to touch, just the other side of the wall.

It occurred to Jude that if the pipes running through the crypts of the two corpses could be dated in the forties or fifties, this would offer a clue as to when the victims met their deaths. As work on this particular tunnel began in 1947, and surely the pipelines predated the train line. By bricking around the pipes, whoever was responsible for walling these two unfortunate victims up, may well have been familiar with the plans to build the subway soon after. At least that was the speculation ongoing inside Jude's head: Late forties, and pipes inside the little fortress walls; pipes here before the fake walls were erected with precisely the same bricks made from clay quarried from local pits. Given the date—some seventy-two or three years earlier, it was little wonder the pipes needed replacing in 2020, triggering this awful discovery.

Ralph took control of the remains of John Doe, tagging his toe bone with a number that was jotted down in a book. So far, just as with City Hall Jane, identified by a number. At the same time, Jude and Sybil took charge of the final specimens. The chain of evidence was all set now. Close examinations would take time, but from all they could surmise ahead of the tests, the two victims had suffered a horrible end. One in which a quick asphyxiation would have been merciful, but no—their deaths may well have taken days in the darkness of their dungeon walls—as air filtered in around the pipes.

Jude noted the time and calculated how much she had left to get to the University of Chicago campus to be on time for Professor Griswald, who'd made it a point for her to be promptly on time, no 'diddle-dallying excuses', to which she'd joked over the phone, "I imagine you've heard them all."

After a brief pause, he had replied, "I put a cover over a Chicago telephone book that designates it as The Excuse Book, my dear, and I tell my students if they have an excuse that is NOT in the book, then I will accept it as a fresh and unique addition to the book! Ha! an excuse. Most then toe the line, ahhh mark, as they say."

Jude was hopeful that Griswald would be helpful in learning more about Poe. She rushed to locate her car in the parking lot, which had been towed, worked on, and returned to her during the day. As she pulled out and onto the street traffic, she worried that she would be too late to get to Griswald on time. He had assured her, if she was so much as a minute late, he'd be gone. "Poof!" was his last word over the phone.

9

When Jude found the building that housed the English Department at the university, she found a catacomb of corridors with professors' names on each door. The corridor was shoulder-to-shoulder, wall-to-wall, giving her a sense of claustrophobia, and she knew that one of her great fears was being locked away in a coffin alive but unable to scream, and now that unease and fear was multiplied by what she'd found in the deaths of Jane and John 'City Hall' Doe. Finally, at the end of the tunnel-like corridor at the corner, she saw Griswald's name on a larger and more ornate door than any she'd seen this entire way. He had the corner office on this floor. She then saw his nameplate also indicated that he was the Chairman of the Department. As she was about to knock, she heard the voice—the same one that had haunted her at her flat, at her job, and now following her here. She distinctly heard it repeatedly saying, "Juu-dithhh, Ju-dith."

She gritted her teeth and wished the sound away, and when it stopped, this made her wonder if she had the power to control the damnable voice in her head. Emboldened and just on time, she pushed on.

Jude heard the same phone voice of the old professor from within shout, "Open! Enter."

She pushed through the door, which opened on a large office with bookshelves covering the walls, filled to the ceiling. The man's large, lovely mahogany desk was stacked with files, papers, and scattered cups and saucers. At first, she could not see the man's features for the lamp and the tower of books that dwarfed him, but he quickly stood and came around his desk to welcome her into his world. She instantly thought he looked like an EA Poe character from the films—Peter Lorrie, in fact. A short, short man with pinched features and glasses too large for his face, the professor's grayed head reached only her midriff, as he was of no height. In keeping with social distancing and masking, he struggled to get the mask on, while offering his elbow as per handshake.

She bumped his elbow and snatched out her own mask, reminded of it by the small man who ran this place. "Please, dear, sit-sit."

She gauged his age at perhaps in his late sixties, but it was impossible to be sure. Griswald offered her a miniature chocolate, which she declined. "Coffee then?"

Jude noted the half-full pot with its green light on. "Frankly, have had too much of the stuff already today, but thanks."

He'd returned to his cushy chair the other side of his desk. Although a small man, he was round and heavy enough to raise a squeal from the chair as he'd dropped back into it. She saw that he had a large window on one side that looked out on the quad below, where trees swayed in an upcoming storm outside. The skies had gone gray and then black just before she'd ducked into the building, and now a heavy downpour pelted the window in what sounded like harsh anger. At least it felt like the storm was personally out to get her as she thought again of the voice calling her name. Was it all part and parcel of the sense of impending doom that seemed to be coming for her? Another fleeting thought had her wondering if she shouldn't find a way to break it off with Meriam to keep her lover safe from whatever might befall Jude.

Griswald had used the moment to study Jude's features. Then he said, "Harsh storm! That rain must be cold, too!"

"Be November soon. Expect the winter days are barreling toward us."

He nodded, took his glasses off, and began cleaning them as he said, "Now about Edgar…"

"Poe, yes." She noted that the man dressed in professorial fashion—Chinos with boat shoes, a knit sweater, and a high collar shirt, while a sports coat with patches on the elbows hung on a rack behind him. He had the long hair typical of an Einstein admirer as well, giving off the impression he was far too busy to concern himself with the time it took to sit in a barber's chair.

"So, what can I provide you with, with regard to Edgar?"

She assumed he had studied Edgar so long and so hard that he was on a first name basis with the man's ghost. "I need to know if you think he was murdered rather than the story that has him dying of some sort of epileptic disorder."

"I don't know how he died; no one does."

"But what do you think of the various theories?"

He scratched the back of his head and thinning hair and smiled. "You are a medical examiner with curiosity about Poe's end. Curious. Can you be more specific as to what you want from me—or rather from Edgar?"

She gave it a moment's thought. "Well, it's about the plot and main incident in his stories, *The Black Cat* and *The Cask of Amontillado.*"

"Two short stories with one common thread, yes. The Cat, Edgar saw published in the August 1843 edition of The Saturday Evening Post. Perhaps you'd like to gaze on the original."

"You have a Saturday Evening Post from 1843 with a Poe story in it?"

"I do." He pointed over his shoulder at a bookshelf.

"What can you tell me about Poe's preoccupation with immurement?"

"Ahh, yes, you're onto the heart of the matter, the act of bricking up the wife, but first, you must realize the tale is an extraordinary study of the psychology of guilt, as similar to his *Tell-Tale Heart* as much as it is to the Cask. That is, it's often paired in analysis with Poe's Heart tale. In both, a murderer carefully conceals his crime and believes himself unassailable, but eventually breaks down and reveals himself, impelled by a nagging reminder of his guilt."

"Yes, the nagging voice in his own head in the one instance, the nagging mewing cat in the other."

"Cat or self-conscience, both represent and carry the weight of guilt on the narrator's actions, his mind. Wears him down like peeling an onion."

"Yes, like Dostoevsky's *Crime and Punishment.* The real punishment is the growing guilt."

"A great novel, but Poe delivers it in a short work!"

"What do you think of the Cask?"

"First published in the November 1846 issue of Godey's Lady's Book of all places, but Victorian ladies rather enjoyed gothic tales, and a few wrote them—under male names, of course. Now the Bronte sisters, they were so far ahead of their time."

"Ahh, yes, far too titillating for females to possibly handle," Jude said, smirking, "given their delicate nature as Freud would have us believe. Ha!"

"Hmmm, yes, Freud, another matter altogether, but Edgar would have read at least some of Freud's early epistles."

She nodded, allowing Griswald to continue. "Edgar's Cask story, set in an unnamed Italian city at carnival time in an unspecified year, paints a picture of a mad man, or madman, taking fatal revenge on a friend."

"A friend who, he believes, has insulted him, from my reading of it."

"More than insult. The friend has acquired all that the narrator had ever wished to achieve, so the revenge is not due to insult in the normal understanding of that word, but rather the man's entire life and prosperity and luck, all of which the madman wanted, you see. And as our narrator has failed in life, he strikes out at his so-called friend, who has succeeded beyond all expectation."

"I see, I think. Do you mind if I record our conversation—homework for later?"

"Not at all, not at all. Go right ahead."

She set her phone to record his words and laid it on the desk between stacks of pages and books through which he met her eyes and laid a large caliber gun on the desk in obvious show of warning. She then said, "Is that necessary?"

"It is if we're to continue, yes."

"I see, I think. Please, sir, go on."

"Well now, where was I? Oh, yes, the Cask. Like several of Poe's stories, and in keeping with the 19th-century fascination with the subject, the narrative revolves around a person being buried alive—in this case, by immurement, as you yourself have named it."

"Oh yes, I had to look the word up, but as it came up in my google search."

"Bah, Google. I prefer a hefty book. "Well, then, as in *The Black Cat* and actually again in a sense in *The Tell-Tale Heart*. Edgar, in all three tales, conveys the story from the murderer's perspective, which is rather telling in itself."

"Why do you think he prefers that motif of the mad narrator?"

"To raise the question, put in the same set of circumstances, might we not all act in the manner of the insane?"

"You think that is Poe's point?"

"In his day, authors stepped into the story and addressed the reader directly, telling them what to think. Poe was among the first to invite the reader to become the character—the insane character, the lying, conniving character, who is willing to lie, cheat, and steal to gain his ends."

"I see."

"In literary terms, we call the execution of a story from a questionable source as a façade story."

"Façade as in a fake wall on a sound stage?"

"Or simply a forked tongue?"

"Good point," she replied.

"No one among us can really know if pushed to extremes—horrid extremes of the mind—what we might do."

"Despite our better angels?"

Griswald smiled at the invocation of angels. "Edgar's 'angel' was a black raven—a kind of recurrent call from the dark side of existence."

Jude thought the old elf behind the desk was sharp indeed, and he spoke as if he knew Poe like no other man living now. She remained silent and listening to the man's melodic voice and the depth of his knowledge.

"Despite his macabre literary genius, Edgar's life was short and largely unhappy. After his young wife, Virginia, contracted a death sentence, tuberculosis, in 1842 and died five years later, the already hard-drinking poet, his heart enraptured by his young, beautiful wife, apparently dove deeper into the bottle."

"He was so attached to Virginia."

"His dream, she was. Well then, seven years later, in the late summer of 1849, he was in Richmond, Virginia, where he proposed to an old sweetheart, Elmira Shelton. This renewed his energies and he again had a reason larger than himself to live. Which makes the notion that he 'killed' himself with drink questionable."

"Most people believe that he did—liver damage."

"Damned by history of a questionable nature."

"Complexities of the mind haunted him and led him to drink, which led to organ failure."

"If you've made up your mind on this, you'd not be asking questions." He fingered the gun and using his index finger spun it like a child playing spin the bottle. "Look here, my dear Dr. Avery, on September 27, 1849, Poe left Richmond happily re-engaged to a childhood sweetheart with plans of marriage. Soon after he is dead.

"I read about that. He left Richmond supposedly bound for Philadelphia."

"The details of his actions and whereabouts over the next few days remain uncertain, but as early as that prior July, he was suffering from cholera and deathly ill with it. Then on October third, seven days later he is in Baltimore when a passerby notices Poe slumped near a now two-hundred-year-old Irish pub with a rather cheeky name: The Horse You Came In On. The bar still claims to have served Edgar his last and final drink."

"Talk about closing time," Jude said.

"Recognizing Poe, an acquaintance, a Dr. Joseph Walker contacted Edgar's friend, Dr. Joseph Snodgrass, who promptly arrived at the scene."

"Slumped near a pub? Not inside over a table?"

"Some had him inside, others outside. I suspect he was ambling around."

Jude pictured a disoriented man weaving about the Baltimore streets of his day.

"Some say he stumbled there from the notorious Ryan's Hall, a bar that doubled for a polling place. Doesn't matter, as Snodgrass found the forty-year-old, well-known author—also well-known for drinking and using opium and laudanum—in what Dr. Snodgrass easily assumed was a highly drunken state."

"I read that he was wearing another man's clothes as well."

"Yes, wearing cheap, ill-fitting clothes, obviously not his. In fact, in his right mind, he'd've never been caught ahhh dead in the rags he had on at that time."

"Very different from his usual mode of dress, black overcoat or cloak."

Griswald nodded, affirming this. "Obviously robbed of his hat as well. At any rate, Snodgrass saw to taking him to Washington College Hospital, where the poor poet slipped in and out of consciousness."

"And where he reportedly died."

"Early on the morning of October 7th, reportedly uttering the last words: "Lord help my poor soul.""

"Do you know how that lament was uttered? I mean the tone, the delivery?"

"Guilt-ridden, one nurse, a young woman whose name is lost to history, reported."

"Hmm, guilt-ridden. Not unlike his narrators in the stories we discussed."

Griswald nodded thoughtfully. "Afraid so. Some said he was in control of his faculties to the end, while others say he was ranting gibberish like a lunatic."

"Which do you believe from your years of studying the man?"

"Which? There is no which—both! Different doctors were in and out and around Edgar over many hours, and like the blind men trying to describe the elephant, no one got his diagnosis right."

After a moment of silence, Griswald dropped his gaze and shook his bushy head to finally say, "It grows late."

Jude examined her watch. It read: 6:13pm, and while the storm outside the window had subsided, a true darkness had come over the campus below them. "I fear I've overstayed my welcome."

"Oh, no, not at all, my dear, and do come back. I've enjoyed our chat about Edgar. Nowadays, Edgar's gotten less and less important in academia, abrogated to the ghetto of being labeled a mystery writer or worse yet, a horror writer, when in fact, he is a true genius of literature who ranks with the greatest classics."

"I can tell you have the utmost respect for the man and his work."

"That I do, despite all his flaws and frailties and self-recriminations, which I find deeply saddening."

"Despite his guilt regarding his treatment of others? His relationship with his parents and stepfather. He was also quite acerbic toward other writers of the day. In fact, his reviews are downright sardonic, and some think satanic."

"He had much to feel guilty over, I am sure of that. As to his reviews, they savaged and torched his competitors."

"I so would love to shake your hand, sir, but best I can do is thank you for your insights and allowing me to record, as I have a terrible memory for things not medical."

"Delighted to help, and my door is open to you, Dr. Avery, anytime if you have further need of an aging dwarf."

Jude was taken aback by his last words. "Sir, I hardly think you qualify as small enough to be—"

"Ah-ah-ah, now, just testing you on social graces."

"And did I pass or fail?"

"If you do not know that answer, only then do you fail."

God, she thought, this guy is a small Confucius. She then stood to leave with as many questions as answers, and Jude still felt unsure what was driving her, but it felt like Edgar Allan Poe himself. At the door, she turned and said, "Thank you, Dr. Griswald; you've been a great help, and I will likely either call with more questions or come back to see you again. That much I know."

"Then you are wiser than ninety percent of my students here." He smiled while saying this, and she'd caught the wry smile from where she turned at the door. "You're not afraid to ask questions—the root of all learning."

Jude nodded and waved a final goodnight, as the professor put away his gun. She honestly feared she was not ready for a Griswald final exam.

The following day at the Cook County Coroner's Office

Jude had to set all aside, as she'd been called to drop everything—hard to do in mid-autopsy on another possible suicide, or was it murder? A young woman who supposedly drowned in her own bathtub, found hours later by her 'asleep' husband now 'distraught.' As an ME, Jude had seen this scenario play out far too often, and many times across the country, the wife-killer got away with his crime for years, until wife number two or three met the same or a similar fate.

In the corridor, she ran into Sybil taking the same elevator, and once inside, the two shared their destination, learning both had been ordered to see Dr. Grant in his top floor suite of offices.

"What do you suppose the boss wants?" Avery asked Sybil, who'd had far more years of experience working under Grant than she had.

"It could be anything from a stolen bagel off his desk to the immurement case," she replied, lifting a copy of the Chicago Tribune to

Jude's eyes. "I had nothing to do with this, so I assume you did?"

"What're you talking about?" Jude took the newspaper and read the headline: EA Poe-Style Killings Discovered Below City Hall. The sub-title read: 2 Victims Punished to Death by Way of Immurement.

"Quite the teaser, eh? Who knows what an immurement is, right?"

Jude thought immediately of Dr. Griswald. "I swear to you—"

"Save your denials for Dean. Don't waste them on me."

"Sybil, I have not spoken with anyone from the press."

"But this university professor you took the case to obviously has."

"He…Dr. Griswald didn't indicate…no, I don't believe it."

The elevator doors opened as Sybil glared at Jude and said, "You mean you don't want to believe it!" Sybil stepped off and tore ahead of Jude for Dean's sprawling office.

"I had no intention of or thought that—"

Sybil turned and pounced and said, "That you could be so naïve ? Did you swear the man to confidence?"

"I did not think—"

"Right, you didn't think!"

"—that-that under these circumstances, that I needed to get his word."

"Well now, you'll have to live with that decision. I had nada to do with it."

"And I take it your visit to the vet with Moe went badly?"

"Moe's dead!" Sybil gasped the last word. "I had to have him put down."

Sybil stormed away, sure to get to Grant before Jude. Jude shouted after her, "I'm so sorry, Sybil."

Jude slowed and then sat on a settee outside Grant's office, and she scanned the front-page story. The only saving grace was that the story in question was below the fold and overshadowed by news of a new surge of the pandemic sweeping across the northwest now—stabbing Wyoming of all places, and badly.

It was true that Dr. Griswald was quoted in the story, remarking on the Poe connection to the awful way the victims met their end. Even so, the article proved sketchy at best. 'The lurid nature of the deaths discovered after some seventy odd years by estimate of the Cook County Coroner's Office has left authorities scratching their heads'.

Upon reading that line, an immediate fear of what Grant was going to say and do hit Jude like an anvil. How would this reporter, some woman named Louise McGrath have gotten that estimate from the County Coroner? Who beside her and Sybil would know? A disgruntled Luther Noble, one of the other deniers? Sybil, no! Ralph or Lionel, who worked closely with Sybil? It could have come from any number of people—hell, even Frank the bricklayer guy, who may've overheard them estimating at the scene.

Jude only knew that she must get her ducks in a row. She now stood, and with paper in hand, entered the lion's den, unsure what Sybil may or may not have said to Grant ahead of her.

Once inside, she could hear Grant shouting at Dr. Shanley. All the support staff and secretarial people were standing and looking awkward, some making excuses to leave even as Sybil was escorted to Grant's inner chamber. Feeling sure to be the sacrificial lamb in all this, Jude took a great breath of air, girded herself, and she reminded herself who she was. In doing so, she could hear her father's voice telling her to stand up for herself, and to not allow anyone to trample on her dignity and self-worth for any reason. And she stepped in prepared to make a strong stand, and if that were to cost her this job, so be it.

Then again, she'd become quite enamored of working on the subway discoveries, the two corpses from another time period. She'd been putting down so much on paper, and she truly hoped for an opportunity to write up a professional paper on the double-murder from so long ago with some semblance of answers. To detail precisely how she had handled it forensically. She hadn't begun yet to scratch the surface, and to now lose it over a stupid fumble, to lose it to Sybil and Dean, made for a mix of gut-wrenching sadness and teeth-clenching anger.

All this time that voice she'd been hearing, that warning of impending doom. Was this it? The reason for the ongoing fear of the unseen events about to unfold in her life. There seemed a connection, and she imagined herself returning to her office only to pack her things and say goodbye to Ralph. Why bother to go in to be berated and sent packing? Why not just go pack? she asked herself. But that other voice—her father's voice—came cascading back through the corridors of her mind, saying, "Get in there and take your lumps!"

10

Once inside Grant's inner office, Jude was surprised to find both Sybil and Dean cordially smiling, but she instantly feared it was some sort of pact they'd made between themselves, one she was not a part of. After all, they had worked as a team for many years, even before Dean had become Chicago's Chief Coroner.

"Sir, I am here as you requested."

Dean lifted a single hand, indicating for Jude to sit. "Make yourself comfortable." She was surprised at his cheerful tone. Open on his desk, however, a copy of the same paper she held in hand. Jude gulped, ready for him to bark out that she was fired.

Instead, he asked Sybil to explain the circumstances to Jude. Sybil paced a moment, then said, "It appears that City Hall, the mayor in particular, wants us to pursue the case of the walled-in couple at top speed and priority, and that they are ahhh happy with the alacrity we have so far shown, and the concern our city has shown, the compassion and empathy for citizens older than imaginable, but still Chicagoans."

"Jane and John 'City Hall', really?"

"That's how the Lieutenant Governor put it," Dean added, shaking his head. "Can never know which way the spin will go until it spins. This one surprised even me."

"I thought…after seeing the article in the paper," Jude began, thumping the Tribune's front page.

"I thought so, too, Dean."

Grant pointed to Sybil for Jude's sake, saying, "She came in here like a fireball, defending you, kiddo. Said if I canned you, she'd quit and walk out herself."

"Don't exaggerate, Dean," Sybil said, turning away and staring out at the city streets below.

"I guess I owe everyone a thank you, Dr. Grant for not wanting to fire me, and Dr. Shanley for standing up for me."

"Still I am upset with you both," Grant said, snarly and grimacing. "Somehow information on the case was leaked, and Sybil tells me you had talked to the guy Griswald about this case, Jude."

"I was cultivating information. I had no idea he'd call a reporter."

"You're still young, naïve. This is Chicago. Reporters are like flies here. For all you know, one followed you to the university grounds."

"I had no sense of that."

"Hmmm, interesting choice of words—no sense of it, eh? Well doctor, you're in the big leagues now, and to keep our official integrity, well it's top priority. But for now, the way City Hall has decided to pump up its image of open transparency and pride-building plans—to Make Chicago Chicago Again isn't it? As a result, you land on your feet. Jude, but even a cat only has so many lives."

"Ahhh, yes, sir. Of course."

"Well, with that out of the way, it is now our job to cooperate openly with the press on this case, and so we do so as much as possible while maintaining our professional acumen and integrity. Is that understood?"

"Yes, master," jSybil said, joking to lighten him up.

"I wish I could run this place like a king, just to get rid of Noble," Grant said, suddenly changing the subject. "He's fighting it. His union rep is an ass and a brash one at that. I could tell from the Luther's body language that he most certainly did steal items off the Jane Doe, but he is a well-practiced liar-denier. Denies it up and down."

"Is there any chance he is telling the truth?" asked Sybil.

"None, and I am seeing his crew today, one-by-one. The weakest link the last."

"Lisa Anderson, the newlywed?" asked Jude. "Why do you call her the weakest?"

"Because she's a woman, and Dean is an old stuff-shirt of a man!" Sybil said and laughed lightly.

"No, not because she's a she; she has some semblance of moral upbringing as opposed to the men."

"Then what you're really saying is that she's the strongest link."

"I suppose you're right—bad choice of words."

"And that all the men are weaklings without morals, and Lisa alone has character."

"I said a semblance. The whole crew, I believe, have been rather infected by a case of Lutheritis or something."

Sybil said, "Noble-disjointedness?"

"Heavens, what to call it."

"Thievery and deception come to mind," Jude replied.

"Hard to believe that all of them would go along with such rotten behavior?" Sybil said.

"We've seen it with whole units of police, even firemen," Dean said, sighing. "It's not a pleasant task, so one of you, I'd like to have in the interviews today. Who's up for it?"

"I have such a caseload waiting on me downstairs," said Jude, begging off.

Sybil leaned in over his desk, her cleavage in Dean's face. "I'm in, coach, but let's get our signals straight."

Jude admired the mutual respect that her boss and Sybil had for one another, and that it was based on truth—the strongest bond in any relationship, and without it, there could be no 'true' relationship. She hoped to have the kind of relationship her two colleagues shared, but she knew she had to build up to it, as Sybil had obviously done over the years. But there were some lines Jude would never cross, and she was beginning to believe that Sybil had, and too that there were scars from having crossed those lines in the past. It made Jude wonder what Sybil cried tears over in her most private moments.

Jude bid the other two forensic doctors good day and good luck with the interrogations, adding, "Get them all to write and sign brief statements. Remember, I am a graphologist as well, and I can spot a lie and a liar in their cursive script."

"Good idea. And hey, that kid who first discovered the female body, the foreman's nephew..."

Dean's words had stopped Jude at the door, where she replied, "Yes, what about him?"

"He went under hypnosis without question, and no hesitation once Dr. Langan got him focused. Says there were several rings around the bones, resting about the knuckles, and he said she had a necklace as well."

"No coaching beforehand of what to look for?"

"No, none whatsoever. Langan is a hundred percent sure of the lad's testimony. Of course, in a court of law, it'd get less credence than a lie detector."

"Or a run at handwriting analysis, I suppose."

"Depends on judge and jury, but afraid so."

"Still, we know then that our instincts were right," Sybil mused.

Jude added, "The corpse of bones, hardly held together in that corset, let that sink in: she was robbed, and to get at the jewelry, Luther or one of the others knocked her loose from the wall shackles."

"Definitely not details City Hall wants to hear about, or to see disseminated to the press," said Dean.

"Yeah, I get that," Sybil said.

Jude, nodded appreciatively. "It'd destroy the image that our city fathers want to project—that our dutiful city workers, to a man and woman, actually—"

"Gives a shit—cares!"

The threesome exchanged looks of understanding, as Dean said, "We keep this little in-house investigation in-house."

"On pain of death, my liege lord." Again, Sybil was teasing the boss.

"You have my allegiance, sire," Jude said, joining in with her own semi-jest.

"Go on, scullery maid," Dean said, now escorting Jude to the exit. "Maid Shanley and I have to prepare for fool's court!"

◆　◆　◆

When Jude returned to the lab, she realized on seeing Ralph working about the place, that a kernel of mistrust and distrust and suspicion was coursing through the corridors and pathways of her mind. Could anyone really know what another human being was capable of doing—or not doing for that matter? Without any evidence or a single clue, she had flash-pictured a Ralph she did not know in a darkened alleyway exchanging details of the case for cash. Of course, it was absurd, but suppose Ralph was strapped for cash. Which she knew to be true, as he'd struggled with getting that education loan. One must ask how far he would go to keep from being evicted. She imagined his pay here was piss-poor.

She then thought of others in the building who could just as easily be trafficking in information to outsiders. Relaying to a newsman who, with a shared grudge against Grant, or the police, or the mayor's people might simply wish to trade in revenge. Not so great a grandiose vengeance that Poe's mad narrator in The Cask wreaked on his victim, but revenge, nonetheless.

"I heard about what happened upstairs."

"Really, you did?" she replied to Ralph, who was going about disinfecting tools and items.

"It's all over the building."

"Really? Travels fast here, the rumors."

"People are saying you're not long for here."

"Don't you believe it, Ralph!"

"Listen, Dr. Avery, none of my business except I like working for you, and I've learned a helluva lot from you."

"And I from you."

"So, so if it'll help, I'll go upstairs and give Dr. Grant a piece of my mind."

"No, no—not necessary, Ralph. Thank you for the thought, but don't, please, act on it."

"Are you sure?"

"Absolutely sure, yes."

Even as Ralph silenced himself and went back to work, Jude wondered if any man could be sweeter. Still, she also wondered who could be trusted unequivocally, unconditionally, unabashedly? The immediate answer is only oneself? And even then, we humans hide ourselves away from truths, and everybody lies. Some for good and true reasons, but many for evil, as if it's a pestilence of the mind.

What troubled Jude so much was not the reality that everyone lies and disseminates, but that she must live life questioning and doubting the actions and motives of others. That life required it of her, and her profession magnified the requirement. Trust was truly a double-edged sword that cut both ways. You must trust others to get by in life, and yet when trust was broken, like ending a relationship, it hurt like hell.

Later the same day, as darkness descends

Meriam had become a close lover and confidant for Jude, but tonight, Meriam could not be with her, something to do with her needing to hunker down at her own place and study for an exam. She was taking classes at the University of Chicago Extension campus, which amounted to a conference room in the local YMCA. It did not sound like the college experience that every young woman dreamed of, but Meriam said it was all that she could afford.

Jude, so taken with her new friend and partner, had toyed with the idea of helping her financially to reach her educational goals. She'd hinted at it after their last heart-pounding lovemaking had ended, after she had caught her breath, but Meriam, too proud to accept charity, had shut her down on the idea even before she could get to the word loan or the part about payback. Knowing that Meriam had refused her help in this regard made Jude sure of the other woman's love for her. She didn't want to muddy their relationship with debt. Knowing tonight that she'd not be seeing Meriam, Jude had phoned Dr. Griswold back, and saying not a word about the Tribune story, she asked if they might not get together again to discuss Poe and the dire business called immurement—walling someone into a death prison.

She half expected Griswald to beg off. She imagined he might prefer to hide from her after giving the Tribune reporter the gist of what they'd talked over during their last meeting. But he surprised her, agreeing to meet her over wine and a meal at Capone's, a distinctly Italian restaurant with a 'gangsta' theme. She thought it appropriate and assured the professor that it would be her treat.

"I don't get out much," he'd replied, hemming and hawing for a moment to add. "Not often given an invite from a pretty lady. All right, I'll do it."

She wanted to say that it wasn't a date, but she didn't wish to discourage him or have him change his mind for any reason. "Eight then. Shall I pick you up at the university?"

"No, no! I will be at Capone's and see you there."

She almost asked if he meant to bring his gun but decided not to. She could almost hear him over the connection salivating, and she wondered how long he'd gone without a good steak. Capone's was known for its filet mignon, and despite the garish photos lining the walls, the campiness had its charm. Shots of early Chicago crime and murder like the infamous photo of the aftermath of the St. Valentine's Massacre; multiple murders ordered up by Capone himself. Still, the quality of the cuisine was impeccable and unassailable.

After a quick stop at home and a necessary feeding of the cat, and an even more necessary shower from the day's work at the lab, she got to Capone's on time, again not wishing to wind up in the professor's excuse phone book! After parking her beater in the lot, and then entering the place, she had to pass a couple taking a selfie with a life-sized fiberglass replica of Al Capone himself. This Capone 'statue' was humorously short, but so was the real Capone. Short but replete with Spaatz shoes, a white-brimmed hat, Cuban cigar inside a wide grin, rotund stomach, barrel chest, and a glowing pair of popping-out-of-his-head eyes, one of them winking.

As Jude now entered the ristorante, a man in black, ostensibly the 'fuzz' or FBI snapped a photo with an old Polaroid. These shots were sold at the door immediately or later at the table by the wait staff who made annoying jokes, labeling one's photo with a gangsta nickname. Jude's was ready and forced on her as she was looking around for Griswald.

"Foxy," the FBI officer who looked to her like a high school kid. "Only six-fifty."

"Is that all?" She paid up and took the shot.

For Jude's taste, the Italian Capone's Ristorante proved a strange mix of no-class and class, or rather a lack of class on the one hand, while the food itself proved superior, first class. For this reason, people put up with the low social ambiance to get to the high payoff of the food itself. It were as if the message was in your face—you give Al respect if you wanna do business here!

Jude had read a review of the place once, and it described the ambiance in similar terms, adding that 'that's how the real Capone was! He killed anyone who didn't show him or his family respect.'

She found Dr. Griswald waiting in the semi-darkened entryway on a bench that had letters printed across its back reading 11th Precinct. Griswald leapt to his feet and warmly greeted Jude, and a hostess in a bunny-styled cocktail dress quickly seated them at a rear booth. The hostess graciously asked if they'd like to order drinks or wine before she should slip away, a nice touch.

They both agreed on the house favorite, a carafe of Rosa's Chablis. "One of Al's mistresses, Rosa" said the demure waitress to fill them in on this fact.

"Is Al here tonight?" asked Griswald? "I'd love to get an autograph." He chuckled at his own words.

The waitress played along. "His spirit is always here." She didn't miss a beat. "So you may get that autograph, sir, you and your daughter."

"Oh, no, I mean, she's not—"

But the waitress had moved away too fast for Griswald to correct her wrong assumption. Almost as quickly as the hostess had disappeared, a waitress calling herself Rosa came to the table with the pink-red wine and some bruschetta to whet the appetite. They soon ordered, and as Jude had expected, the professor ordered the most expensive item in the way of steak on the menu. Jude gave in and made it two filet mignons.

While they awaited the meal, sipping at the wine and dipping the bread in oil and having a bite, the conversation moved toward what Jude had come for. "I've learned one thing about you, Dr. Griswald. That is, you can't be trusted."

"I am not surprised to hear you say so."

"No one at this table should be surprised. I had not thought it necessary on our first meeting to swear you to secrecy. That our talk should remain…confidential. But I am asking that tonight that you respect that condition."

"I was approached, offered a chance to discuss what was already general knowledge, the two bodies found in the subway." He shrugged as if it was nothing.

"Promise me no more reports in the newspapers. It very nearly cost me my job."

"I do not understand why it—"

"It just is, Dr. Griswald. Respect my wishes."

He pulled at his goatee, nodding. "I will respect your wishes."

"At a future time, I may ask that you go right ahead and speak to whomever whenever about the case, but that time is not now."

"I see, ha! And you think you can buy me off with a steak dinner." The old professor laughed, but it was not malicious, rather lilting in fact. "And you can!"

"So, will you promise?"

"You're seriously worried about what an old man has to say to the press in Chicago? Rather quaint."

"I'm new in town, remember? Will you please humor me?"

"Promise you this?"

"Yes, please."

"All right already. I promise."

"Promise me what?" she turned the tables on him. "Exactly what're you promising? I want to hear it."

"I said that I promise, and you have my word—"

"You can make the promise, but can you keep the promise?"

"Yes, damn it, I can."

"Say it then."

"Say what then?"

"Say all the words necessary to calm my fears, sir."

"I promise to keep our talks private—between you and me alone."

She breathed a deep sigh. "Was that so hard?"

"Apparently, yes. Thanks to your bullying, Dr. Avery."

She paused, listening to the sound of Mario Caruso himself, singing a heart-wrenching love-gone-bad Italian melody from the days of Al Capone's reign of terror in Chicago. Then she realized the extent of the entertainment: the music was piped in to accompany a 3-D hologram of Caruso on a small stage at the other end of the restaurant. She pointed this surprising feature out to Professor Griswald, who turned in his seat to watch, mesmerized.

"How they so easily bring back the dead nowadays."

"No one is safe from being disinterred."

"Appears so."

"Not anymore. So why not exhume Poe's body for modern analysis?"

"Ha! To determine if that thing rattling around in his skull can be determined a stone or a calcified brain tumor?" he asked.

"Stone? Tumor?"

"Edgar was exhumed some twenty-seven years after his death."

"I didn't see that anywhere in my readings, but then who's had time to scour everything on Poe?"

"You can be forgiven. It's a cryptic report about one of the workers who helped in the exhumation."

"But who had him exhumed and why?"

"Baltimore."

"The city or the Lord?"

"The city decided after those many years that their by-then legendary literary hero needed a decent stone marker and burial, so the ceremony was on. In moving the body, by then hardly more than a set of bones."

"I see."

"One the workers reportedly said to a reporter that there was a solidified item inside the skull. There was no brain left—"

"First organ to decay."

"So, what was it the man heard 'rattling around' in Edgar's head."

"Rattling around? That's how he described it."

"Are you suggesting that Poe died of a brain tumor?"

"I am, and he may have been living with it for some time, but if he'd taken a blow to the area where the tumor resided, who knows what actually killed the man?"

"Cooping atop the tumor, you mean?"

"It is suggested, yes."

Their meals arrived, and the conversation stopped as they enjoyed their steaks and sides. Jude had no memory of seeing a man enjoy a meal as the professor did now. She got the impression that it would be unsafe to disturb him until after he'd devoured everything on his plate. So, she focused on her own meal.

After they had both filled themselves and sat back, going back to their wine and pouring from the carafe for them both. "That was a fantastic meal," Griswald said as he dabbed at his lips and chin. "Thank you."

"The food here is all that it's cracked up to be."

"Indeed. Now, back to Edgar and the mysteries around his death."

"I'm waiting," she replied.

"Poe's death has left us with a mystery that has lingered for more than a century."

"No death certificate seems unusual."

"May or may not have been filed, a possible oversight."

"Or some sort of devious plot to have someone else buried in his name, while he returned to Paris and lived out his life there in exile?"

"You truly have been scouring the conspiracy theories. It would've taken quite a few people to make Edgar a 'disappearing' act."

"Just saying, no death certificate—even in his day they were routinely filed."

"Meanwhile, the local newspapers in more than one city he called home reported Edgar's cause of death as 'congestion of the brain,' a well-worn euphemism for alcohol poisoning in his day."

"I have to tell you that I came across a bit of shock in my research on your Edgar."

"I suspect your stumbling on the fact that shortly after Edgar's death, a certain Rufus Griswald, Poe's literary rival, wrote an obituary characterizing Poe as a morally bankrupt, drunken womanizer. I should have forewarned you of my ancestral tie to Edgar."

"You're related then to the Griswald who wrote the first biography of Poe?"

The small man across from her toasted with his wine. "It should matter not a whit, and as to my great-grandfather' father, well his biased portrait these days only forms the basis of Poe's image in the public mind at large, and those who benefit from Poe being an addicted and afflicted soul, a huge exaggeration, most likely."

"Kind of like that awful red and black labeled wine that has an image of Edgar on the label, you mean?"

"We have to thank real scholars, who have corrected the image created by Rufus Griswald, who I loathe although, of course, I've never actually met my ancestor." He paused to laugh at this. "But I know the man well enough to ignore his assessment of Edgar. Myself, I believe scholars who came later."

"Who've concluded that Griswald's version of Poe's debauchery was highly exaggerated."

"Precisely. Aside from alcoholism, historians and biographers have suggested alternative causes of Edgar's death. These range from lesions on the brain, epilepsy and tuberculosis to cholera, syphilis and even rabies. He had a cat, after all, and rats abounded in US cities then."

"As now," she said, recalling what Sybil Shanley had said of Chicago's rats. "What do you make of the cooping theory?"

"Another popular theory…holds that Poe may've been a victim of so-called cooping, yes. A common practice at the time."

"Supporters of the cooping theory point to Poe's unfamiliar and ill-fitting clothes," she challenged Griswald. "As well as the fact that citywide elections were being held in Baltimore the very day he was found."

"True, yes, and furthermore, he was found at an Irish pub that functioned as both a bar and a voting station."

"So that too is a possibility, that he was force-fed alcohol to the point of poisoning or destroying vital organs, liver, pancreas, vessels."

"In my family, another story has been handed down through the generations, Dr. Avery."

"Really? A story handed down?"

"Through the generations, yes; a different one indeed, one that could have been written by Edgar himself, but Rufus Griswald wrote it first."

"Enlighten me."

"I said story, but in fact, it is a confession. A deathbed confession."

"Go on, sir."

Dr. Griswald leaned back in the booth and breathed deeply, as if more oxygen was needed to get this 'confession' underway.

"Our family story has Edgar and Rufus absolutely at one another's throats."

"I saw something regarding their literary rivalry."

"Literary rivalry, yes, but even more so literal hatred; hatred over large matters like money and reputation. Who got the editor's ear, who got the cover of a magazine, whose story was featured, and only then to the mundane matters."

"Such as?" she asked.

"Such as their very penmanship. Frankly, as it has been told many times to me, Edgar needed Poe to hate, as hate kept him interested in this world, and Poe was also feeding on this personal animosity to the level of…well like Ahab's hatred of the white whale."

"Jesus, that bad, eh?"

"Each time either of them published, the other would write a scathing and brutal review of the other's work. It meant nothing if either man lied as long as he crippled the story and the pen—ahh, reputation behind it."

"That sounds so very petty for men of…of genius."

Griswald laughed at this. "My dear, Dr. Avery, the brain is an old house with many additions built onto it. Since when does anyone, however talented or skilled, control their OCD or madness?"

"Wild-horse emotions, my dad called them. So a buckets of bad blood between them."

"This was bad ink, and of course, both men had ink coursing through their veins."

"So, what is this family story? Does it have a plot?"

"It is a tragedy like Hamilton and Burr, the two men simply could not abide the sight of one another. I mean to the point of perversion. Could not abide knowing they were in the same orbit of acquaintances, vying for the same opportunities in the field of letters."

"Letters?"

"Books, publishing, my dear."

"Ahh, yes. I kinda get it too, and I like that turn of phrase, that the other was in his orbit, on this planet."

"Finally, as it was told to me by my father, and he by his father before that Rufus Griswald, and not a politician, paid the hooligans at this Irish pub to snatch Edgar and give him a good, thorough cooping treatment. In other words—"

"To not spare the booze."

"Correct, you are, Dr. Avery."

"But then, did your ancestor, did he mean to kill Poe in this fashion? Intent, I mean to say."

"I think he would've liked to've had Poe boxed up or walled in like one of Poe's stories. But no, as the tale is told, he'd felt great remorse on learning of Edgar's death only days after this insidious conspiracy had unfolded against Poe."

"So there's the plot, but to be clear, are you saying that Griswald's intention was merely to disgrace the man?"

"He called the local newspaper to tell them and Snodgrass where to find Poe."

"And if the papers picked it up, that he was aimlessly wandering the streets in a full-blown state of inebriation, in those days…"

"Why then Rufus's star would rise with the publishers, while Poe's would drop precipitously, as his disgraceful, public show of alcoholism could well put a final end to Edgar's career."

"But if he felt remorse, and Rufus hadn't intended the kidnapping plot to end in Edgar's death…then why does Griswald stand for the eulogy just to-to condemn the hell out of Poe before the coffin?"

"No, no! He did not attend a wake or the burial. He made his eulogy an open letter in the literary opinion page of the local paper to figuratively brick up Edgar in a wall, to do more than merely disgrace Poe publicly on his time, but to wall him off from future generations of readers. Rufus believed that in doing so, that he himself would be remembered far longer than his literary rival."

"I see, after all, he was a model of morality, eh? But he didn't figure on Poe's immorality that Rufus himself had exaggerated to result in even more fascination with Edgar as a fascinating and complex author and poet, heralded rather than despised."

"Backfired, and had the opposite effect, his petty plans."

"Exactly, thanks to readers who love the lurid tales of Poe's life as much as the stories he's left for eternity. Good heavens, readers to this day, do not shun the man with the gothic and dark reputation. Instead, they cannot get enough of Edgar and his work,"

"People, even kids intent on video games, they do eat his works up, so to speak." Jude covered her empty plate with her black cloth napkin.

"Ironic, yes. Karma, I'd say."

"But sir, can you…do you believe the story passed down through your family is true?"

"It's part of my heritage; yes, of course, I believe it happened thusly. Edgar had problems, health issues plaguing him, and he was sick to begin with, so my ancestor sped up an inevitable death likely by many years. The cooping episode was the catalyst to an abrupt end to the genius."

"I've known a few geniuses, and I find there is one type that cannot stand being made the fool of. Nor can he abide a competitor getting the upper hand."

He laughed lightly as if struck by a memory. "Some of my students, for instance who must at all costs arrive at the answer to a question first."

"Fascinating to hear your family's tale."

"Frankly, we normally keep it under wraps. Who would believe it? That sort of thing."

"You should consider writing a book about it, Professor."

"Who has time? Besides, who'd believe it?"

"I think I do."

"Really, on hearing it for the first time?" Griswald appeared genuinely shocked.

"The thing you said about Griswald wanting to box him up, coffin him in, wall him up, sounds, well, rings true."

"Yes, well he was by all accounts a sour, bitter, and vindictive soul."

"I've had cases like that wherein a man is filled to the brim with hatred for his divorced wife, or two neighbors hating on one another to the core for years, until awful things happen. I interviewed this man who killed his next-door neighbor, and all he felt was the void left then with the object of his hate gone! The murderer missed the common bond of hate they shared—like a rope or lifeline that staved off depression and boredom so long as each was pulling at his end of the rope."

"Until the rope unraveled, they had a mutual hatred society going…hatred nurtured for years."

"Not just the imprisoned killer, but the hatred displayed by the dead victim as well."

"As if trapped in the allure of it all—this undeniable emotion."

She nodded solemnly. "Seems they hold a mirror to one another, the hater and hated stuck in a cycle like a revolving door."

"We do not study this emotion—hatred—enough in this world, scientifically, I mean in order to understand its depth and power over a man or a woman."

"Hell hath no such fury, yeah." She paused only a moment. "Tell me, what do you know about this immurement punishment? Where did Poe get this dark idea from, which apparently Griswald knew of too."

"Vestal Virgins in the Roman Empire faced immurement as punishment when they were found guilty of breaking their chastity vows. That's how far back it goes."

"Rome, really?"

"Immurement was a well-established punishment for thieves in Persia, and as late as the twentieth century, some ambiguous evidence exists of the practice of coffin-type confinement in Mongolia."

"Really?"

"Isolated incidents of it, not continuous traditions to be sure, and yet, it finds its way back. It's attested or alleged from numerous other parts of the world as surfacing, and some of these notable incidents are included in Shakespeare and other early writers' works that Poe would surely have read."

"I see, and so too Rufus Griswald."

He nodded, nursing his glass of wine as if it were his last. "Instances of immurement as an element of massacre, you know, within the context of war, or revolution, are documented. Immuring living persons as a type of human sacrifice is also reported, for example, as part of grand burial ceremonies in some cultures."

Jude took a deep breath, while picturing a line of sacrificial people. Rather than enjoying a quick end with sprayed bullets, they're marched into a wall to be shackled and bricked over. Just then Dr. Griswald continued lecturing her. "As a motif in legends and folklore, many tales of immurement exist. In the folklore, immurement is prominent as a form of capital punishment, but its use as a type of human sacrifice to make buildings sturdy—"

"Hold on, to make something like the pyramids sturdy?"

"In the sense that the gods would then bless the structure, yes— brick some poor devil up in its walls."

"And there's evidence of this practice in Egypt as well?"

"There've been many tales of skeletal remains having been, from time-to-time, found behind walls and in hidden rooms and on several occasions remains found in such a condition, yes, and it points to the practice."

"Assertions or fact?"

"Hard evidence of such sacrificial practices exists, as does the use of this form of punishment."

"Wonder how much it accounts for all those people who go missing without a trace."

"Like your two victims found in the subway, yes. They must surely have had family and friends who knew it was odd that they'd fallen off the face of the earth. If you wish to give me a ride back to the university, my office, I can provide you with some books on the subject— homework, as it were."

She nodded at the suggestion and having covered the bill on the table with cash and an ample tip, they left Capone's. Outside, they located her car in the lot under the orange glow of sodium vapor lights. Another indication that the city had for too long let her infrastructure go. The drive to the University of Chicago held each of them silent, quiet with their own thoughts. Jude went over all he'd said at the restaurant, imaging it out in her head.

11

Once ensconced in the old professor's semi-darkened office, Dr. Griswald went about his shelves in search of specific items for her to borrow, insisting they were out of print and invaluable to no one but him, and that she must return them once finished with them. After stacking several books on her lap, he opened a huge old dictionary that sat on a pedestal in his office, the sort of thing Jude had only seen once before, in a library run by Catholic Nuns just off the military base where she was a resident for a time, as her father'd been stationed there—Fort Bragg, North Carolina.

Griswald began reading from the enormous dictionary, saying, "Immurement, from the Latin im for IN and murus for WALL, literally wall in or a walling in. A well-used form of punishment in ancient times, and not at all the same as being buried alive—wherein you died of asphyxiation, relatively quickly. While a coffin might be used, it was actually more humane punishment, rather than encasing someone in a wall. In the walled off area, death came far slower with starvation and dehydration."

"Yes, well that much we learned from the autopsy and common sense."

"Science and common sense run along the same course."

"Aye, they do. Much of it."

"Well, I thank you for the ride back and your ear. I've never wholly shared the family secret. I've never revealed it to anyone else—have no children to curse with it." He laughed.

"Perhaps a good thing," Jude suggested.

"Perhaps, yes, and perhaps your suggestion that I write a book on the matter is a good idea. Would be a rather thin volume, but there is no end in sight to the Poe mystery."

"And if your title and maybe sub-title hinted at a final answer to the mystery of his death, who knows. Could be a bestseller." Jude stood, three of his books in hand, and said, "I'll see you home."

"Oh no, I walk from here. It's not far, and I need the exercise to walk off that scrumptious meal."

"So, you live hereby in Hyde Park. Rather dangerous, the entire South Side, by day much less by night."

"I'm a fixture here. No one bothers with an old English professor. Ha!"

Jude caught the slight hint at the depth of his self-denigration, and she wondered just how badly this so-called Griswald curse had harmed the little man. She stifled her curiosity over the question and instead bid him goodnight and a hearty thank you, when she saw his hand go up as if to stop her, but it went to his side as fast as it'd risen overhead in a gesture that seemed to say wait.

"Is there something else, Dr. Griswald?"

"Perhaps, I will take that ride you offered, after all." He signaled his stomach. "Rather imagine I over-indulged."

The entire way to the car, Griswald looked nervously about as if seeking something in the dark, reaching-out-at-you shadows that colored the nighttime campus. A huge oak cast a monstrous shadow across the parking lot. "I should think by 2021 that they'd have improved the lighting on a campus this size on the South Side of Chicago."

"Talk is all they do around here."

She realized only now that he was clutching to what appeared a crumpled note in his right hand. It made her wonder anew at his sudden about-face on taking the ride home. She again asked if he was okay as they entered the car. He seemed a man either on the verge of a heart attack or was suffering the aftereffects of a meal not well received in the digestive tract. "Acid reflux?" she asked. "I have some pills in my purse."

"No, no. Not that."

"I can feel your sudden agitation, sir."

"I just…well. It's bad news. A note left on my desk in my absence."

Jude had seen neither the note nor his reaction to it. "Oh, sorry to hear that. If there's anything I can do…" she let the sentiment linger. "Family?"

"No, no. I have none. I am the last of the line."

"Yes, of course." He'd earlier confessed to having no children. "Troubling news from one of your students, then?"

"Could be, that is…yes, unsure."

"You're unsure who the note is from? Perhaps that reporter, Louise what's-her-face."

"I don't wish to pursue it further, Dr. Avery. Please, it's merely about my rent."

She knew a lie when she heard one. His tone and tenor gave him away. "Tell me where to turn." After a moment's silence, he replied, "Left at the next stop sign."

"I would've thought you'd own rather than rent." She tried to make small talk.

"I invested badly and did worse in planning for my retirement years."

"I see. Sorry to hear it, sir."

"Had I been wiser, more prudent, I'd have better circumstances now, and to make matters worse, the chancellor, the board, and the president are all urging my retirement."

"But you're the chairman and needed in the department," she replied, trying to buck him up.

"They want me out. End of story. Want it official out, Jude—may I call you, Jude?"

"Yes, of course."

"That leaves me with a single cheque drawing social security."

"What about your retirement income?"

"None, as I failed to participate in the retirement program here. I am one who earns and spends." He shrugged and pointed to the curb, saying, "Pull here.

Griswald groaned as he climbed from the car and made his way up the steps to a two-flat where window lights beckoned. Although he never turned, Jude waved him off. Again, she noticed his clutched hand with the crumpled note in it as it went into his coat pocket.

Jude pulled away from the curb and abruptly hit her breaks as she watched a black cat casually walk across the path of her car. She wondered for a moment if the old superstition about a black cat crossing one's path tallied the same if you were in a car when it occurred. It'd been a long day, and she was anxious to get home and find some respite from the day. While Dr. Griswald proved an interesting character, a third-rate Obi-wan Kenobi character, she found him both fascinating and tiring at the same time. But for now, she just wanted to get home and free her mind of all worry.

The following day at the Cook County Coroner's Office

There remained much to do with the couple from the subway walls in terms of tests for toxins and identifying clues from the collected DNA. The picture of the couple in the tintype, which had seemed at the time of discovery a great and useful find below the corseted corpse had instead only emerged as a mystery within a mystery, as the tintype technology was a hundred years old by 1947.

Still, if the people in the photo were from her family, it could eventually help. Were they her parents, maybe even her grandparents? The couple in the photo both stood in the range of five feet four inches, typical for men and women of the day, as even a six-foot fellow back then would have been considered unusual, a giant even. Abraham Lincoln, during his entire presidency, was considered freakishly tall, a giant. Of course, the stove-top hat only added to the image, but most men of European and Irish and Scottish ancestry were in the range of five four to five six or seven at best.

Jude and Sybil determined color of skin and eyes as well. He was blue-eyed and she brown. They were both of Scottish heritage according to their DNA, not at all unusual for early Chicago days. The couple were close in age, approximately early twenties, with their whole lives ahead of them. More and more, the 'wall people', as the couple were being called, became the couple in the tintype—at least this was so for Jude.

"So much pathos."

"What's that?" asked Sybil of Jude.

"She had their picture on her person when placed in the wall, that picture of herself with him. It was no doubt her only solace if it could be called that." Jude imagined Jane Doe being walled in, deep darkness ascending with the last brick, her last opportunity to look at the tintype before she could only clutch it to her breast until her dying breath.

"Whatever is going through your mind, Jude? You seem a million miles away."

"Silly thoughts, I guess."

"What kind of silly thoughts? What with us holding scalpels over this desiccated body on your slab?"

"You'll think me foolish."

"When have I not thought you foolish?"

"All right, here's what's playing in my head." With that, Jude shared her thoughts on Jane and John Doe as lovers, newlyweds in the photo."

"But that doesn't jive with the timeline at all."

"I know, but what if—imagine if they'd just gone to Maxwell Street or some carnival and the only photos taken were throwbacks, tintypes? What if someone was still using the old technology?"

"You are going to have me contemplating writing a gothic novel based on this case, this Doe family. A lurid novel with an even more lurid cover. Not for forensic journals," she said emphatically, but for a sensational, juicy novel of love and hate that'll be a bestseller."

From Sybil's tone alone, Jude believed Sybil to be less than serious, and thus asked, smirking, if she had a title for the story.

"Dying Breath, of course."

"A real bodice-ripper, eh?"

"Exactly."

"Good luck with it."

"And you, Jude? You've been taking copious notes on your tablet."

"Yes, so? I always do in every case."

"Come on, you're planning to write the case up for Forensics Today or a medical journal, right?"

"Okay, yes, I've been giving it serious thought, but will have to see."

"It is an unusual case; enough to catch the attention of any editor."

"On that much we can agree."

"Frankly, I prefer writing fiction."

"And you do it so well, Sybil."

"To do a work of the imagination hundreds of pages as opposed to six or seven of factual material. I've had to write journal entries, but oh how that bores me, although I read as much as I can."

"To stay current, yes. As to imaginative work, maybe I should try that some time; however, hundreds of pages sounds daunting—perhaps too daunting."

"Not if you take it one step—one scene at a time."

"Really? You don't plan it out till the end? I thought mystery writers write to a preconceived ending, the end scene!"

"No, never." Sybil had written and published a few short stories.

"How then do you know where you're going?"

"I don't—so neither does the reader. That's how it works for me—organically grown from scene one and on it flourishes."

"Creativity—fascinating thing in itself."

"Speaking of creativity," said Ralph, carrying an Apple computer over to them and flashing the image on the screen. It was a 3-D image of the finally completed facial features built over Jane City Hall Doe's skull. Dr. Louise Stroud had done a remarkable and stepped-up job, and she'd not been given a copy of the woman in the tintype to work from, as that would unduly influence the results.

"It's her—our mystery lady in the old photo."

"Hmmm…not quite, I'd have to say, Jude." Sybil looked up at Ralph. "What do you say, Ralph? Is there a resemblance?"

Ralph was slow to answer. "Could be her, but maybe not. Hard to say."

"Don't want to blunt your enthusiasm, Jude, but I think Stroud's bust and the face in the tintype are two separate ladies."

Jude, with Ralph's help, had gotten the male skull to Dr. Louise Stroud only yesterday. It seemed a near sure thing that the second skull would be reconstructed in the image of the man in the photo to Jude's way of thinking. But now she wondered if it hadn't been wishful thinking. Still, no way to be certain until the man's skull was finished by the artist at Quantico. "What do you bet Stroud's been rushed by the governor and the mayor here, and maybe Dean as well, and a rushed job, it could be off."

"Accept it, Jude, the tintype is of another woman, and so…likely another man as well."

Jude immediately responded to Dr. Stroud's email and attachment, thanking her profusely, and adding, "Please send us finished work on the female skull as soon as possible, as we are in hot pursuit of identifying family members who may have additional documents and photos to match her, as we are in the process of link-DNA analysis with the deceased."

Jude had ordered the link-DNA analysis for both the male and the female in an attempt to locate descendants rather than long-dead ascendants, ancestors. This was done in the hope that Jane and John of City Hall had a family story—like Griswald's—to the degree that a pair of family members had disappeared without a trace."

"Way back when," Sybil had said of the plan to use the links.

"Way back in the tree branches." Jude noted again the uncanny re-created features, regardless of the ill-fit to the photo found below the corseted victim. The work of a true sculptor, Dr. Stroud, working from the skull up. "I so admire that talent," she said to Sybil and Ralph, who'd remained mesmerized and looking over Jude's shoulder at the image of the deceased young woman.

"Dr. Grant's going to wanna see this," Ralph put in.

"Yeah, sure. Run a copy and get it to him, please."

"You got it, doctor."

"Dean'll take it up the chain to the mayor," Jude said. "Maybe if they put the image out on the nightly news, we'll get lucky and someone will recognize her."

"Meanwhile, fingers crossed on finding a match with the ancestry plan."

"Link-DNA searches have caught killers hiding among us, it's reunited countless siblings and family, but this would be a first, I think—kind of using it in reverse."

"Searching through the living to find the dead, yes, rather than the other way around."

"Your old professor friend, Griswald, would likely find this search of great interest." Sybil said and smiled wickedly at Jude, teasingly so.

"I've not told you of his latest revelation—that he is in fact a descendant of a man who may well have been responsible for Edgar Allan Poe's death."

"He told you that?"

"He believes it with his every fiber. Says he may write a book on the story."

"And he shared the story with you?"

"He did."

"You must be a charmer. Still, you do realize he could just as well be making ahhh, make-believe for an audience of one—you!"

"It's a compelling narrative, and he only told me about it because I had discovered his namesake was in fact a chief rival to Poe."

"Rival, just how? In drinking? Bingeing?"

"No, not at all; they were hardly drinking buddies."

"What then?"

"They appear to've been in a kind of literary war between them-selves."

"Sounds interesting, but Jude, we both know people who've spent their entire human capital on one fixation."

"Like Dr. Griswald, you mean?"

"Like an author whose every book is to push one agenda."

"Like for instance?"

"Justice, rule of law, death to evil, end times—"

"Not sure I follow you, Sybil."

"Damn, like for instance, you ever go to one of those Comic Cons?"

"No, should I?"

"No, you miss the point. Okay, for that matter a Horror Writers of America gathering—where everyone is vying for an Edgar, no wait—that's the Mystery Writers of America award? A goofy-looking, playful statue of Poe."

"I don't see what—"

"Let me finish. I go down to the vendors room and art dealers are there, and the trinket and ring sellers, and once there, I swear you will find the most OCD people on the planet, people who make a living off stuff like Jack-the-Ripper exclusively—an entire kiosk and every item within has to do with Jack this and Jack that from a beach towel to a cigarette lighter, books, films, music—all Jack shit, understand?"

"And you think Griswald's preoccupation with Poe is the same thing?"

Sybil didn't slow to answer. "And-and even make-believe people and monsters, another booth will cover—I dunno, Sherlock Holmes, or all Frankenstein; zombies here, vampires there, and the Werewolf at the next—from paintings to toothbrushes—vampire toothbrushes."

"Sybil, I think your comparison is skewed. You write mystery, crime stories and horror."

"Skewed, eh? And you don't think Griswald is fixated on Poe after all you've told me about the man?"

"All professors of literature have their concentration—Emerson or Hawthorne or Hemingway or Faulkner."

"Or Victor Hugo or Dickens. I know that, but to be so fixated as to believe oneself a kin of Poe."

"No, he did not claim kinship to Poe, but to the man who did Poe in, and it was kind of sad, how he told it."

"Sad, really? How sad?"

"Imagine yourself having to live a life then of remorse over the actions of an ancestor?"

"I think we can all relate to that!"

"Sybil, you can be so exhausting at times."

"The famous author Nathaniel Hawthorne could relate. He did it."

"Whatever are you talking about?" asked Jude.

"His grandfather hung witches at Salem, 1692. Changed his name, added an E at the end to distance himself from the direct line. Refused to accept guilt by association, and yet he seems to have himself done so."

"That proves my point," Jude said, smiling.

"How so?"

"Here was a man who was not fixated on his family history—made a change!" Jude hosed down the floor around her slab. Then she added, "Look, I kind of like Oswald Griswald." Jude thought of the night before, how much she had enjoyed the professor's conversation and company. Her last thought was seeing him go up those stairs gingerly, creakily to his empty flat just off campus. There was a sad element about the fellow, but he seemed to come alive when the subject was Edgar.

Sybil nodded appreciatively at Jude's final words on the subject of Griswald. She begged off, saying she had some things to clear off her desk, and she left Jude's side in the lab, returning to her nearby office. Jude realized it had grown late, and given the short fall days in Chicago, it was already getting dark outside as well. She felt a stir of sexual desire rise in her as she and Meriam had earlier spoken on the phone, agreeing to a night out and a romp afterwards. Romp had become their euphemism for making wild, unbridled love to one another. To make it even more tantalizing, their shared lovemaking had the 'feel' of unequivocal, unconditional caring for one another's needs.

Sybil had, earlier in the day, noticed a change in Jude and had then asked about the spring in her step and the glow in her eyes, but Jude was not at all ready to confide in Sybil about her newfound love. As these thoughts tumbled about her mind, and as she was de-gowning and tossing protective medical gloves and other items into a bin destined for the incinerator, Sybil rushed back in, gasping and saying, "Sorry to be the bearer of bad news, Jude, but it's Dr. Griswald—medics were called out by his landlord. Found dead. Possible suicide. Pills scattered everywhere."

"No! It can't be. I-I just saw him last night."

"I'm sorry, dear." Sybil hugged her. "Damn, bad things happen."

"No, he-he had plans. We talked about his doing a book on his family history, the connection with Poe, and how he could prove it. Why then kill himself?"

Sybil put her at arm's distance and stared into her eyes. "Jude, he set you up for a fall, this old man."

"What're you talking about?"

"Go on google. Search his name. He has done all manner of articles and papers on Poe, enough to make a book, and he's gone on about that connection he believes his family has with Poe, and he's often revealed that story to the world, and he lied to you about it. Must've given him some perverse pleasure to do so."

"It can't be."

"The story, the same one he told you; told you he'd told no one else."

Jude pulled away, stunned. "I guess I am the fool. But why lie to me about it? And you, Sybil, why didn't you tell me?"

"I didn't know how, and I didn't know you were going back to see him again, and damned if I knew he was a candidate for suicide."

"Mark Twain was right. We have two enemies in this world. The one who talks behind your back, and the other who runs in to tell you."

"That's not fair. Besides, I didn't rush in to tell you."

Jude stormed out and went to her office. She dialed the central nervous system of the coroner's Office—the switchboard, it was still called. Where all in-coming and out-going calls originated. "When did the call for a man named Oswald Griswald come in?"

"Half an hour ago. Medical unit from Rush-Presbyterian Hospital called us as they wished to take the body to holding at their morgue until someone told them otherwise."

"Was the transportation green lighted?"

"No, Dr. Grant's at the scene still."

"Contact him; tell him I'm on my way."

"Yes, doctor."

"Tell him to hold the body."

"Will do."

◆　◆　◆

Jude's hands shook as she drove to the professor's flat, a block off the university campus. When she turned onto the small cull-d-sac, she saw the coroner's van—and leaning against it, Noble and his crew in various stages of boredom and smoking. How is it that man still has a job, she wondered.

Nearby, she saw Grant's black sedan. When she got out of her car, a used Mazda 2, Noble's people, Lisa in particular, turned their backs on her passing, none giving her the least respect. Luther flicked his cigarette butt onto the pavement just ahead of her. Obviously, Grant had given them a talking to for all the good it would do. So far as Jude knew, none in the unit had owned up to having robbed Jane 'City Hall' Doe. Instead, they had lawyered up and were being backed up by their union rep.

Jude went up the steps, recalling how difficult these stairs had been for Griswald, but then he'd had a few drinks at dinner. She stopped at the porch, turned, and realized she could see the professor's office from here. The row of houses faced the campus like a line of sentries. The windows like so many eyes looking over the greenery of a campus that could well be used as backdrop in a Harry Potter film.

She turned and entered the place of death, her heart heavy.

Inside, she hailed Grant who said, "You shouldn't be here, Jude. I tried to get word to stop you from coming. Sybil called me, told me you have a connection with the deceased. Our policy for years disbars you from having anything to do with a case in which you have a personal connection to, or interest in, a victim."

"Victim, then you've determined he didn't kill himself?"

"Victim of suicide or homicide is what I mean. We don't know yet. Sybil tells me you were fond of the old gent."

"He was helping me with the Jane City Hall case."

"Really?"

"He's…he was a Poe expert. I was picking his brain for…for help in understanding Poe's fixation on walling people—characters in his stories—up in walls."

"You'd best leave the scene, Jude—for sake of policy and your well-being."

"Dean, Dr. Grant, do you think it was suicide?"

"Too soon to tell. We'll know more after autopsy. He has a number of bruises, but he was found sprawled on the hardwood floor, as if slipped from his easy chair."

Jude was surprised at how neat everything in the flat was. Everything had a place, all squared off and relatively sparsely furnished, but nothing like the chaos of the man's office.

Grant was saying and Jude half hearing, "I've asked Sybil to stay late; she and I will make those determinations as quickly as we can. But the old fellow, Jude, well, he left a suicide note."

"Oh, I see. Typed on that old Remington?"

He turned to look at the aged typewriter. "No, no ribbon on that thing. I shouldn't be talking to you about any of this, but the note is in cursive."

"Hmmm, handwritten…"

"And ahhh, he mentions you in it, Jude, the note, so…another reason for you to go home tonight. Take your time to take all this in."

"Mentions me? In the note?"

"I would not make that up."

"Yeah, sure, okay but what did he say about me in the damn note?"

"He said he was sorry that he'd had sexual fantasies about you, something of that sort." This hit her like an anvil; at the same time, Grant blushed as he said the words. This resulted in her flashing on her boss as an old-time conservative cowboy actor in his not wishing to upset the little lady.

"That truly doesn't sound like the man I interviewed twice. Before that, I did not know him. What two, three days ago?"

"You really need to get out of here, Jude. Policy, like I said."

She wanted to lash out at this policy, so she lashed out at him instead. "Looks like you have Luther Noble on the run. How can you trust that he didn't produce the note?"

"Not sure he can spell or write."

"Lisa and the others can write, right? And they act in lock-step." She then stormed out, paused, glared at Noble, came back down the steps, and marched to her car, as Noble and his 'guys' laughed, as if overjoyed about her having been ousted from the scene.

Jude backed her car down the street, cut into a driveway, and executed a three-point turn and raced away for the university. It occurred to her that she wanted a sheaf of paper with the professor's handwriting on it. Then it hit her. The crumpled note the old fellow had jammed into his coat pocket. Where was that coat now, and was the note still inside the left pocket?

Parked in the campus lot, she quickly pulled her iPhone to eye-level and dialed Grant. He came on and was fussing that she must 'go away' when she shouted him down. "The oxford sports coat he wore last night! There should be a note in the pocket, outside left. He was upset by whatever was on that note."

"Oh, I guess." Grant paused. "There, back of the couch—fallen."

"The note?"

"Give me a moment." Dean took enough of a moment, before saying, "Ahh, have it, but it's crushed into a ball. Hold on."

"Tweezer it open. It has to have prints on it other than his."

"I know how to handle potential evidence, Dr. Avery."

"Then please, read it aloud to me."

"Not policy."

Fuck policy, she wanted to scream at her boss. "Dean, come on, please. This is me."

He paused then began reading. "I will strike tonight in the name of The Raven."

"Raven, the Raven—another aka for Poe." Jude then added, "Dean, compare the handwriting to the suicide note."

As he paused to do as she suggested, Jude slid from the car and leaned in over the hood, waiting for what felt like an eternity."

During this long pause, a chilling wind hit her, foretelling of the coming winter. Young people hurried between buildings even now, this late. Finally, Grant came back online. "They look similar, but we'd need to run them by Sheila Lowe to be sure."

"I know enough about graphology, Dr. Grant, to tell you tonight if it's the same hand or not."

"How many times do I hafta tell you, Judith, you're not on this case."

Jude recognized the name; Lowe was an expert on handwriting analysis. "All right, but I'll get more examples of Griswald's handwriting for Sheila to work with."

"Your help in such a way could taint the investigation, don't you understand? It's nothing personal. All the same, did the old guy share any handwritten documents with you?"

"Yes," she lied, justifying this with the assumption she'd have something from his office in five minutes.

"Handwritten?"

"Yes." Minimal lie, soon to be a truth.

12

Jude Avery hung up on her boss and rushed to Griswald's office, hoping the corridors would be empty this time of night, and they were. The office door surprised her, as it stood unlocked and slightly ajar. She wondered if this was normal, a lock issue or something amiss? As Griswald would surely have locked up on leaving, and yet she did not recall his pausing to do so when they'd left together the night before.

She cautiously entered, one hand on her pepper spray. Of course, without the professor in his office, at his desk, sipping hot tea, the place was an eerie, dark cave. And the cave made her feel in danger, as if someone were here in the darkest corner, watching her. Just paranoia, she told herself, her thoughts fighting back. She couldn't find the wall switch for a light, so she rushed to the desk, lit the old reading lamp, and took a breath, still clutching the pepper spray. Unlike Sybil, she did not wear her service gun on her everywhere she went.

The lamplight helped, throwing the office into a semi-light, but at the same time, the areas where the light did not reach seemed to've become in sharper darkness still. There seemed a fight between light and dark all around her.

Corners of blackness that she'd not noticed when Griswald was in this room with her. Two previous nights in this same weak light that now appeared portals into an abyss prepared to swallow her up. Odd how light and dark worked on the mind, she thought, but she got busy searching for some instance of Griswald's handwriting. In action, much of the sense of being in a haunted office, the place where the dead man had spent most of his last years. This pushed her to rush in her search, but she was having trouble finding any handwritten notes atop the desk.

She began rifling the desk which she found surprisingly enough unlocked. In fact, jimmied open. On the floor, she saw a broken letter opener with the sculpted head of Edgar Allan Poe at her feet. Someone had gotten here ahead of her. She tightened her grip on her single weapon. In the desk drawers, which she pulled out, one after another. Rifling through files, she found nothing handwritten. She cursed the bad luck, when in a closed tin box with the image of Poe on it, she found a small, key reflecting light. "Perhaps to his file cabinet," she said aloud to combat the silence.

Jude went to Griswald's wall of filing cabinets and gave the key a try. No good on cabinet number one, which was not locked and the drawers were relatively empty. Not likely anything of value inside. Cabinet number two like the first had no key receptacle. By now, Jude wondered if the key was useful at all; still, like the story of the three bears, she went to number three and bingo, keyhole. She inserted the key and turned it. The final turn of the key, unlocking all the drawers, startled her a bit, as each lock on each drawer popped in staccato fashion.

She imagined that if Griswald had wished to hide something, such as his handwritten manuscript, it would be in the bottom drawer of the locked cabinet. She knelt to look inside, wherein she found more handwriting than she needed. Griswald's fat handwritten manuscript in a file—hundreds of pages. The cover page had his name below the title—How Edgar Allan Poe Died—the final analysis.

The author's name, Oswald T. Griswald was struck through and corrected as Dr. Tristan Tremain—a pseudonym for sure. Was the old professor planning on using an AKA, fearful perhaps that no one would believe his truth if he used the infamous Griswald name? She also wondered, Had he held the script here for the day Griswald could get it digitized and sold?

"Oswald's book," came a voice from behind her.

Jude felt the blow to the back of her head, and she saw true blackness as she slipped into unconsciousness, as this shadow person pried all the loose pages of the book from her hands and from beneath her. The shadow turned her over, gathering the last page in a rush to race off.

◆　◆　◆

When Jude awoke, it was to an awful pain in her head, her hand going to the swollen lump above her left ear. She was disoriented and at first unsure where she was in the darkened room, as the desk lamp had been turned off. In short order, she realized she'd been knocked senseless, and to determine how long she'd been out, she checked her watch. Through blurry vision, she read the time as 10:37 PM, and as she'd entered right around ten, she concluded she'd been unconscious for perhaps twenty minutes, twenty-five at most.

She tried standing but nearly fell in the effort, grabbing a file handle, the file coming out with her weight pulling it to its end with a loud metallic scream. She let go of the file, fearing it might well topple over on her. She balanced instead against the desk, knocking over a stack of books to the floor.

She ran through a series of questions for herself, beginning with who to call, results of a call to Sybil—a tongue lashing for certain. Dean—a tongue lashing and then a firing; after all, she'd failed to do as he'd said, to go home. Meriam—it'd worry her to no end. Ralph—yes, Ralph who'd do all in his power to help Jude and make no judgments.

For this reason, she dialed Ralph for help, describing her situation in broad strokes and her condition even broader, and finally providing him with the location and room number. She did so breathlessly fearful of going back into unconsciousness, as blood ran from her head wound. She recalled that Griswald's office had its own small half bath, and in the dark, she located it, closed the door, and switched on the light.

She almost screamed at her unrecognizable appearance, and in a silly moment worried about Ralph's seeing her so disheveled, hair matted in blood, her strands like those of a Medusa. In the mirror she saw that her wetted hands held a wetted paper towel against her auburn hair, red now with blood, as whatever the shadow man or woman had beaned her with had torn a gash in her scalp. She might require stitches, but for now, she found what she needed to clean the area as best she could. That it was all important to her regardless of all other considerations.

Once or twice, nausea from the pain attempted to put her down again. After cleaning her wound, she realized it was still bleeding. She slid down the wall at her back and dialed Ralph again and said into the phone, heavy in her hand, "Better hurry..."

◆ ◆ ◆

When Ralph arrived at the darkened office, he shouted out for her name. A custodian insisted on accompanying Ralph to the office, saying he'd heard some awful noises coming from inside, but that he wasn't about to go it alone. After flicking on the lights, the maintenance fellow actually rushed in to lift the two small trash cans and to empty them into the huge can he wheeled up and down the halls here. Force of habit? Ralph wondered, when the custodian said. "Your friend musta' skedaddled outta here. No one here but us and the mice."

"Wait, what's behind that door?"

"Toilet—oh yeah, 'nother trash can too."

"She's in there!" Ralph rushed through the door and found Jude unconscious and bleeding from a gash to her head. "She's in need of help. Call 911."

"Thought you was a doctor?"

"Med student, never said doctor."

"My phone's on my desk in the basement downstairs. You call!"

"Use the phone on the desk!"

"It's not on the desk! Covered in blood."

"SOB hit her with the office phone. Damn heavy object."

Ralph sighed heavily, worked a wet cloth onto Jude's wound and applied pressure with one big hand and dialed for help with the other.

"Don't call, Ralph," she managed to say, having come to. "No doctors, no reports."

"Dr. Avery, I have no choice. Your head. There could be intracranial bleeding, swelling."

"I'll take that chance, Ralph."

"Not with me you won't. He stepped away from where she'd remained prone on the floor, fearful of going out again should she push it. She listened helplessly as Ralph called for paramedics from the closest hospital that he trusted. "Stat!" was the last order Ralph barked into the phone.

While awaiting paramedics, she saw that the cussing custodian was complaining about Griswald's being the messiest man he'd ever run across. Hoarder, I guess," he was saying when he moved about the area at the filing cabinets. "Papers every damn where." Jude watched from a now sitting position, the toilet door open, lights on in the office, as the custodian picked up debris where he stood, about to discard it, saying, "If it's on the floor, it's in the can!"

Jude yelled across at the man to bring her any papers found in the vicinity of the filing cabinets, adding, "Please and thank you."

The custodian's an old 'codger' who looks the part of a Dickens character, Jude thought, watching him through a haze of pain. "Sir," she called him at one point and it made him beam to be called sir. Indeed, as if he'd stepped out of Oliver Twist, as he grunts and hems and haws. However, he did as she requested, like a man used to taking orders with both alacrity and disparagement.

When she got the two pages in hand, she realized that they'd come loose from the manuscript she'd been robbed of. As she studied the handwriting, certain it was Griswald's script, she asked Ralph to bag it and enter it into the chain of custody. "Someone assaulted me for the professor's life's work."

"Don't talk now. Save your energy, Dr. Avery." Ralph then asked the custodian for a plastic bag, as there were a number hanging from his large container just outside in the hallway. Using an oversized, see-through bag, Ralph did as told, while urging with Jude to stay still and lay back.

"I'm all right, Ralph. You needn't worry."

"Do shut up, doctor, and preserve your strength. You'll need it. Heed me, doctor, please."

"It's looking that bad, eh?"

"Who'd want to harm you?" he wondered aloud, then realized he was asking questions and telling her to remain silent at the same time.

Jude thought it was charmingly cute how Ralph was fussing over her. She started to say something, but he gestured in that universal gesture for silence. "Just wait for the stretcher."

"What exactly happened here, anyhow?"

She took a deep breath. "Other than getting crowned with maybe a flashlight, I dunno."

"From a cursory look around, my guess, this guy used the desk phone."

"You sure?"

"Carefully detached it and clubbed you with it. Blood's kind of a giveaway."

Just then they heard distant sirens blaring, getting closer, closer and closer still, until the racket came to a sudden stop, at which moment multicolored lights danced in through the windows, and every interior wall and surface was dappled, painted in Jackson Pollack fashion by the swirling lights. "Medics are here."

◆　◆　◆

Jude had pleaded with Ralph to keep the incident between them, "No need to disturb Grant or Sybil or anyone else," she'd said, but Ralph refused to agree to doing so, and in fact, before it was over, he'd gotten hold of her phone and had called not only Sybil Shanley and Dean Grant but Meriam Oglala as well. Ralph had done so on seeing how often Jude called this Meriam person, and how frequently Meriam called back.

The doctor examining Jude Avery's abrasion and sewing up the laceration assured her that she'd be fine, but at the same time, he insisted she remain overnight for observation. She argued but it did no good. It came down to Dr. Mort Castle threatening her with, "Should you leave, young lady, and should this thing turn any more serious than it already is—"

"I'm fine, I tell you!"

"—and, and should it kill you, Dr. Avery, we will not be responsible, and to assure you of that, you will have to sign a release form. But if you were my daughter or sister, I'd put you in restraints."

"All right, okay, but overnight only, and then I am out of here."

As Dr. Castle left, her visitors began to pour in. Sybil, followed by Dean, both wanting to know what precisely had occurred, after, of course, asking how she was doing and feeling. Jude was actually a good bit touched by their sincere concern. And genuinely surprised, not so much by Sybil as by Dean. However, fatigued and frustrated by this turn of events, and feeling and looking awful and pitiful as anyone in a hospital gown, Jude reluctantly tried to explain why she'd gone to Griswald's office. "It was to fetch a handwriting sample, that's all." When pressed by Dean as to why she could not have taken his orders, she looked away to the window that overlooked the rooftop of the first floor of the hospital. Nothing to see there. She finally told them of the manuscript she'd seen and had in hand before she was knocked unconscious and robbed of the book.

"Where's Ralph?" she asked now. "He's got two pages of the book, a sample of the professor's script. The thief and Griswald's possible murderer dropped two sheets. Guess he was in a rush after attacking me. Where's Ralph?"

"He spoke to us on our way in. He's gone for a Coke and a cigarette."

"He's to enter those two pages into evidence."

"He's doing that now," Dean assured her. "After he explained it to me, I sent him to immediately take those for processing. I also have a crime scene unit combing over Griswald's office, and they're finding a lot of blood—yours."

"You lost a lot of it," added Sybil.

"Afraid I couldn't help bleeding from one end to the other. I've never bled like that ever in life."

Sybil was holding Jude's hand now, and she replied, "Head wounds like that can bleed more than people realize. By the way, did you get a chance to pepper spray the guy who attacked you?"

"Your canister was found on the floor alongside your purse," said Grant, the caliber of his annoyance ratcheting up. "You should never have been there."

"At the moment of finding the book, I had to release my grip on the spray—pocketed it in my blouse, I thought. After being struck—Ralph says it was the desk phone—everything went black."

As she finished, Meriam rushed in, gasping, but she halted on seeing Sybil at Jude's bedside, holding her hand. Jude called for Meriam to take her other hand on the side of the bed where she stood. "It's so wonderful to see you," Jude assured Meriam. "As for these two, Merr... my boss, Dr. Grant and my colleague Dr. Shanley. Sybil, Dean, meet Meriam, my dear friend."

After a round of cheerful introductions and handshaking, elbow-style, Grant and Shanley excused themselves to leave Jude and Meriam alone. No words were spoken, but the other two sensed that Jude and Meriam needed privacy. Jude had what amounted to a bandage turban on her head. "Did they have to shave your head? Are you all right, Jude? What happened? I got this strange call, and I almost didn't believe the guy, but he said you were here, so I came as fast as I could. Did you fall? Was it a car accident?"

Jude did not know how much to tell Meriam and what not to tell her. She feared if Meriam knew the extent of sudden danger around her lover, the death of Griswald, a questionable suicide, possible homicide, and her being attacked at the professor's office, that surely Meriam would race off never to be seen again. All that she had shared with Sybil and Dean, professional crime fighters, and how they had taken it in with bated breath and gasps, the danger she'd lived through this night, then how to explain it to Meriam? What kind of reaction would she get from Meriam, a civilian, and a kind, sweet soul? All these questions sparred with one another all at once in Jude's medical-examiner mind, deep inside her aching head wound. Questions became squirming, living organisms that swirled in her head in a cocktail of doubt and disturbance. At the moment, too, she had Meriam's tearful cheek in her lap as the sweet companion leaned in from the hospital chair to Jude's breast. Her ear against Jude's heart.

"I'm going to be fine, Merr—the doctors tell me it's nothing. Be up and running again tomorrow at the crack of dawn, yelling for my release!"

"You do seem hale and hearty." Meriam spoke without raising her head, as if in prayer. "For that, I am relieved and beyond grateful."

"Thank you, honey."

"I care a great deal for you, Jude. I'm not sure you realize how much."

"Good, then you can go to my place and feed Squeakums tonight, and I'll find you there in the morning."

"Oh, no! I am staying by your side right here, all night. Not leaving you out of my sight."

"That's really not necessa—"

"Horse hockey, not leaving you alone in this place."

"This place is a hospital. I'm perfectly safe here."

"No sense in arguing with me, Jude." She dug in on Jude's lap as if she meant to sleep in this position. Then she raised up and stood at bedside, wiping tears with napkins found on the nightstand.

Jude smiled and indicated with her open arms that she wanted Meriam closer, and without a word, Meriam understood what Jude beckoned for. They hugged, and Jude kissed her lover with all the passion she could muster. When the embrace was over, Meriam, in her

Native American accent urged her to get some sleep, adding, "Sleep and know you are not alone."

Meriam began a lilting, mesmerizing chant, low and gentle, and to the sound of her love's care and concern, Jude slipped into a slumber with a Mona Lisa smile upon her lips.

The following day at Rush Presbyterian Hospital, Chicago

Jude awoke to find Meriam had gone but not for long, as she cheerfully entered with a large brown bag carried flat like a pizza box. "Carry-out breakfast and coffee for two and a Tribune," she said, and Jude noted the newspaper under her arm. "From a Starbuck's inside the building."

"Oh, thank you! I'm famished!"

The couple had a cheery meal of cinnamon rolls and cream cheese on bagel nuggets. But as quickly as her coffee was downed, Jude rang for the duty nurse, Kathrine, and asked that release papers for Avery be put on priority."

Katherine smiled and nodded and said, "Will do all I can to speed it up, Dr. Avery, but I can't work miracles."

"Meaning?"

"Dr. Castle's in surgery. Greatly in demand."

"But he said last night—"

"Possible he'll make rounds by one."

"That's crazy, he's said last night that—"

"We need his go-ahead, and we don't normally see him until well after lunch."

"Look, I'm anxious to get home, feed my cat, shower, and perhaps make it to work by this afternoon." Jude wasn't sure that Nurse Katherine even heard her last words, as she'd rushed out, escape her only option left with hours of delaying tactics, Jude imagined.

"What exactly do you do for Dr. Shanley and Dr. Grant?" Meriam asked between sips of her cooled coffee. When Jude hesitated, Meriam asked. "Does your work, the job you do, does it have anything to do with your injury?" She gingerly touched Jude's bandaged head.

"I suppose it's time you know."

"Know what? Tell me, Jude."

"I am, well actually, all three of us are medical examiners, Sybil,

Dean, myself. Dean is the head man for the Cook County Coroner's Office."

Meriam's forehead creased. "Oh, dear, then you are a doctor not of the living but…I see."

"Tell me you're all right with that." Jude wondered if Meriam had any lifelong superstitions or prejudices about people who worked with the dead, other issues about the dead, possibly ancestral norms and customs, lines that a medical examiner crossed. After all, she was a Native American, who were rather well known for commuting with nature and their ancestors. Even as these thoughts shot through Jude's mind, she wondered if her own biases weren't in the way here.

"Am I all right with who you are and what you do?" she asked. "I am, of course."

"But you're troubled by it?"

"I am, I suppose. Look, I've seen a few recent headlines mentioning this man, Dr. Grant. We get the Tribune at the library every day, and now I recall. Two bodies found bricked in a subway wall."

"I'm involved with that case, but Grant's taken the lead as spokesman…PR."

Meriam stood and reached over to the newspaper she'd earlier dropped on a chair, and raising it, opening it to page two, she asked, "And this—even this morning—'M.E. Questions University of Chicago Prof's Death'"

"Let me see that."

"Just a minute." Meriam kept scanning the story, making Jude wait before folding it neatly for her and handing it over.

"You can quit babying me now."

"I enjoy babying you. So, last night, your accident as you called it, was no accident?" Meriam asked point blank.

Jude was still reading the report on Griswald's death. She wondered how the reporter got it that the death was questionable, possibly more than a suicide.

"I get it that you don't want to talk about it, Jude, but when you are in a relationship with someone who actually cares about you, and wants you to be safe, then I am sorry, but you have to be honest, or we don't have a relationship, not without trust, you see."

"It's just that I don't wish to unduly worry you, Meriam," Jude spoke from behind the newspaper. "That relationship highway runs both ways."

"Enough with the protecting me, Jude!" Meriam slammed the newspaper down and glared at Jude. "I'm not a child to be coddled."

Jude smiled at this sudden remark. "Hey, we cuddled all night, remember."

"You know what I mean!"

"All right, all right."

"I'm sorry, but you can't ball things up and hide them from me."

"No, I'm sorry. My bad. I should've let you know what was going on sooner."

Meriam pursed her lips and shook her head, saying, "Yes, you should have."

"Start over?"

"From what the nurse says, we'll be here through lunch."

"At least."

13

Jude finally escaped the hospital once all the release forms were signed, but it was after two PM. More than once, she almost bolted for a stairway door like they did in the movies, but she feared leaving in such a manner would cause problems for the nurses, and overall, they'd done a great job in caring for her, so she had instead waited and waited. Meriam had finally had to leave ahead of her or jeopardize her job at the library, which aside from her scholarship also paid her bills. They had spoken of Meriam's goals and her schooling, and Meriam bemoaned the size of the loan she'd had to take out to continue her education, despite having won a scholarship.

Jude had gone directly home, having called for an Uber ride. Once inside her flat, she even welcomed her noisy upstairs neighbor whose heavy foot had always been her number one negative about this apartment. The neighbor from hell, he wasn't, but he was annoying. For this reason, she'd been looking for a place closer to work anyway.

Her first responsibility was to Squeakums, who desperately needed attention, feeding and a change of litter. After seeing to the cat's needs, she warmed up a can soup for herself, and made a grilled cheese sandwich slathered with mayonnaise, tomato, and lettuce. She flicked on her TV and listened to the news and weather, realizing it was growing late, and she had to get her prescription filled.

The mundane necessities of life seemed for a moment overwhelming, and she wondered if the still nagging pain in her head would ever completely subside. The thought of having to go out to the pharmacy felt like a great burden after the long day of frustration she'd endured, and so she instead opened her cell phone and logged into her CVS account and asked if her prescription was ready, called in by the hospital. As they had her card on file, and as they delivered for an extra charge, she finalized the transaction and found the shower, Squeakums accompanying her as far as the shower door that closed on him.

The evening went uneventfully with the prescription delivery, an ice pack on her head, reruns of Law & Order, and phone calls coming in from Sybil, Dean, Ralph in that order, and finally from Meriam. All checking in on her. The peaceful dark outside her window, the quiet evening, even her upstairs guy doing no pacing, got her mind off everything, and yet the calm clearing of her mind set her brain racing—the mind listing all the bad that'd occurred since the day they discovered the first body behind the subway wall.

It all seemed so twisted, so tortuously gnarly, and the events after the discovery so curve ball crazy. She enumerated each occurrence in list form in her mind, and then she found a notepad and began jotting down each event. The list took on the character of an episodic mystery on cable TV, starting with episode one: the discovery of Jane Doe City Hall, the stolen items off the corpse, then the discovery of the tintype that the victim may well have hidden on her person, possibly in her corset, or had the killer who'd bricked her up meanly shoved the tintype into her shackled hands or bossom as he finished his ungodly work.

Then came the news that the foreman's nephew, Eddie, first to discover the body, had said under hypnosis that items had been about her neck and fingers—jewelry. The foreman had said somewhat offhandedly that the workmanship of the wall that killed the lady was good masonry work. When Jude had pressed the point, Frank called it "Expert work, very clean lines."

Then to compound the amazing discovery of the decades old body, they found a second in the same condition nearby—walled up, murdered. This all around the time of the building of the tunnels, the1940s. Far and away from the time of the last use of tintype in photo making.

She listed these facts, including the fact that the man's nephew, under hypnosis, had indeed seen a broach and a necklace, and what appeared to be a wedding ring. Grant had told her in his last call that those involved in the theft were given a chance to return the items to his office by noon tomorrow or face charges, and that they were already terminated. The lot of them.

"Hold on, you fired all of them? What if one of them had not participated in—"

"The rule is simple under my leadership they take an oath: 'I will not lie, cheat, or steal, or tolerate it in others.'"

Grant proved a true taskmaster when it came to honesty in his department.

Two of the stolen items matched the jewelry worn by the woman in the aged photo—the necklace and the broach. Jude jotted these facts down. She then added the identifying features of the reconfigured skull, and how that image of Jane Doe of City Hall had gone out to the networks and the papers, and social media, despite the lack of resemblance to the lady in the tintype. Anyone in the nation, certainly in Chicagoland, would by now have seen the features of the lady in the Tribune displayed with a story by Louise McGrath. Alongside this recreation of the features from the skull, Grant had decided to have the papers also display the tintype with the male in the frame with the woman who may or may not have been the victim's parents or grandparents. It made sense, timeline-wise. In the olden days, a woman who loved her parents kept photo mementos of them close at hand. No telling whose choice it'd been to wall up the victim with this heirloom—the killer or the lady herself? The question made the mystery of the small, framed depiction of a couple dressed in clothes befitting the 1800s even more intriguing.

Finally, they at the Coroner's Office were working on a DNA link via the victim's genetic material to hopefully locate further any living descendants. Jude listed this alongside the fact they were doing the same with the John Doe of City Hall. With all this going forward at the lab, and all the open public relations through Dr. Grant with the approval and support of the mayor's office, all of City Hall remained abuzz about this particular Jane Doe, despite the fact that many a Jane Doe was buried every day in the Chicago Potters Field—designated for all unidentified bodies that passed through the hands of the office.

It'd been about then that she had called on Dr. Oswald T. Griswald the second time, and as a strange result, possibly having nothing to do with the Jane and John Doe cases, the poor man was dead. Be it suicide as his note suggested, the one naming her as an object of his unrequited love? Or be it a staged suicide? The result was the same in so far as Griswald had lost his life—and she was hit hard enough with a blunt object that she might well've bled to death if Ralph not called for an ambulance. The first thing the medics did in the ambulance was to hook her to a plasma IV. Jude prayed that it wasn't too late, and the IV would assist in clotting and the replacement of platelets would slow her bleeding.

She then tried to recall how she had come across Griswald in the first place. She had Googled the question, hadn't she? Several experts came back responding to her inquiry about who was the most widely held expert on Poe in the Chicagoland area. When it came to Poe research and knowledge, Griswald's name came up again and again. He was Chicago's premier Edgar Allan Poe scholar and expert, and if anyone would know about walling people up, well…while a longshot, after her reading, research, and questions left unanswered, she had decided why not talk to this man?

And so here she was and here she remained with more questions than answers, except for one: someone seemed hellbent on getting his hands on Griswald's unpublished 'final analysis' of Poe's death, the story he'd shared with her—his family history.

Jude set aside her now pages of chronology of the crimes—both those committed at the turn of the century, and that which she herself may have inadvertently played a part in—Griswald's murder. The likelihood that the two instances of murder—if Griswald was proven murdered—had anything to do with one another seemed remote at best. Perhaps they had no tie whatsoever, no connection. It was highly unlikely, and yet, she felt a nagging at the back of her mind that in some distant way there might be a thread of tissue connecting these events.

Alone except for her cat, she said to Squeakums, "I should get back on the computer, maybe duplicate my question about Poe—now that Griswald is gone. Who stands to take his place in the pantheon of Poe experts?"

The question lit a bulb in her head, a faint memory, something Sybil Shanley had put there—something about OCD types in the specialized field of horror literature and art—the true 'dark arts' and those vendors at the Horror Writers convention and Comic Cons, yes, and how cutthroat might some of them be?

Jude went to her workstation and computer, opening it and going to Google. At first thought she might simply duplicate her question. Then she halted, as her cat had leapt onto the station and placed a paw on the keyboard, as if to say no. "If the person who attacked me," she thought out loud for the cat's sake, "if he or she knew of my interest, and that I had chosen to speak with Griswald, he or she may have been among the several other names that'd surfaced during my initial inquiry. You are so right, Squeaky!" She lifted the cat to her nose and nose-kissed him. She then put him at her feet, where he curled around her bare toes.

Talking to herself now, she typed out the words rushing into her head: With Griswald gone, I could announce his sad passing and ask the question anew, saying I am working on a dissertation and had been left with questions Griswald had failed to answer. Possibly, my attacker, Griswald's killer, was a competitor in the field, the field of Poe literature and possibly would kill for his own theories to survive those of Griswald and the Griswald family curse.

This notion at first seemed wildly far-fetched, she thought. But she couldn't stop thinking of what Griswald had said of the vendors at conferences, echoed by Sybil Shanley saying the same of this class of people so absolutely fixated on one literary character, historical event, personage, or even fictional beasts: trolls, unicorns, incubi, and elves. Griswald had laughed when he spoke of the Lucy Wistera Society, explaining that there was an association devoted to the one character in Bram Stoker's Dracula who had slowly weakened and succumbed to the vampire's repeated, nightly visits, likening Lucy's death to a debilitating disease.

"Suppose for a moment," she said to herself and to Squeakums at her feet still, "that another professor, a doctor of dark American literature, say even a Hawthorne enthusiasts who's also as heavily invested in Poe's literature, as well as the tales of Poe's demise, would he stop at nothing to preserve his own theory of the crime? To perpetuate the sales of his own pet theory and writings? His buried dissertation?"

It was a leap, and she knew it, but there felt a compelling pull to the crazy notion that The Raven was an aka for a chief rival to Griswald and his claims, down to his so-called family curse. Jude no longer succumbing to the dead professor's every word, no longer in his 'spell' could well imagine how the old fellow used that family curse story on others—even for a steak meal at Capone's where the clientele certainly knew him.

While Griswald had told her that he'd never confided the story of his ancestor having a hand in Poe's death, apparently, this was a lie. He'd broached the possibility of this tale being true in articles he'd published online. It'd obviously been his life's work, spent running down details and facts that would support the story. He had a manuscript awaiting a typist in hand the night he humored her with the lies she had fallen for. She recalled suggesting he write a book, how the suggestion had drawn a laugh and a shake of the head, alongside a denial that 'anyone would believe it.'

Apparently, someone did believe it. She wondered now if that someone hadn't been in a nearby booth at Capone's, secretly listening in. She had noticed no such person, but a feeling and an image of a dark man flitted through her psyche.

She realized now that if she went back onto Google and asked the same question, seeking an expert, that this dark shadow man would know that she was trying to ferret him out, and she was neither brave enough, nor crazy enough, to want him coming after her a second time. She instead had a better idea. Turn back the clock. Turn back time on her computer to the night she had first learned the name Griswald. She calculated the date and time as best she could. It was helped by her email sent to Griswald that first contact, which she stared at now. She felt a new wave of regret, remorse, and downright guilt at the man's ever having come into contact with her; perhaps he'd be alive today if…

She successfully turned back her computer to the day she needed, and in the Google cloud, she found the back and forth she'd had with others online. There were ample interested parties who genuinely wanted to help in her 'dissertation research' and while several seemed a bit pushy and arrogant, one stuck out as being self-deprecating and anxious for her to contact Dr. Oswald Griswald, saying as a former student of the man, that he in fact had never had a better adviser and counselor and genius to work with on his own dissertation on EA Poe. The man's name was Aaron Fiske Jr., currently a professor of American literature at Northwestern University in Evanston, just over the city line north.

Had Fiske anything to do with the old man's demise? Could he have gone unrecognized at Capone's that night? Wouldn't Griswald have seen his old and doting student? Maybe Fiske knew nothing of any of this, but he might know someone who did—another student, a teaching assistant to the old man, as TA's were assigned their positions to earn while they learned. Could Griswald's TA have soured on a demanding 'boss' and done away with him, and knowing of the Poe manuscript gotten away with it, leaving Jude in her own blood?

Most people saw only the surface of a university campus—like the superficial surface of a bookstore. Push the image of a happy place, smiling busy people on the quad and in the commons, on the parkways throwing Frisbees for fetching dogs, kids on bikes, others rushing to class, and see nothing of the inner turmoil and emotion among faculty, staff, administration, custodial staff, and the families they all had to feed.

Few saw, and fewer still understood, the nerve center of such a setting. Few saw the politics involved in climbing the ladder in a college or university, especially an Ivy League one like Griswald's or Northwestern—named for its location just North of Chicago. Few knew the pressure to publish, for instance.

It was not unheard of for a person, even a well-educated person, to kill either figuratively or literally—should figuratively fail—to get ahead in academia. Sometimes it was for social advancement which also meant money, marrying the right person, pulling the right strings, and in academia—publishing. Someone may well have wanted Griswald's manuscript to slap his own name on it, or to deep-six it, burn it, and why? To protect his or her own theory of the mystery of Poe's death? To bury Griswald's theory with Griswald?

While this might sound farfetched to outsiders and even to law enforcement, perhaps even to Dr. Grant and Dr. Shanley, Jude sensed it was true. She based it on what had happened when author Patricia Cornwell had applied her knowledge of forensic science to unmasking Jack-the-Ripper, as in fact, her book Jack The Ripper—Case Closed was viciously attacked, not only by legitimate reviewers for legitimate literary and structural reasons but by almost all who'd already made up their minds on who the Ripper was and why—many of whom were selling their own theories via their own books.

Even more vociferous than other authors, however, were those making a living off the Ripper's identity remaining the mystery it was. Venders, ghost tour companies, guides in London who hawked the streets where the Ripper did his killing and mutilation. This included people selling Ripper wares from pens, pins, aprons, and Jack-the-Ripper pillows, ties, underwear and socks. None of these people wanted Cromwell and forensic science methodology to expose the real life serial killer—arguably the most famous of serial killers, the Ripper by name! Not any more than they wanted Hasbro to create a Jack-the-Ripper Clue board game or computer app. Cromwell's book, cogent almost at every turn of the page, meant one thing to a Comic Con vendor who specialized in Ripper wares: an endgame to their game and income.

With these wild thoughts fluttering through her mind, she continued her timeline of events up to the moment she was attacked and left for dead. She had not given her new thought life until now, *If I pursue this, will the man who attacked me attempt it a second time?*

Before she closed her computer—now her 'time machine,' she studied two other names besides Aaron Fiske Jr., both of whom felt like possible over-the-top contenders for a fixation on Poe and possibly Griswald. One was named Abdula Asim, a student on the university campus and living in the foreign student dormitory. The third name was Jacob JaCovey Stone. Stone seemed the most erudite of these English majors. Stone had a flare for dramatic wording, to say the least. He was Griswald's teaching assistant or TA. He joked in his reply to her question that while Griswald lectured in English, he did so at such an elevated, linguistic-gymnastic performance that it was up to JaCovey to 'translate' what the hell Griswald was saying.

There seemed an unspoken disdain in that description of the professor, but Stone ended with, "However, no one in all of Illinois, much less Chicago, knows more about EA Poe as does Professor G. He's linked to Poe so closely that the man is on a first name basis with Edgar. By the way, if Poe had been a British author, surely he'd have been posthumously knighted."

That last line about knighting Poe seemed a bit extreme. Perhaps Stone was indeed OCD when it came to Poe and the theories of his demise. At any rate, Jude had three men now marked for investigation: Jacob JaCovey Stone, Abdula Asim, and Aaron Fiske Junior. All her suspicions hardly buttressed, built rather shakily on a shallow scaffolding and having no basis in fact, yet. Yet, she repeated in her head. Just based on a deeply held conviction of emotion driven by the still dull throb in her head. A conviction that the little professor, despite being penniless and about to be put out by the university he'd given his life over to, was not suicidal.

Her head throbbed more with each conclusion about both Griswald and herself. The pain pills as dosed out seemed only of a peripheral help at best. She was wondering again if she shouldn't have stayed in Castle's care a day longer. Then again, perhaps a good night's sleep would help greatly, if only. "If only I can get to sleep, sensing someone in the world might be coming for me."

That sense of someone coming for her kept Jude restless and wakeful into the 13th hour and beyond. She realized that she'd gotten to the point where she'd talked herself into being unable to get back to sleep on awakening at 2:23 AM, and at the same time, the pacing overhead beat out an uneven rhythm that was no help either. She put on some soft, bluesy music that promised to capture her mind, provide support for her T-cells, and lull her into slumber.

Meriam had called around nine to say she had a last-minute call to go at once to see her mother in Upstate New York."

"Upstate New York? I thought your mom was in North Dakota?"

"She's a shaman, gets around. Mother's a guest of the Mohawk Indians. There's a gathering of tribes, a celebration of fall crops, but Mother's fallen ill. I have to rush to mom's side. No other way."

"And your father? Is he there too?"

"Father died several years ago, cigarettes and firewater induced cancer."

"Damn, I am so very sorry," Jude had said. "Take all my best wishes, prayers, and vibes to your mother for me, Meriam, and be careful. I think I love you."

"And I you."

On hanging up, Jude took stock. Just after learning that I am a medical examiner and was nearly killed by some maniac with a desk phone, Meriam has to take a vacation from me? True or not, the thought floated into her brain and took up lodging there.

And so, Jude was alone in her place, alone with her cat curled up in bed, trying to calm her mind and get much needed sleep. But it wasn't coming. Restlessness in the middle of the night. She climbed out of bed without disturbing Squeakums. While she paced the floor, she wondered if Meriam was really on her way to Upstate New York, and if so, was she flying, taking Amtrak, Greyhound, or what? She tried desperately to put the worst of the worse thought out of her mind. That

Meriam had made up a story, a lie, to make for distance and to take a little think time for herself.

More pacing. She had read somewhere that if a person could not sleep, then get up and do something, anything from doing the floors, the dishes, stacking books alphabetically on shelves or shaving one's legs, after which going back to bed was a kind of award or reward, and having tried this before, and finding it had worked, Jude was now cleaning her bathroom tub and toilet.

Soon after putting away the Scrubbing Bubbles, she was back with Squeakums and with some soft music playing low, the easy-listening kind, she was back to the Land of Nod.

14

"The game's afoot, Watson!" Jude called out to Ralph on her return. "And hey, again thanks so much."

"For what?"

"Saving my life!"

"Oh, I hardly think—"

"No, no false modesty. You could've easily done me wrong!"

"Never!"

"Had you done as I'd pleaded. Had you taken me home to convalesce right into a casket."

"It was nothing."

"Ralph, you infuriate me! Nothing, really?"

"All right, I done what I done, now you have me blushing, Dr. Avery."

"I think, my friend and savior, you've earned the right to call me Jude now."

Ralph looked around as if fearful someone overheard this. "Oh, no, I can't; not here in the lab, Dr. Avery. It'd look, well, not right—you know, to others."

"Ralph, what do we care what others think?"

"But it's proper. Best leave it as is."

"As is—saw that sign on an old typewriter in a pawn shop once. A Remington."

"As is, as in, I mean."

"As in?"

"I get away wid calling you doc from time-to-time, as is."

"And you're happy with that alone?"

"Not a matter of happiness, certainly not mine. I mean look at me. I mean, I'm your assistant and you, you're Dr. Avery. It is what it is."

Jude thought she heard something in his voice like a plea to really see him. She blurted out, "You do know how much I appreciate you, Ralph, don't you?"

"Yes, of course, I do."

Their eyes met as she studied his expression and found it unreadable, inscrutable. He then said with a half-grin, "You could lobby for my raise."

"I will!" She slapped him on his expansive back with her gloved hand. "I owe you big time."

"You needn't feel obligated. I'd've done the same for anyone in distress, Doc."

"Even Grant?" she joked.

He snickered at this and said, "Even Dr. Grant, yes."

She nodded. "I know you would."

"Not sure what you were doing at the university in a dead man's office, dead of night, but I assume you had a good reason to be there."

"Dead of night? It was early evening! Dead of night is like twelve to three."

"Okay, my bad."

"Besides, these pages you took care of while I was going in and out of consciousness, Ralph, might have all the answers we need to determine who killed Professor Griswald."

"You still won't accept it as suicide?"

"I didn't know the man long—not at all, but he did not present, in my opinion, any sign of depression or suicidal ideation."

"What signs? We all know people who committed suicide that showed no signs, Dr. Avery."

"There are moments, the blank stare, called a blank affect. A person in deep depression, feels he has no effect on anyone or anything; then there's the confused thinking, slurring words, loss of sleep, bloodshot eyes, general sadness in body language presenting."

"Maybe if you spent a lot of time with a person, you might start noticing something's not right, but suicidal thoughts in another person? I dunno, unless you're trained to see it. Otherwise, who knows what a person is going through?"

"True enough for most folks, Ralph, but I am trained to see it when it's before me, and I saw not a whit of it in Griswald."

"But Dr. Shanley and Grant, they're closing it out as a suicide. The man had alcohol and had downed a half a bottle of sleeping pills along with an overdose of blood pressure tabs. That's too much to call an accident."

"And possibly too much to call a suicide."

"How will you prove it?"

"Not sure, not yet. Maybe begin with interviews of those who knew him best—others in his department, colleagues, students."

"That's a lot of time away and on the campus."

"I'll need help."

"If you trust me, I'll be of help."

"I do. I trust you implicitly."

"Thank you, Doc. Of course, I'd have to do it on the clock here, given my studies."

"We'll go together, cover as much ground as we can today."

"Very well. You mean now?"

"Now, yes."

◆　◆　◆

A canvas of the English department at the university revealed a strange phenomena that Jude had not expected to find. A university department devoted to communication, literature, language, linguistics, and writing had the nature of a series of caves rather than offices, and each 'cave dweller' did more grunting than speaking. She and Ralph had come across a departmental secretary, Susan, who was bubbly and bright, if young, who'd earned the nickname here as Suedini for her ability to keep the place operating smoothly, to get next term schedule out, along with this term's grades to the registrar on time, and to act as secretary for all the instructors under the English Department's wide umbrella.

Suedini pulled off lists of professors in the department who specialized in American Literature along with graduate students concentrating in the same area. "As for dissertations, that sort of thing, you'll want to visit with Ms. Elanias at the library. She's the chief reference librarian here."

"Miscellaneous? Are you sure?"

"No, slow that down." Suedini giggled at this. "Miss-miss E-lani-as."

"That must get the students confused—sending them to Miss Elanias," Ralph blurted out, smiling then for Sue.

Smiles and chuckles followed before the 'Health Department' officials waved Suedini off. Out of her earshot and on the stairwell, Jude said, "Of course, dissertations, why didn't I think if it?"

Ralph shrugged. "I dunno."

"We need to see what the library may be hiding."

"Cradling, you mean?"

"That too."

Soon they were across campus at the huge, expansive library and asking for Miss Elanias, not knowing what to expect. Someone had to go get her, as she was 'lost in the stacks' and 'meantime, can I be of service'?

"We need access to dissertations," Jude replied.

"Ahhh, the place where dead books go," the young librarian said with a grin. When she saw that neither Jude nor Ralph were amused, she added, "I mean the Manuscript Mausoleum. Only Miss Elanias can help you there."

"We'll wait here then."

After a moment, another librarian guided the now infamous Elanias to her visitors. She looked like a female version of an elderly Hollywood Morgana, a witchy woman of devious means. White haired, keen-eyed, observant to all things around her, Elanias must be on the verge of retirement, Jude thought. The medical examiner sensed Elanias was sizing her up, even as Jude was sizing up the hunched over matron of this place—the head reference librarian here in her cathedral of books, her castle and fiefdom.

"Can I help you, dear?" she asked Jude, giving a nod to Ralph, who towered over everyone here.

"I am curious to find any dissertations—serious ones—done on Edgar Allan Poe."

"Oh dear, not Poe again." The elderly lady shook her head. "Seems every college student wants to do a research paper on that overrated poet, Poe. I can only imagine what the professors think when seeing yet another atrocious paper on Poe."

"We're not here to do a research paper on Mr. Poe, Miss Elanias, but rather to determine who has spent most of their blood, sweat, and tears on a dissertation, as opposed to a ten-page freshman hiccup."

"Ha, hiccup research paper. I rather like that characterization, dear. But then who are you, again?"

Jude introduced herself and Ralph once again as with the city's Health Department.

"I see," she said, nodding. "This way, then. Now," she continued talking, her back to them as they followed, "you can take only three dissertations at a time, and they must be returned within a week's time—two if you'd gotten them through inter-library loan, but obviously that is not the case here."

"A week? That's awfully tight. What if I told you that this has to do with a case of murder?"

"Murder?" She stopped in her tracks and turned to stare anew at Jude. "Who are you? You're not students, nor are you from the Health Department, now are you?"

"We work for the," Jude began, about to push hard the Health Department lie, but she sensed it wouldn't help to lie with this woman. "That is, we work for Cook County."

"The county, really, and in what capacity?"

"The Coroner's Office, gathering background information on a case. Ever watch House, the TV show? Background info."

"I've never had much use for televisions, so no. This has to do with Oswald, Dr. Griswald, doesn't it?"

"It does."

"I read in the paper where they're saying it's suicide."

"You knew him?"

"Well, yes. Wonderful, compassionate, caring man. Always delightful. And as for suicide, no! Impossible. Not Oswald."

"Then help us. I am trying to prove exactly that."

"My dear," said Elanias, snatching out a handkerchief and softly catching a tear. She put up a stern, arthritic finger to her lips, indicating quiet as Jude was about to speak further. "You, you are advocating for Oswald. You have me now on your side. This way."

They followed Miss Elanias through a door she alone had a key to. Unlocked, it opened onto a room full of stacks, rows of metal shelving, cheaper by far than the maple wood shelves the public saw the other side of the door. Lights on now, Jude and Ralph marveled at the stacks of boxes filled with dissertations over the lifetime of the University of Chicago.

The silent, lonely and semi-dark space felt like the back room of a museum, wherein all the enormous collection of art and artifacts were badly stored, only because there was no room to display it all in the public areas. Here the paper and boxes rose from the floor to the ceiling, collecting mildew.

"It's all rather daunting, but it is catalogued here. In a forward corner, she sat at a computer and typed in the search question, asking for any dissertation done in the last ten years on Poe in this collection. Several came back. "May I see the cards?" asked Jude. And authors' names? thought Jude.

"Yes, of course." The librarian stood, giving Jude the office chair.

Jude pulled out her list of three names that she had narrowed from her own computer, and sitting now, she read, "Fiske, Asim, and Stone among the names listed."

"Remarkable," said Elanias, leaning in over Jude.

"Why so?"

"All three, close in years, have done their graduate work on Poe under Oswald's tutelage."

"And all of them left their findings here."

Ralph, as impressed as Elanias, let out an appreciative grunt.

"I'll want to take away all three dissertations, but I may need more than a week, ma'am," Jude said, a plea in her voice.

"Well now, that goes against rules I put in place in 1968 when the Vietnam war was raging."

"Can you bend those rules for the sake of Professor Griswald? All three of these men who wrote these papers, they would have likely had your friend Oswald as a professor at some point, and he is on all three dissertation committees."

"Of course, he would be as the unquestioned expert on Poe."

"And Professor Griswald would have been one of those who green-lighted the research and followed up with a thumbs up or thumbs down on its completion, moving the author along to his PhD or disallowing his going forward in the event the dissertation was flawed."

"They're given a chance, of course, of rewriting."

"Or taking a walk?"

"I suppose, yes."

"What happens to a dissertation that does not pass muster?"

"It never gets here to the Manuscript Mausoleum as we often refer to this place. Dead Letter Office, some call it. Book graveyard."

"Why do you call it that?" asked Ralph.

"No one reads dissertations. The island of misfit books, you might say."

Ralph tried to whisper but given his voice that seemed impossible."If all three of these guys got passing grades, no motive to kill the teacher."

Elanias gave him a queer look.

Jude covered with a weak come back, "Maybe someday soon, Ralph, your dissertation will be finished and done with." She then said to the librarian, "Ralph's in medical school, working on his own dissertation," Jude explained to Elanias.

"It makes my skin crawl to let three dissertations go out for an indefinite amount of time," she said with the tone of the wounded. "But I do respect the legal and the medical profession, and I do know the work of the medical examiners is a medicolegal necessity, so it's twice the respect."

Jude jumped on this, saying, "Great, good, and thank you, Miss Elanias, for your help and cooperation with law enforcement, and I promise you no harm will come to these loosely bound books we take under our care."

"Old metal snaps come away easy. You must take care." She sighed heavily. "I do it for Oswald. You wouldn't know it to look at me, but he and I were once...well, water under the bridge, as they say. Sadly, his preoccupation was his occupation, and his fixation on Edgar as he called Poe, well it became too much to bear, even for the most patient person on the campus—which is me!" She ended with a light laugh. She then took Jude's hands in hers, and she shakily said, "Those bastards on the Board of Directors wounded him badly. They're after all of us."

This sounded a bit paranoid, but Jude asked, "Us?"

"Seniors—wanting to wipe us all out of our place here."

Jude saw tears welling up in the little, elderly lady. "Dr. Griswald mentioned that to me, but are they asking for you to retire as well?"

"They've made it clear. Anyone over seventy—get off our campus!" Her voice cracked on her last words. "I'm sorry." She sniffled. "I shouldn't've said…shouldn't bother you two with my troubles. Like Oswald…gave my life to this place. Oh, I didn't mean that how it sounded."

"No, no need to apologize, Miss Elanias."

"They made a big deal about my only having a master's degree. After all these years. My experience alone is worth several PhD's, but they'd already made up their minds, and I think they'd voted even before I was given an audience."

Jude was moved to give the lady a hug, and she said she would if it were not for the pandemic, which while on the run, remained a danger.

"Thank you, my dear, I appreciate that. I am sorry that I took your hands in mine."

"Well, it has gotten far better."

"That it has."

"Tell me, how old are these men—I assume men—on the University board?"

"There is one woman, but yes, all are relatively young, certainly younger than Oswald or I. Myself, I condemned them, but Oswald refused to become as bitter as I had."

"Do you have anything with their names of those people on the board?" Jude wondered about another path to The Raven. Might he be a mad university board member?

"I have their letter asking me to resign my duties. Signed by them all."

"Signed by, by each one?"

"Yes. I suspect they were out to drop an anvil on my life—same as Oswald. We, he and I, discussed this, as he'd gotten the same letter."

Jude thought about the note that Griswald had crushed into his pocket from The Raven. She wondered if Dr. Sheila Lowe and perhaps even she herself could match one of those board member signatures to the Raven's note. Perhaps the lone woman on the board even. "Please. May I borrow that letter?"

"The original is in my lawyer's hands, but I have a copy."

"You're contesting it?"

"I damn sure am!"

"Would you make a copy for our investigation? I agree with you that Dr. Griswald was not suicidal."

"We were sharing the cost of the lawyer that our teacher's union found for us, and last time I spoke with Oz…oh, I called him Oz, well…last we spoke, he feared the union lawyer was paid off by the board to put up no real fight!" She led them out of the room, locked it after them, and led them to the to her desk and a nearby Xerox copier.

Jude, dissertations in hand, thanked the librarian profusely, while Ralph took the heavy bound manuscripts into his care. Meanwhile, Jude signed a form allowing her to borrow the dissertations, a form with a date written across it for return of the materials.

"They are, after all, one of a kind," Elanias said on returning from the copier with the board letter in hand, saying, "To add to your load. I hope to God you two can clear Oz of this heinous suicide label they've painted across his legacy here at the university."

"We just want to get at the truth, dear, and we will. I promise you."

Miss Elanias watched them leave, her heart palpitating. She had never allowed such a free-wheeling loan with the dissertations before. Her rules applied to everyone. From the custodial staff to the university president. One or two at most at a time, one-week rule, even if requested through intra-library loan. Her heart was fluttering, like a caged bird struggling to get free.

♦   ♦   ♦

"We have a treasure trove or a stack of useless junk here, Ralph," Jude said as they stashed the three bound manuscripts from the library into the trunk and came around to the doors and climbed into their respective seats. With Ralph driving, she looked over the single sheet two-sided letter from the board to Elanias. She found the language erudite academic, as if written to impress easily impressed donors, and still the tone was rather abrupt as well. She then scanned the names and signatures of the board members. "Bingo!" she said.

"What's that?" asked Ralph, rounding the last foot-path-sized road out of the campus and turning into traffic.

"Damned if Jacob JaCovey Stone is on the board that wanted to get rid of Griswald. I think I'll start on his dissertation first."

"Quite the coincidence, another Poe expert on a committee that held sway over the old prof."

"Quite—agreed."

"Of course, a backstabbing letter is far from a murder and an attack on you, Dr. Avery."

"That's an understatement."

"I'm famished is an understatement too. Can we grab a bite at a drive thru?"

"We'd best get back to HQ."

Ralph growled, bearlike, at this suggestion.

"Last drive thru I got in took me twenty-nine minutes!"

"Okay, got it. It's no bigly."

She thought it cute, the big guy using the term that Webster's had accepted as a real word just last month, bigly.

15

The rest of the day kept Jude busy as information from Trident Optimization Laboratory, TOL had been rushed to the Cook County Coroner's Office. Trident had good news, as they'd found a match in linked DNA with a young woman whose DNA was a sure match to the lady in the corset. This living ancestor's name was Gwyneth Cordellia Marshall, her married name. Her maiden name was Sturgess.

Sybil had gotten word first, while Jude and Ralph had been at the university and library on campus. Sybil, who'd covered for Jude's absence, had already called in an expert on DNA links in criminal cases, Sheila Lowe, the same Dr. Lowe who was a graphologist, as she was also an ancestry expert. Lowe would begin the arduous research necessary to work backwards in time, starting from Gwyneth Sturgess's parents and grandparents to determine if the identity of the lady in the subway wall could be determined.

"This is great news, a hit!" Jude said, overjoyed that TOL had made this connection between the corseted Jane Doe and the family Sturgess. "Still a long way from establishing Jane's identity, but it is a first step toward that day if!"

"Yes, if we can get more time out of Dean, and if we can get the family to cooperate."

"Yeah, could go either way, I suppose."

"Yeah—they might be greed-driven, craven jerks, whose first question to us is: 'Will there be any kinda reward, or just maybe—"

"Maybe they are overjoyed to be tapped to help us out here?" Jude's smile lifted her features.

"Just don't go all Pollyanna on me. Promise!"

The two lady MEs exchanged a look and a nod. "Worth a shot."

"We need to talk to this Gwen Sturgess."

"See what she's made of."

"And what she might know about her family tree."

"History's like a dropped anvil for some, kiddo, so hold your emotions from your sleeve."

"History's an open book to others," countered Jude.

"Sheila Lowe works back through the family tree, does her magic, and voila-presto-digitizes? It is seldom a straight line. And we already have a roadblock."

"Roadblock?"

"TOL no longer has a working phone number or address for Gwenyth Sturgess. We have no idea of her whereabouts."

"Shit." Jude's buoyance deflated. She plopped into a chair and groaned.

"True that. I'll have Lionel get on it. If Sturgess can be found, he's the man to find her."

"You think so?"

"Has a gift for it. Needed his help once, personal matter, locate my deadbeat husband during a difficult time for me and my daughter, Anastasia, alone."

"Dragged his worthless ass into court. My assistant is to me what Ralph is to you, indispensable."

"Fingers crossed till then."

"So, what did you learn from your trip back to the university?"

"Some interesting threads."

"Really, enough to darn a sock?"

"Ha! Not sure if the threads make a sock, let alone a sweater, but worth looking into...further, I think."

"Good, I think, but you should be carrying now, kiddo—your weapon—at all times. If whomever were to decide to take a second go at you, well...no one wants to lose you to some crazoid killer."

"Crazoid? Is that even a word?"

"Crazy and oid, yeah, I think. I am serious about you packing, lady."

"I have my lady Glock in my locker. Had it with me at the university the whole time today, but I am not going to be wearing it in the lab—no way."

"Understood, but when moving about Chicago's mean streets...." Sybil let her advice hang in the air, letting it sink in. "Whoever this freak is, the one that beaned you so badly, he's dangerous."

"I have no doubt of that."

"So, you say you got something out of the campus romp?"

"In my office, and I have a lot of pages to dig through." Jude pointed toward the indoor window that looked on her desk and still sparsely furnished office, as she'd still not requisitioned all the shelves and other items she wanted, eschewing the paperwork involved. Sybil stared at the foot-high stack of bound dissertations, even as she asked why the place remained so bare.

Jude shrugged this off, saying nothing, as Sybil pointed to her desk through the glass. "What the hell's that stack of eight-by-eleven books?"

"What indeed. I told you, dissertations—all on Edgar Allan Poe."

"And Dean's having forbidden your having any more to do with this case I guess it didn't register in your head? On account of the blow to your noggin? Are you wanting to get fired?"

"I want to determine the truth. It's our job. And Griswald didn't off himself any more than did Jeffrey Epstein."

"Oh, please."

Jude pointed through the glass to her desk. "There's three dissertations on Poe, written by three men who by varying degrees think they are the chosen ones to determine precisely who Edgar was and why and how he died at so young an age?"

"You sure he was all that young? I mean in his day young and old were relative."

"Forty in fact, January 19, 1809 to October 7, 1849, Baltimore, only two years after his beloved Virginia Clemm Poe passed in 1847."

"Sheeze, you really have been studying up on Poe. But really, do you for a moment believe that you can find answers to forensic questions in a stack of dissertations, really?"

"Griswald put his stamp of approval on all three, and yet each varies from the other on who did Poe in and why. All three heavily researched, and all three in that turgid and bland language of academia. I have only scratched the surface of each—read the precis."

Sybil grinned on hearing the word. "Oh, the preee-cis…wow that! Gawd, I do not miss being a student. All those fanciful words like paradigm for template or predicate for verb."

"Worse still, the things are chockful of enough passive constructions as to lull you right off to sleep."

"Good! Then you have every reason to read them! Ha! Help you with your slumber problem."

"What slumber problem? I don't—"

"Ahh-ah-ah! That disturbing voice in your head, one that calls your name. I hadn't forgotten about that."

When Jude only frowned and said nothing on the subject, the two of them now going into her office, Sybil said, "I think I have a solution to your hearing voices calling your name, Jude."

"Really? Seriously, I don't need your making light of—"

"No, seriously-seriously! There's a condition many people suffer from, from time-to-time."

"Yeah, schizophrenia. I've already looked into it, and Thorazine may be in the offing."

"No, hear me out!"

"I'm going to see a doctor about what I can do about—"

"No, no!" Sybil laughed at this. "It's not schizoid behavior at all."

"How would you know?"

"Well…be honest, my mother had a true case of schizophrenia—which is a rarer condition than people and Hollywood thinks."

"Really, your mother?"

"Trust me, once you live with it in a loved one, you know it when you see it."

"Then what the hell is in my damned head? I feel like this oppression, like someone or some ahh thing, maybe some damned human demon is coming for me. Like what I imagine a precognition event feels like. Opposite of a dé-jà-vu thing. That's out of the past; this feels out of the future."

"Shut up and listen, if you want me to tell you what's going on in your head."

"What do you mean?"

You keep showing me this flat aspect. Staring off into space. At first, I thought it straightforward depression, but then no!"

"You can't possibly understand."

"Are we BFFs or not?"

"Yes, but still."

"Not so much, since Meriam came into the picture, eh? Hey, kiddo?"

"Doesn't have anything to do with Meriam, and you and I are as tight as ever."

"Then why won't you confide in me anymore about what is troubling you?"

"When I am alone in my shower, or alone in bed, I'm hearing voices—one in particular, calling my name. Creepy-sounding too."

Sybil breathed deeply, nodding. "I think I do understand."

"How could you possibly—"

"Part of it is being alone too much! Come here." Sybil gave Jude a warm hug. "Now sit down and let's talk, 'cause I think I can help."

Jude slipped from the hug and found her desk chair, as Sybil sat across the desk from her. Sybil wasted no time getting back to the subject at hand.

"Alone in the shower, eh, and alone with the ceiling fan humming overhead?"

"Well, yeah."

"Do you hear music as well as voices?"

"No, mostly just the voices, like whispering, unintelligible until one voice stands out, calling my name."

"Honey, have you ever heard of a condition called pareidolia?"

"No, never, what's that?"

"Since you mentioned the sounds you've been hearing that day we talked, I've been doing some research."

"Yes, and?"

"Unfortunately, it is a naturally occurring condition that a helluva lotta people over generations have been institutionalized for, but it's not schizophrenia."

"Oh, great. I'm going nuts, but it has no recognizable name?"

"No, no! The diagnosis for generations has been falsely treated as being schizoid but—"

"Can you be more confusing?" Jude sarcastically asked.

"Pareidolia, it's a normal condition in which one hears patterns in sounds, that is random data and we auditorily interpret these patterns, some of us, as music or conversation, and sometimes both. Key words here being patterns and interpretations—our brains at work."

"I don't get it, Sybil."

"Common sources are ceiling fans, rushing wind, air-conditioners, laundromats, white noise generators, the drone onboard a plane, the clickity-clack of the railroad tracks. Had a bout with it myself when I had to submit to an MRI."

"Really? Are you making this up?"

"Have you ever submitted to an MRI?"

"No, should I?"

"They cover your ears with headphones and shove you into a tube, headfirst, and still the noise fires through your brain, your entire being! After a while the repetitive noise, for me, turned into 'Sybil, Sybil, Sybil'. Two syllables. Made me feel like Johnathan in Rollerball, the movie…ugh!"

"The origin of all the fear and dread that I've been nightmare-sweating over? A damn fan or drone of a shower?"

"Relax and enjoy the experience; it's harmless—there's even a visual form of pareidolia."

"Visual form in the para-id-olia thing, this human experience?"

"Yes."

"Give me an example."

"Come on, Judith Avery, haven't you ever looked at your meal and find it staring back at you?"

"Walleye, yes, Haddock no. At that high-end restaurant inside the Hyatt, yeah."

"What the hell're you talking about?" Sybil's features pinched with her question.

"They leave the head and eye on; stares right through you."

"Oh, yeah, right. Okay, better example: You surely must've heard of this housewife, Di something or DD something, when she picked up her cheese toast, she was shocked on seeing this lady looking back at her."

"Lady Di? This some kinda joke?"

"No, it was in the Tribune. At first it terrified her to see the face of a scary woman in her cheese toast. Scared hell outta her until she realized it was the Virgin Mary, known for good and not evil, which realization mellowed her out."

"Now you're just mocking me!"

"As God is my witness, word got around, it soon began to spark more attention, and eventually, a Trump casino at the time paid thirty thousand bucks to exhibit the toasted sandwich in their lobby."

"Stop it!"

"For many, the woman's soft image in the now molding toast, her full features and serene expression, did recall famous depictions of the

Virgin Mary. But I saw it in the newspaper, and I thought the curled hair, the pursed lips, and heavy eyelids more closely resembled another Madonna."

"The singer-actor?"

"Rather than Jesus' Madonna with Child, yeah."

"So, it's…if this is true about this para-whatever?"

"Google it. People see lots of pattern shapes in clouds, uncooked potatoes, and banana peels from Jesus and JFK to Marlon Brando on a bagel, and Tom Brady on a potato chip."

"I just see dragons and panda bears and unicorns in clouds." Jude, finally resigned to the phenomena, added, "Aha, like the oft-seen man in the moon, the face on Mars' surface."

"Now you've got it!"

"So, you're saying the sound I hear is a rhythmic pattern of noise that my mind translates into my name being called."

"Exactly. No brain damage, no schizophrenia, no aliens nor demons involved. And no precognition."

"I just became…felt oppressed over what I feared and failed to understand."

"Fear is real and understandable in a person who doesn't know what's happening in situations she cannot control. But maybe now, you can control it better, and thus, sleep better."

"It was the name calling out of the blue, like a witchy warning, and that's been due to my wild interpretation of a rhythmic noise? Is that what we're saying here?"

"Yes, simple as turning off your damn ceiling fan, my friend."

"That's a huge weight off my shoulders. Thank you so much!"

"No bother."

Jude lifted one of the bound dissertations. "While we wait for Sheila Lowe to get back to us, I have some reading and skimming to do."

"Staying late then?"

"I am, yes. Calling out for Chinese or a pizza and going to dig through this stuff on Poe."

"I'll stay then and help as much as I can."

Jude smiled at this and lifted a second booklet and tossed it across the desk for Sybil's perusal, to which Sybil responded by opening and glancing at the name Abdula Asim. The two began reading each obscure, unpublishable work, but Jude stopped Sybil before she got too far in. "Hey, about the voice in my head that has been ahhh chasing me around from home to wherever."

"You heard it in the subway at the wall that first day?"

"I did, yes."

And when we went to the second subway scene?"

"Yeah, but now I know it was the sound."

"The noise of the approach of the trains."

"And those going off and away. Now I know, that is, thanks to you, so I want to thank you, seriously. Like I said, it's taken a great weight off my shoulders."

"Sure, glad I could be of help. Now, back to work. What are we looking for?"

"A level of passion that—"

"Passion, I like that, but in a dissertation?"

"Takes passion for a subject to write a damned dissertation. But I'm looking for a level of the stuff that could mutate into obsession."

"A subject we all grapple with, ha!"

"An obsession so strong as to cause the author of the dissertation to lie, cheat, and kill for his belief."

"His belief being?"

"What lies tucked into his premise and position on the subject of the piece."

"Pretty dull precis here. An abstract, my prof called it. Why do English teachers have so many different terms for the same damned thing?" Sybil said. "Yeah, I recall that term now from my university days."

"I am going for what lies between the lines, no matter how dry and boringly written the abstract. Abstracts are necessarily summation and short. Read on."

Each fell silent again and pursued the elusive goal: To determine the level of passion each of three authors held for his position on the death of Edgar Allan Poe. One, penned by this Fiske guy, was direct and a poor imitation of a Hemingway style. It gave a nod to all the many theories circulating, before settling on organ failure due to drugs and alcohol. No surprises. The dissertation in and of itself did not rise to the level of passion to bring on hatred for Griswald.

"A style so easily mimicked that they hold an annual contest in Key Largo for the new Hemingway," Jude said of Fiske's work. "Anyway, my level of enthusiasm to like Fiske for smashing my head in just feels mild-to-middling at best."

"Could be you're reacting to his style and not the substance, maybe?"

Jude ignored this. "Nope, putting this one aside."

They'd talked of ordering a pizza or sandwiches, but neither one had actually stopped to make the order, instead, each had become engrossed in the reading. Then Jude's cell phone rang, a lilting tune, and it was Meriam. "Hey, I thought we were on for tonight."

"Oh, where are you?"

"Your place. Me and Sqaukey." Meriam had taken to calling the cat with her 'pet' name.

"Can you feed him, change his water out? Afraid I'm going to be working at the office late."

"Sure, sure. On a call?"

"No, just paperwork here at the lab."

"Gotcha. Understood. Disappointed, but I get it."

"Love ya, later."

"Later, love you back." Mental note, ask after her mom's health next time, Jude thought.

Sybil's ears had perked up on hearing Jude's last words. "So, you've made a friend, this Meriam, eh?"

"Yeah, it's been good so far, the relationship."

"Good. Glad for you."

They got back to the final and large three dissertations penned by Aaron Fiske Jr., Abdula Asim, and Jacob JaCovey Stone, a name that Jude had said sounded rather pretentious, one of those elite names where the long-standing family names of two lineages were combined. JaCovey and Stone. Sybil had scrunched her face up at this. "The privileged wealthy. Wonder if the family bought him a seat at the table there." She derisively added, "No doubt they call him JJ."

"On the board of directors, really?"

"I was referring to his test scores, just getting into the prestigious University of Chicago."

Another hour passed when Sybil cleared her throat and got Jude's attention.

"This dissertation by Abdula Asim, very likely a foreign student from all the dropped its, the's and these's," Sybil said, scrunching her nose. "Poe continues to have international appeal."

"Articles they're called."

"Articles?"

"Yeah, words like a, an, the, that, maybe which, I dunno, I forget, but second language students have trouble with 'em.

"Well, anyhow, Asim comes off blustery and adamant and self-righteous, yeah, but he seems to have a patina of careless abandon of a confused premise largely entangled in serpentine sentences that ramble into pretzel-lized thinking."

"Your reading that from the dissertation committee's report card, aren't you?" Jude took it from Sybil. She'd scanned portions herself, and with Sybil grinning, Jude wondered aloud, "How did this ever get past the sponsoring committee to award a PhD?"

"Three men on the committee, two to one vote, it's no more surprising than a supreme court vote."

Jude scanned the attached appendix for the decision, as she had with Fiske, who'd gotten a quick pass with three positive responses on a second go-round. "And that one dissenting vote against, came from Griswald."

"Seems your friend Griswald was a real task-master."

"But is that enough of a motive to kill the old prof?"

"Nahh, cause the damn thing didn't get his vote, but it did pass!"

"With an Asterix attached. One of the three dissented."

It was growing late when Jude took up the third unbound book, held together with three spaced pins in three-hole-punched sheets, split it between Sybil and herself. She gave the Sybil the second half to explore, while she took on the first half. Scanning as with the others, reading more diligently in parts, skipping over the dull areas, which was most of it, she took in a deep breath of air and said, "This one's it. This has got to be our man, someone who had the most to lose if Griswald's book was published."

Sybil frowned at this and shook her head. "To attack you for the manuscript, damn near kill you? Who…I mean what could motivate a man to do that, and as for murdering Griswald? And how in the hell can you take that leap based on this?" Sybil held up her half of the manuscript and dropped it on the desk with a thud.

Jude jammed her index finger into the typed pages on her desk. "This is the guy, I'm telling you."

"How can you know that?"

"There's an old saying among the Buddhists—"

"Oh, really? You have a Buddhist's motive—M.O.?"

"The Buddhists say that 'desire is the root cause of all evil.'"

"Desire? I thought it was money! Greed."

"Greed is a desire. Desire, a passion unchecked, uncontrolled Buddhism teaches, yes when passion becomes obsession."

Sybil gave this a moment's thought. "I am learning so much about you."

"I'm not a Buddhist. I just read about various cultures and religions—kind of a hobby."

Sybil nodded, stood, stretched, and paced about her chair, as there was not room enough to pace the small office. "Well, yeah, we've all seen obsessions lead to murder. Remember that case where a guy killed a woman in a library over a goddamn ink pen? Offered to buy it from her, but she wouldn't part with it—some sort of heirloom, I think. Anyhow, he killed her for that damned pen."

"Proves my point—a life for a pen. What about a life for a theory on the true cause of death in the Poe mystery? Is it worth someone's life to control a narrative?"

"Hmmm…if Trump taught us anything, 'control the narrative' for good or bad."

"Theory of Poe's death narrative could translate into not only money, but standing within the academic community. Asim is likely long gone from UC, Fiske as well, but Stone, he is on the goddamn board of directors, somehow!"

"Well, Stone is convincing despite his overburdening vocabulary."

"Stone writes he died of a brain tumor. His evidence, the medical details."

"Which are, while not extensive, have the veneer of rational reasoning, and he has interviewed some sound medical professionals for support of the brain tumor theory."

"So, it is a believable theory of the crime? And you are a medical examiner."

"I mean I'm believing it from reading the dissertation, weighing up Stone's research—and if it is true, yes, and wouldn't a tumor explain his melancholia and why he wrote such sad and dark poetry, and ahhh macabre stories?"

"Griswald may well have stolen this research from Stone. Dates align as such. Griswald told me about this possibility of what actually killed Poe. I mean, suppose Stone, having risen through whatever cutthroat means to the board of regents at the university was himself preparing to publish either this, his dissertation, or an updated version?"

"Kind of a leap, kiddo."

"Academics have to publish or perish, as they say, and just suppose he caught wind that Griswald was readying his final book for publication with a major publisher? Suppose he is The Raven, and suppose he'd sent more than one threatening note to Griswald?"

"That would constitute an obsession."

"People have killed for less."

Sybil nodded. "Far less, agreed. But can you prove it?"

"Right now? No, but I intend to."

"Well do it through science and the lab, okay? I don't want to be visiting you in a rehab center ever." Sybil stood to leave, but first she came around the desk and said, "I'm going to hug you, if you don't mind."

They hugged, and as they did so, Jude saw that Meriam had arrived and was standing outside at the window to her office, watching them. She could see from the look on Meriam's face that the younger woman was upset at what she was witnessing. But Meriam suddenly pasted on a smile and lifted a brown bag—Chinese food as an explanation as to how she'd gotten this far past all the checkpoints to the labs.

Meriam opened the office door and cheerily said, "Brought you a bite! You need to eat! And hello Dr. Shanley."

Sybil returned the greeting and holding her phone up, she said, "I'd like to join you two, but I've got a call. Someone's died. Lionel just buzzed me."

"What a surprise," Jude said to Sybil as she left, and then to Meriam, who was unpacking the lunch items—little boxes with metal clasps, "And what a surprise you are!"

"It wasn't easy finding you, but a nice guard brought me down the right elevator."

"Flirting with the guards, eh?"

"I am a sucker for a man in uniform—or a woman in a lab coat!"

Jude smiled and exaggeratedly displayed herself in the lab wear. "Technically, the guards're supposed to frisk you."

"That might've been fun." Meriam stepped around the desk to kiss Jude. Jude, caught off guard, said, "Whoa, whoa…not a good idea in my workplace. Cameras everywhere here."

"You didn't seem to mind when Sybil had her arms around you."

"That was only a hug between friends, co-workers. Nothing more. And please tell me you're not the jealous type."

"I'm not, but I sense there's been or was there…"

"No, purely professional here. I'd've been fired from here long ago if she hadn't come to my rescue. Close yes. Close friends."

Meriam breathed deeply, plopped into the chair across from Jude, and said, "Good, that's good to know. When I first saw her at the hospital, holding your hand, and now hugging you, well, what's a girl to think?"

"You've been watching The Bachelor again."

"Big Brother," Meriam corrected her.

"We've not known one another for long, Merr, but I want you to know that I am not seeing anyone else. And you?"

"No one, no."

"Then for the time being, we're talking being exclusive, and if that ever changes, you let me know, and I will grant the same respect to you." When Meriam hesitated, Jude added, "Deal?"

"Deal."

"Shall we enjoy our feast then. Ahhh and you've learned my favorites! Moo goo gai pan!"

16

The following day at the lab, Jude was again ordered up to Grant's office—the high tower, or so she'd begun to think of it as. She had no idea what the situation might be, and once she got there, she found Sybil again had been called in with her. "I have some strange news to impart, doctors."

"What is it?" asked Sybil. "The suspense is killing me."

Jude was unsure if this was a time for levity, but at the same time, she envied Sybil's ease with Grant, while she herself felt a complete uneasiness in the man's presence. She hoped one day to change that.

"I have results back from Dr. Lowe," began Dr. Grant. "It's regarding Luther and his team. Appears, according to Sheila, that Luther and his entire team failed in her reading of their handwriting. Says there are spikes and emotional clues all over the place in every sample. Luther, maybe another, intends to challenge it—not surprising."

"Challenge the handwriting analysis part, you mean?" asked Jude.

"Precisely. We took the samples without informing them that their written statements would be analyzed. But hell, we offered either a video of their verbal statement or a written statement, and they all chose writing it out."

"Aha, afraid their body language would give them away, I imagine," Jude said, hoping to impress Grant.

"The whole lot of them were found lacking?" asked Sybil.

"Lying is the word, Sybil."

Jude frowned. "Not one telling the truth?"

"I've interviewed them individually, some with union rep, one without."

"Lisa newlywed Anderson? Did you get invited to her wedding?"

"Yes. You?"

"No. I did not."

"Yes, well, she claims that she took nothing, and when Luther offered her money from pawning the loot, she refused it."

"Will you keep her on?" asked Jude.

"No, no she lied about it in our initial interview, so it's time to begin reading resumes and hiring new staff, and I want you two on the hiring committee this time around."

"But we're stretched to the limit already with our normal load and working on the subway murders, Dean!"

He put a hand up to Sybil. "You're both done with the subway murders."

"But our time's not up! You said two weeks!" Sybil said.

"I'd give you that time too, except for the change in stance on the walled-up twosome."

Jude shrugged. "Change in stance? What's that mean?"

"Means that City Hall's had a change of heart toward the whole matter."

"What the fu-hell, Dean?"

"Hard to explain, but some butthead PR advisor over there has convinced the mayor that as long as the mystery couple remain a mystery and are not identified, then the bricklayer killer will never be known, so the mystery falls into the infamous variety called unsolved mysteries, and that puts a whole new patina on things as far as City Hall sees it."

"Patina? You're confusing the hell out of me," said Sybil.

"Me too. This is something like making hay out of a bad situation?" asked Jude.

"Like making lemonade out of lemons, but the lemonade is laced with cyanide, I guess."

"Come out with it, Dean."

"City Hall sees more of a future in keeping the mystery alive than in resolving it. Cold case extraordinary so to speak. They're talking T-shirts, hats, baubles, keychains, and a citywide contest to name the lady in the corset and her man. Winner gets, I dunno, so many free rides on the subway?" He gritted his teeth. "So crazy, I know, but that's the latest from the man!"

"This is what's come of putting the image of the young couple in the tintype on the front page of the papers and on the nightly news?" asked Jude, alarmed.

"And the image of the woman's reconstructed features?" added Sybil.

"Maybe we should have withheld it all from the public to begin with." Grant clenched his fists and his teeth, clearly unhappy with the orders from on high.

Unable to let it go, and with Sybil pacing the spacious office, Jude ranted, "You're telling me that our illustrious mayor and City Hall, the infamous machine, due to all the 'fun' the general population is now having with the mystery of a John and Jane Doe, that they've decided that to solve the question of who this highly unfortunate couple are without question…that they find that'd be counterproductive to the party atmosphere the double-mystery has created in the fertile, collective imagination of the people, whose theories have run rampant at this point, which came about in large part to our caving into City Hall from the beginning?"

"Hold on there, Dr. Avery!"

"My point is that this party city latched onto the PR that we put out, the PR which was supposed to 'deal with it' and 'get out in front of it' to keep Chicago's reputation as a deathtrap out of the collective conscious of its people—or some such nonsense?"

"Sybil, you were here when—Jude wasn't here when—but you recall when that alligator—big ass one—was found in the lagoon in Humbolt Park?"

"Is that your answer? To change the subject at hand?"

"Absolutely not. The same thing happened with the alligator!"

Sybil turned to Jude and told her of the time when, "Vendors circled the little lagoon at the park to sell hot dogs, sandwiches, and funnel cakes, and people came from all around to view the gator in the water, six-foot long gator, by the way, swimming about and occasionally making landfall."

"The crowd cheered for the gator," added Grant. "No one wanted animal control to capture the monster. They were having too much fun, you see, and, actually, CAC failed to bag it. Had no experience at it."

"We flew in a gator hunter from Florida," said Sybil.

"Hurricane Wayne Caine, Florida gator guy."

"And he got the job done while a huge crowd of bored Chicagoans looked on," finished Sybil, a light laugh escaping her.

After a moment of silence to let all this sink in, Grant passed along the information that Jude and Sybil were to, "Chalk the lady in the corset case up to a lost cause—a cold file too cold, a brick too far. "I know I'd given you two weeks, but that's damn near to a close now…doesn't cost us anymore time, money or energy to-to—"

"To let it go, just like that?" Sybil's face had turned ashen and angry.

"And see the 'unhappy couple' are walled up again, a second indignity, reunited in a Chicago Potter's Field?" asked Jude. "I had thought we could do better than that."

"Your dedication and idealism is appreciated, ladies, doctors, and duly noted. Best you might do at this point is to take up a collection," he abruptly replied, then tried to take it back, then decided, "Hey, it's not a bad idea. Fact is, City Hall could turn that into a Go Fund Me account as part of their carnival act and the two Does can have a proper burial."

"Yeah, why not. The mayor can work on that," Jude muttered, frowning.

Sybil remained unhappy with this as well. "You promised two weeks, Dean, and damn it all, I am taking every minute of it. Fire me if you want, but that's how strongly I feel about this 'unhappy couple.'" Sybil stormed out.

"I think she means it," Jude said.

Dean frowned and shook his head. "Stubborn lady, she is."

"I find stubbornness a good quality in a person who's right."

"*Et tu, Brute?* Going to disobey my orders?"

"Sybil is your Brutus, not I. Look, we just want to give it more time, Dean, ah, Dr. Grant, you know, to continue and hope that one of several ancestry DNA companies finds a match to the mysterious couple's bloodline. We've already put it out there. We should at least wait for results."

"That's a longshot and you know it. Even if you did find a long-lost cousin, what are the odds that that person could know of anything about the fate of the lady or the gent in the wall?"

"Longshot or not, it's a shot we agreed was worth taking, and we should at least determine if we missed or hit our mark." Sybil had often coached Jude on how Dean liked sports metaphors, and in particular hunting, fishing, and shooting.

"All right, tell Sybil you two have the rest of the week. Three days!"

"If we can spare these poor people from any further indignity, being buried without anyone knowing their names, in some shallow grave in a Potters Field…"

"You're still talking? Go!"

She started to do as told when he shouted, "Hold on, Judith. Look, if you do strike on a big fish, I'll fight City Hall on behalf of us all. Now go take your longshot and get out of here."

She was about to leave when he stopped her again; this time shouting, "Wait. What you said about the suicide note, Lowe says it is in Noble's handwriting, and she has no doubt of this. The old fellow had not become infatuated with you, after all. Nor did he say that he offed himself."

"I knew it. I'd say Luther Noble has been using drugs or has a brain tumor. This is going too far, what he did."

"Another nail in Luther's coffin. He'll never work in this state again handling bodies."

"I hope he doesn't find work at an animal shelter either!"

Grant snorted at this as if she were kidding. "And another thing, the small Post-it note, the threat from The Raven, Lowe says it reeks of someone of a narcissistic nature, self-absorbed, possibly enjoys fetishes of some sort."

"Fetishes, self-absorbed, narcissistic? Sheila got all that out of that cryptic bit?"

"Every loop, every swirl, every dip and rise, she tells me, speaks volumes."

"I've been following up a lead on who might've had a motive to see the old man gone, sir."

"He may well have offed himself, Jude. The fact he did not write that note doesn't negate the possibility of suicide."

"But—"

"The scene, despite Luther's childish prank, still screams death by his own hand, so far."

"But if it was staged?"

"Tests show his system was choked with his prescription pills and a fair amount of alcohol."

Jude recalled how much Griswald had drank at their dinner. "I didn't know him, not really, and I only spent a total of maybe six hours on two occasions with him, but I never got the impression he was suicidal or depressed."

"People are devious, especially when it comes to hiding such emotions."

"But he was joyful at the prospect of publishing his life's work. In passing, he told me it was with Simon & Schuster, and as NYC publishing goes, well you don't get any bigger than that."

"Did you check with the publisher to determine if he actually had a contract with them, or was this wishful thinking on his part? Rejection letters have offed more than one writer, I suspect."

"I hadn't time to call them, but I will."

"Why don't we clear it up here and now?" Grant buzzed his secretary and asked her to get a managing editor or director at Simon & Schuster for questions from the Office of the Coroner, Chicago in the case of Dr. Oswald Griswald."

They waited for the contact to be made. Grant handled the questioning after giving the lady, a woman named Hamilton, the circumstances surrounding the death of 'one of your writers.' He followed this by again naming Griswald, middle initial T.

"Yes, well, after a quick check with our two acquisitions editors interested in all things Poe, I am told that no contract was issued, but that is because there were unresolved issues over the advance. You may want to talk to Dr. Griswald's agent."

"But you were in negotiations for the book, correct?"

"Yes, isn't that what I said?" replied Hamilton in annoyance.

"Iyyy guess so. His agent's name, a phone number?"

"This is not Google. But it's Mortimer Spencer, good agent, brings us talent."

"Do you have a number for him?"

"Ohhh, do hold."

After a short pause, Hamilton's secretary came on with the number."

"Not so much as an RIP out of the old girl," Grant said of Hamilton.

A quick discussion with literary agent, Mortimer Spencer, made it clear that he had arranged to have the book transcribed at his own expense, as he believed in its premise, and that Griswald had a possible bestseller on his hands, but that Griswald had not as yet forwarded the handwritten manuscript for transcription, which Spencer, again said he was so excited about that he'd made arrangements to personally pay for.

"So, all was in limbo."

"How strange that he hadn't seen to getting the book into your hands, then," Jude said, interjecting as the phone was on speaker.

"I'm just devastated the man is no longer with us. I so wished to represent his book. I had S&S on the hook for the enticing idea of just how Poe was killed. Perhaps we can still negotiate a deal with a surviving relative."

"Afraid there are no relatives," Jude said.

Grant glared at her and thanked the man and said goodbye and hung up. "This whole thing is like a set of stairs to nowhere."

"Oh, I think there are stairs involved, and I think they will lead to a killer."

"But again, you're not on the Griswald case."

"It's going to be swept aside as a suicide, and this asshole, this monster's going to get away with it, and he's going to go on to become the damn president of the University of Chicago some damn day at this bloody rate."

"Who're you talking about?"

"I have a suspect."

"Jude—policy!"

"All right, I will turn over what I have to Sybil."

"Do that! And no more pursuit on the Griswald affair. Orders! I did the initial workup myself at the request of the current president of the university, and I can tell you, between myself and Sybil, nothing's being swept under any damn rug!"

"Aren't you even curious as to who I suspect?"

He grinned wide at this and replied. "All right, to whom has it come around to for you? Since, you've found an individual motivated to force-feed Griswald his own meds?"

Sarcasm, she thought, unsure how to answer this.

"All right—a name," Grant yelled. "And we never had this conversation, understood?"

"Stone."

"Stone who?"

"Jacob JaCovey Stone. We can prove he's The Raven. If we can get a handwriting sample from him."

"I'm sure you've got Sybil looking into this. I'll talk with her. You are to stay out of it now. From this moment on."

"I hear you, sir."

"Yes, but are you hearing with both ears?"

"Hook, line, and sinker, sir, yes, sir!"

She turned then and left, thinking Grant knew Stone was her subject of suspicion all along, that Sybil had already shared what she'd learned from the dissertation. She imagined Stone was well connected, that he'd had a leg up from the bottom of the university ladder to be on the board at a relatively young age and as a former student in Griswald's classes, English 150, 240 and graduate classes after that.

It seemed fairly obvious to Jude that Griswald, having been on a panel of three to approve or disapprove of Stone's dissertation, that Stone may well have believed that his former professor had stolen or plagiarized much from the Stone dissertation. And perhaps he was right on that score for all Jude knew.

A check back with Miss Elanias could determine if Griswald had checked out the dissertation himself for an extended period of time—enough time to make a copy to work from in crafting his own book, combining the family history tale of an ancestor setting Poe up for a beating about the head wherein a tumor lay in wait to take Poe out.

She had promised Grant that she would relent and rely on him and Sybil going forward with respect to the Griswald case, to steer clear of this case so there'd be no appearance of misconduct or ethical and procedural missteps.

At the same time, she was dying to corroborate the pieces of the floating puzzle bouncing about in her mind. One piece particularly nagged at her. A what if question. If Griswald had, after disapproving of Stone's dissertation on the first go-round and the second, had still then later checked it out with Elanias's blessing for however long her dear friend wished, breaking her own rule for him, what did that say about the whole affair? Had he used portions of Stone's work to entice that literary agent, Spencer?

She then thought that her fertile imagination could fill that dissertation room at the university. That perhaps she was, as Sybil said, 'reaching.'

Jude must soon return the three dissertations that she'd taken with her, but she'd had Ralph make a copy of Stone's book, hefty as it was, as it might well prove to be evidence in a possible case built against the man. On returning the Stone book, she'd have a look at Miss Elanias's meticulous records on who, other than Jude, had borrowed Stone's dissertation. But what were the chances that Miss Elanias had kept no record of Griswald's checking it out? Breaking her rules for her 'special' friend.

17

Later in the day and as hours had passed working on routine autopsies, Jude came to a point of exhaustion and saw that it was only four PM. She'd had time to give all the loose threads her attention in the subconscious mind, even as she'd worked over several bodies today. She stripped away her protective gear and dumped it into the medical waste management container, slipped through the corridor and found Sybil in her office. "I have to return the dissertations to the university library. Wanna join me?"

"I want to find an answer to our subway darlings, Jude. And hey, you're not supposed to be anywhere near the Griswald affair. Dean called down and insisted I do not share information with you on the case."

"Sybil, we're way beyond sharing now! You sat up with me last evening reading the damn dissertations, remember? And we agreed that Stone—"

"That was almost twenty-four hours ago, kiddo! In this place, this work environment chained to the politicos? That's like forever ago. Now just bring those stacks of paper over to my office, and I will see to returning them."

Jude was about to explain her notion that Griswald had quite possibly stolen information from Stone's work, another nail in the reasoning that Stone had motive. But she sensed that Sybil was prepared to go no further out on Jude's limb with her. Grant had seen to that. She instead decided to keep her new suspicion and plan then to herself. "Look, I signed the books out, and the head librarian there is expecting me to keep my word—return the dissertations on time. If you come along with me, I am sure you could then sign out Stone's at the same time."

Sybil gritted her teeth, took a moment, and said, "Fine. To do this by the book like Grant said, I need to sign the Stone book out. Then tell them it's being held in evidence in the Griswald case."

"Tell who?"

"The acting university president, a man named Charles Stueben."

"Who will in turn inform Stone, no doubt."

"Grant believes that if Stone had anything to do with Griswald's death, this will smoke him out."

"Smoke him out, eh?"

"Think what we will of Dean, he's not taking kindly to one of us being accosted or abused by anyone."

"Then he's setting a trap. Why didn't he tell me this?"

"Policy! You are not to go near this case again. As is, you have compromised it, Jude. You surely understand that much."

"It wasn't like I was sleeping with the victim or related to him!"

"Jude, you were admittedly, the last to see him alive."

"How does that make me a—"

"Suspect!" Sybil finished for her. "You said it yourself, desire, greed, avarice it all comes down to desire, you said, and none of us—not one of us—knows how far another of us is willing to go to scratch a crazy itch. I know and Grant knows you had nothing to do with the professor's death, but a canny lawyer, I dunno, like the ones who represent abhorrent people for the root of all evil, money, they could take your sudden interest and pursuit of Griswald as some sort of sick fascination with Poe and in some mad, passionate moment you overpower the old man and shove pills down his throat."

"Did you guys find evidence he was force-fed those pills?"

Sybil shook her head. "You are a sharp knife, kiddo."

"I wanted to ask Dean this, but he barked me out of the room for far less."

"Bruising around the mouth, lips, couple of cracked teeth that were recent and uncared for, while he had, for his age, well-cared for choppers."

"I knew it. Stone got to him that very night—The Raven, not at his door but behind his door."

"You're something else, Jude."

"Well, maybe he was hiding inside the apartment, with the drugs at the ready, when Griswald entered, which means premeditation."

"Your imagination is miles ahead of the lack of evidence."

"Kinda what you might call pre-medicated premeditation."

"Cute, but it's all speculation, and the detectives we sent out to interrogate Stone and others, they came back with a solid alibi for JJ Stone."

"Let me guess! Home with wife and kiddies?"

"The family vouches for his time, yes."

"The entire night?"

"Yes."

"But we know how often family close ranks to lie, cheat, or even steal for a loved one—even an outlier like this man is likely to be."

"And your definition of outlier?"

"Aberration in this case, deviant, quirky one!"

"Asim and Fiske can be ruled out, if we can get handwriting from all three of your suspects. But you see, again protocol comes in here, Jude. A half decent lawyer will contest how we arrived at Stone's doorstep. They will want to know each and every clue. If we tell them the truth, our case against JJ drops like a stone, as you were not only compromised by being a suspect yourself, but by going on this ahhh fishing expedition that led to Stone."

"I see, and I get it, but our last case together, we broke a lot of legal barriers together, Sybil, but in the end, the results are what mattered."

"Hell, we went across several jurisdictions, and we faced the same kind of legal challenges, and in the end, we might well have lost due to our recklessness."

"But we won because the evidence was overwhelming, and in this case—"

"In this case, it's not overwhelming—at least not yet. It's why we are trying to, as Dean calls it, 'smoke' our prey out."

"All right, you take the dissertations back, and I'll step away from it entirely."

"Smart move. Kiddo, this is entirely different from our beating down that snuff film murder operation. That stuff being uncovered, the victims being nuns and veterans and kindly old ladies and dogs and cats, well face it, an old English professor's murder just doesn't get the attention of the higher ups, the press, or the people."

"But two dead people found bricked up in the subway does."

"Now you're seeing the picture come into focus."

"Does Dean see it that way? If he does, not so sure I want to continue here."

"Dean has seen it all. He's written four books chronicling his cases, and there've been some bizarro-buzz attached to them all. One involved a little-person killer working with his normal brother."

"A midget killer?"

"No, a killer midget, but he preferred being called a 'little person' or dwarf and not—"

"I get it—politically correct dwarf killer."

"Scalped people."

"Oh, sheeze."

"So, no, Dean is not unfamiliar with red hot cases, and this one involving your professor pal, no not a red hot or even a warm case that'll garner attention and more awareness of the role we fill and the job we do."

"If that is the case, why'd Dean take the less-than-flamboyant case in the first place?"

"The president asked him to."

"The president?"

"The university president, Charles Steuben."

"They go way back, do they?" Jude risked the question.

"They do—were college buds, undergrads in the same fraternity at Northwestern."

"Do tell. So, it was to be a controlled, hush-hush affair, a quick assessment of an old fellow's suicide, and to not reflect badly on the institution. I get it."

"It started out that way, but after you were clobbered, and after I talked to Dean, he's taken a sharp turn in his assessment of the whole matter."

"Good to know. I'll get those dissertations in a box and over to you."

"Best plan for now, and I hope you'll give us here at Cook County more credit, and that you'll stick with us. Either way, you're a bright light around here."

"Awww, making me blush."

"Cheeky, yes, but sharp."

"You could say the same about one Dr. Sybil Shanley."

"Jude, to be honest, you remind me of myself at your age."

"Yeah, heard about your near-death experience in a grain elevator once."

"Grain under the bridge. Later," finished Sybil as Jude exited.

As Jude traveled back to her office to pack the dissertations for Sybil, she thought how modest Dr. Shanley was, and how different from Grant. She did not care for the limelight, a fact clear enough after their teaming together to end that awful snuff film case that had begun here in Chicago but had led to Los Angeles. The other case that Sybil had alluded to, Jude had read about. Sybil had brought down a serial killer who tortured his victims by repeatedly asphyxiating and reviving them, using a body bag as his torture chamber. Sybil had buried the bastard in the end under a mountain of wheat grain in a silo. She hardly wanted to talk of it, ever. She remained true to form, a foil for Grant, a man who loved to talk of his exploits in the field.

I guess the two balance one another out, Jude thought, "demure vs. narcissist, but which kind of doctor to the dead then am I? What kind of medical examiner do I fall into, which do I want to be?

Lost in her thoughts, she did not see the man approaching her at warp speed, as if trying to catch her. She only saw a blur at first until she realized it was Luther Noble. Jude expected a blow as he'd rushed up to her in this corridor like a madman. "Dr. Avery, I wanted to say I'm sorry—extremely sorry—for all the stupid, dumbass things I've done to make your life hell since you arrived."

"I-I…" Caught off guard, Jude could only stutter.

"I was never like that before, not toward anyone, and I was always a real professional at this job until you…well, until I got it in my head to get your attention anyway I could, anyhow I could, and it got away from me. Feel like a schoolboy with a crush, and my actions cannot be excused, but I wanted you to know how deeply sorry I am now."

Jude was unsure what to say. Was he sincere, or was this part of his plan to get the best severance deal possible? "Your obsession, writing that stupid suicide note, removing items from victims, that dead man's hat, Mr. Noble, it has gotten your entire team fired. I feel awful about that, and I am sorry for that, but that was neither my doing nor my call."

He nodded, a MAGA hat in hand, crushing it, when a lone tear rose and fell, followed by a second before he wiped his eyes with the cap. "I am sorry. All I wanted to say before they bar me from the place entirely. And you know, when I heard you were hurt, put in hospital by some guy, it tore me up. I just want you to know, if ever you need a friend to talk to and maybe have a cuppa joe with or go to a concert with."

He's actually still flirting and asking for a date, she realized. "I appreciate that, Mr. Noble, but that's out of the question, and always has been."

"I just mean as a friend only."

"You should know that I am bisexual."

His eyes widened. "That don't matter to me. I got gay and bi friends."

"Well then, maybe someday."

"Ha, yeah, someday in hell, you mean?"

"Someday after we have all healed. Now I hafta get along. Work awaits." Jude was desperate to extricate herself from this corridor and this man.

"I get it. I ain't thick, but if ever you need muscle to help in a move or to put some joker's lights out, you call me." He handed her a freshly minted business card that read above his name, phone number and email: The Altruist Company—We provide for your every need."

She wondered, wherever did he find the word altruist, although holding her tongue.

"Going into business for myself. I'm my own CEO, and it's kinda, well weirdly thanks to you."

"Don't thank me for your getting fired."

He ignored this. "Got a partner, but I'm top man, the boss of us, as they say. My partner, she's good with numbers, so she's secretary-treasurer combined."

"Not Lisa!"

"Yeah, Lisa. Back of the card is her card."

Jude stared at the backside. Same except Lisa's name appeared instead of Luther's. Jude lifted the cheaply made biz-card into the air, twirled it between her fingers like a magician, nodded, and said, "If I ever need you, sure."

"Luther Noble stands ready to deliver."

She scrunched up her face, gave his words over to a scary as hell image, and said. "Gotta go."

"Yah, sure, and have a nice evening, Dr. Avery."

"In the arms of another, yeah, I intend to."

This image, painted to further discourage Luther, appeared a failure as well, as he seemed to relish the idea of Jude and Meriam curled up, woman-y-woman, as he shouted goodbye after her.

Had the man really been interested in her sexually the entire time of his harassing her in ways that were so extremely far from exciting her sexually? After a year now—treating her as an object of derision and displaying deviant behavior on the job, in the workplace—that he was in fact treating her as an object of affection in his fevered brain, when all he created in her was a sense offended revulsion? Had he lost all judgement, common sense, and normalcy?

When she got back to her desk, and while packing the dissertations inside a file box for Sybil, she asked the same question of Stone with regard to Griswald: Had he lost all judgement, common sense, reasoning, and rationality, along with all normality, this man Stone?

Jude took a deep breath. All that she knew, all that she had uncovered, everything pointed to this man Jacob JaCovey Stone. But Sybil was right. She had to let this go and trust that she and Grant would see to Stone. In the meantime, she'd do all she could to learn more about the couple found behind walls in the Chicago subway.

18

The following day, Jude felt energized and glad to distance herself from the question of suicide versus homicide in the Griswald case; it was a weight lifted off her shoulders, or so she had come to feel, having taken a new attitude toward it. Besides, time now was of the essence to learn as much as possible about the subway couple. To this end, she started making calls to all three of the link DNA ancestry companies that she and Sybil had sent samples to for a search of the nation for any blood relative to the murdered pair. They had a female cousin of the lady in the corset, Sturgess, but thus far the woman had not wished to 'participate,' actually using that word. Jude wanted to scream at the woman that this was not a game show but real life—participate! And thus far nothing in the way of a match of the male's DNA.

After her calls, it was a waiting period, but she hadn't time to simply wait. She got on the phone and called a woman named Lauren McDouglas, a Sturgess cousin—the cousin many times removed from the corset lady if the charting could be believed. When she got the woman on the phone, she introduced herself and told her why she was contacting her.

Jude had her mental fingers crossed that McDouglas would take a positive and responsible role in the investigation, unlike Sturgess, who had at one point informed Sybil Shanley that she, "Simply did not want to get involved in a murder investigation that spanned over seventy years." As if time had anything to do with responsibility and caring for a lost family member, Jude thought, and her thoughts giving way to the fact she had no family, and it angered her to see people with family who took relatives for granted. Sybil had sent Jude an email plea, as Lionel had magically gotten an email on the lady in question. Sybil shared via inner-office email what she'd written to the McDouglas lady. The plea to Mrs. McDouglas read:

I know living in Denver, Colorado, the notion of helping us out here in Chicago may be daunting, but I am prepared to do all I can to gain your help, and please let me explain why the identities of these two people is so important to us here.

Sybil read the list enumerating why McDouglas needed to do the right thing. Still no response after several days. Silence. Crickets.

Angered by these facts, Jude managed to get McDouglas's phone number, and she did not hesitate to call, as time was running out for the 'unhappy couple' as the wall people were now routinely being called.

The voice at the other end of the call did a lot of hemming and hawing that amounted to the stranger in Colorado as having, "No time but three children instead, since I am the only parent as their fuckface father has abandoned us for some whore, and I damn well have my hands full with life now, today, having somehow survived the pandemic, no job, no help from family members, and really, this is some kind of sick lottery to win! I saw that story about the subway bodies on YouTube, and now that it's somehow got something to do with me because six years ago I did a DNA search for family? This is nuts, and my aunt Savanah says we should let the past bury the past."

Jude apologized for the hardships the single mother was experiencing, sounding like she'd just hang up then, but she then explained what was about to happen to the remains of the walled-in couple in stark terms. "Have you at least discussed this with your relatives other than this aunt? Is there one or more who'd like to help us out here? We had first approached a Gwenyth Sturgess."

"She's useless. Gives not one damn for anyone but herself."

"Ha! Yes, well, I didn't want to say anything as I don't know her. She turned us down."

"I've just met a few cousins on my ancestry chart, but only by phone. Gwen didn't want to be bothered. I don't know how the others might feel about this…this surprising development. How can you be sure the Jane Doe in Chicago is really related to us?"

"The same ancestry link company that found your relatives says so. Do you trust them?"

"Yes, yes, I do. I have plans to meet some more lost relatives. One of these days, but money's tight and none are close."

"Would you share this news with them. If you allow me your email address, I can forward photos of the reconstructed features of the deceased. It's very important to us here at the Chicago Coroner's Office, and frankly, our bosses have given us a deadline that ends in two days."

Silence at the other end. "Woman to woman, Mrs. McDouglas,

your maiden name being Sturgess and being related to a family called Hightower, suppose this woman is a great grandmother to you or to one of your cousins?"

Finally, Lauren McDouglas, nee Sturgess said, "All right, send the images, and I'll share them with my newly found family members."

"And your mother, father, grandfather?"

"Grandpaw is gone, but yes, will share with mom and dad."

"Are mom and dad close by to help with the kiddies?" Jude asked.

"They're back in Illinois, actually, Alton. We're making arrangements for me and the kids to move back home to be near them."

"Excellent news. Maybe in some small way, we here can help, maybe set up a Go Fund Me for you."

"That's sweet, Doctor ahh…"

"Avery, Dr. Judith Avery." Jude thought of Griswald's family curse tale of woe and Poe. "Please ask your parents and cousins if they had ever heard of an ancestor whose disappearance from Chicago remained a family mystery. This lady in our care, she fell off the face of the earth for no known reason, and coupled with the pictures, who knows, we might have a match, and someone in your family may wish to take custody of the remains."

They said their goodbyes, and Jude had renewed hope about determining something substantive about the unfortunate, 'unhappy couple.'

Still desperate, the clock ticking, Jude decided she'd call the ancestry link companies again this afternoon about the John Doe found in the subway wall. So far, no hits, only because, so far, his DNA hadn't been run through the system.

Jude was back to the waiting game, and it was excruciating, but to spend it without going bonkers, she busied herself with the day-to-day, normal work of the next autopsy. As she did so, she recalled how the subway bodies had shaken up the routine that first day of discovery, and she felt badly that the most curious case of the year, so far, could go the way of routine as well, ending in the dreaded Potters Field, where bodies were treated like cordwood to simply be disposed of in the quiet of night.

◆ ◆ ◆

Later the same day, Jude began to wonder if anyone, during the time that the subway couple went missing, reported their disappearances? Finding police records on such an event from so long ago without a specific date seemed improbable if not impossible, but what about archived stories in the newspapers? Surely two people going missing in such a manner would raise some reporter's antennae, perhaps? But again, with no specific date or the names of the deceased, where would one start a search? The time frame she had to work with was a wide at best, but it had to coincide with the building of the underground tunnel. Using that date, it could help guide a good researcher to a possible story on two people who'd gone missing.

Jude got on her iPhone again and called Meriam, laid out her suspicion that perhaps a news story might have come of missing persons in between 1947 and 1950, and she asked if Meriam would undertake it as a research project. Meriam agreed without hesitation, excited at the prospect of helping to solve the mystery. "I can go downtown to the Tribune and search their archives. I do it all the time for my school papers."

"Excellent, but there is a catch."

"What catch?"

"Deadline."

"When?"

"ASAP."

"Understood and see you tonight."

"Bye with love."

"You too."

After a brief moment's thoughts devoted to Meriam, Jude's phone, still in hand, rang. It was bad news. No match had come up on the John Doe at one of the ancestry link companies. Soon after a second call came through from a second DNA lab to report the same bad news. "Maybe this guy had no children" said the caller. By end of day, Jude heard from the last of the three companies specializing in link DNA connection. Again, it was a no show. Mr. Unfortunate remained altogether unknown. Disappointment flooded her bones, and she suddenly felt a wave of fatigue and frustration wash over her.

Tick-tock, tick-tock, she told herself, as she peeled away her protective clothes, gloves, mask and visor, preparing to limp home, saddened by the lack of progress, and sure that nothing would come of Lauren in Colorado or Meriam at the Tribune building. Dejected, she sent an email detailing the failed day, sharing it with Sybil.

She found her car, revived now by the guys at Hindman's Autobody and Engine Shop, their jingle in her head: 'No chewing gum, no band aids or rubber bands here at Hindman's,' and they somehow made that rhyme. The drive home had her ears ringing until she turned on the radio and found Mick Jagger and the Stones banging and wailing out the lyrics to You can't always get what you want. She cursed at the Stones and turned the radio back off. "Life just sucks at times," she muttered to the empty car as silence enshrouding her again, except for a distinct humming noise leftover from the job the Hindman boys did on her car.

In a mile or so toward home, weaving in and out of traffic, she heard the hum-ditty-hum-ditty take a turn somewhere inside her ear, transforming into her name, Juuu-diiith, Ju-dith, Judith… Somehow knowing it was all in her head, that it was the idle brain deciphering rhythmic data, did not entirely convince her, and knowing failed to soothe the nerves, despite all that Sybil had told her about the 'common' condition. What'd she call it? Pare-something? Whatever, I'm too young for strange mental conditions to overtake me like this, she told herself. Cursing this now, she snatched the radio back on and found Neil Diamond's classic A Beautiful Noise being belted out. Perfect.

◆ ◆ ◆

When Jude arrived home, it was her and Squeakums alone in the place. Meriam had not arrived as yet, despite the lateness of the hour. After caring for her cat, Jude set to making dinner for the two of them, and while the stew she'd prepared simmered, she took a hot, simmering shower. Nearly ready to step out, she found Meriam, nude, stepping in. Smiling and laughing, they showered together, Jude soaping Meriam from head to toe. Soapy kisses followed. Roaming hands followed this.

"Oh, no! Hell!" Jude yelled.

"What?"

"Dinner! I forgot! Left it on!"

"Let it simmer. I need you here!"

"No, it's likely simmered away by now!"

"More reason to leave it and focus on me!"

Ignoring Meriam's plea, Jude stepped from the shower, wrapped herself in a huge white towel and rushed to pull the stew pot off the burner before the bottom of the pot might burn through. Too late, the contents ruined, dry as a dessert landscape on top and glommed like Gorilla Glue at the bottom. "Damn!"

"Domino's Pizza delivered to the doorstep sounds good," Meriam assured her, entering the kitchen and putting her arms around Jude, whose back remained to her.

Jude went to make the call. Meriam, also in a towel, followed her into the bedroom and sat alongside her as she ordered. As soon as Jude was off the phone, Meriam said, "I've got some news for you, sweetheart."

"Good news, I hope. I am due for some good news."

"You got it coming, all right."

"You had luck at the Trib?"

"I did. Missing Persons story big as life at the time of the groundbreaking for the city tunnel, October 1947. Big on account of its being a huge deal at the time."

"The tunnel or the disappearances?"

"The disappearances. Well, the tunnel too."

"A huge deal?"

"Yes, on account of the missing lady was high society. First story I found was in the society pages, and the story blossomed from there as the weeks went on, until it made page two!"

"Names, Meriam, names?"

"She ran off with a commoner named Johnathan Brawley, a carpenter and wainwright, whatever that is. Haven't had time to Google it."

"Her name?"

"Hightower, Elizabeth Sanders Hightower. There was speculation they'd taken a boat to Canada to escape her parents, and of course, to be married, live happily ever after. It was all for love, so romantic."

"But no one ever heard from them again, ever, right?"

"Can't be sure of that, given what little the stories provided. Made copies for you."

Meriam dug out her cell phone, while saying, "Took pictures of article right off the old microfiche file."

"Microfiche—I thought they digitized all that years ago!"

"Like so much in Chi-town, they started that project, but when funds dried up, you know what's first to go—library funds!"

"Especially archived material, I suppose." Jude took the phone in hand and blew up the first article to readable size. "It's got to be her."

"The society page photo was hard to make out but look at the one in the paper proper—she's poured into that party dress. Her waste is tiny, likely due to a—"

"A corset."

"And Jude, she is the spitting image of the reconstructed skull you guys put in the newspaper the other day." Meriam slipped her arm over Jude's shoulder where the two toweled women sat on the bed.

Jude repeated the name, "Elizabeth Saunders Hightower. Hightower! Scored one huge, big point! I talked to a descendant today named Sturgess who has Hightower relatives. She was a DNA match to the subway lady—maiden name, Sturgess. Coincidence, I think not with a DNA link."

"And the man who disappeared with her was Johnathan Brawley. A jack-of-all trades, and a day laborer type, that is, according to the story, and the reason her parents objected to the marriage, and likely why the love birds chose to disappear, or so multiple acquaintances said at the time. That was one theory—runaways! Eloped!"

"Eloped, eh?"

"She was attending a dress-up party, a sort of masked ball, when she slipped away from the man she'd come with, a guy she was slated to marry. After that night, she was never seen again. Like that TV show—Vanished."

Jude, staring at the duplicated photo of the lady in the wall, was still stuck on the word eloped. "How romantic that she and Brawley eloped! And she was so pretty."

"Given where she wound up, I don't think romantic quite describes it."

Jude sighed. "Brawley, nice, strong name—Johnathan Brawley—rings a good, strong bell, that name. Let me take it all in, that we may well have the names of our two City Hall bodies."

"Underneath all your bravado. Dr. Avery, you really are a romantic yourself."

"Oh, stop it."

"Anyway, this news could well end the mystery. Please your boss and City Hall."

Jude, in her excitement had completely forgotten that City Hall no longer wanted the mystery solved. From the crestfallen face she made over the thought, Meriam squeezed her hand and asked, "Is there something wrong, Jude?"

Jude breathed deeply and informed Meriam of the new direction that the mayor and even the governor were so happy to go with, how City Hall no longer wanted the mystery of the unfortunate and unhappy couple disclosed. "Crazy as that sounds," she finished.

"That is an unbelievable shocker! After all you've done, working this case, and now they order it dropped?"

"Yes, as the mystery of the walled-in couple is the latest distraction from real issues."

"Jude, to hell with that. If they want to pull-a-Trump, let them do it with someone else's case!"

"Someone else's ancestors."

"You've got to fight it, Jude. Will you?" asked Meriam, confused.

Jude said, "I shouldn't've told you this, but now that you've helped out so much, well—"

"Shouldn't've told me!"

The doorbell rang. "Pizza guy already?" Jude bit her lower lip and glanced at a wall clock.

Meriam rushed to the door to open it, still in her towel, but Jude caught her up and stayed her hand on the doorknob. Shakingly frightened, she angrily said, "No! Can't be the pizza! They're never that fast. Do not open it!"

"Jude, you're shaking! It's all right."

"Could be Stone again! Don't open it."

"Stone? Who's that? Jude, it's the pizza guy."

"Let me see. Give me a minute to look out the front window."

Meriam called through the door. "Who is it?"

"Domino's. Delivery!"

"See, how would this Stone person know we ordered from Domino's?"

"He may've tapped into my phone for all I know." Jude then shouted through the door. "It's paid for over the phone! Just drop it and go!"

"You gotta sign!" came the high-pitched male voice on the other side of the door.

Meriam from a side window looked out on the porch and saw that it was indeed a young fellow with a Domino's uniform and cap. "Jude, it's okay!" she said, coming around and tearing the door wide open. The delivery boy's mouth fell open, the pizza box shaking in his hand, as he stared at the two beautiful women in towels.

Meriam laughed now, and Jude relaxed and began giggling herself as the door closed on the shaken driver. "Wait, you didn't sign!"

"Free pizza then!"

"No, it'll come out of his paycheck!" Meriam snatched the door back open to find the delivery boy still frozen there. "Give me the check, Jerry," she said, reading his nametag.

"S-sure, you guys having a slumber party kinda thing, huh-eh?"

"How'd you guess?" Meriam signed for Jude, adding a fifteen percent tip, and sent him on his way. Meriam smiled to see his step sending the signal that he'd been happily stunned. Over his shoulder, he called out, "Ask for me by name next time! Ups my pay!"

The ladies giggled over the real reason Jerry wanted to return to this street address again.

◆ ◆ ◆

After gorging on the all-vegetable pizza, Jude insisted on a robe and slippers and to make a call to Sybil Shanley with the news of the Tribune story, while Meriam only wanted to make love. Pulling away, Jude continued reading instead.

The story had gone on to conjecture that something untoward could well have happened to the couple as there could not be any corroboration from Canadian authorities that such a couple had ever come across the border by land or by lake, and the nearest cities in Canada had nothing to add to such reports.

It was suggested that the couple could have spiced and peppered the groundwork for the story, that is laid the trail to Canada in an effort to throw off any human bloodhounds sent after them, After all, West instead would make sense, as even as late as the forties, so many Americans were migrating to the far-flung western states. The fact her parents were wealthy, Jude imagined they could afford even the Pinkerton Agency to find and return their 'little girl,' who'd disappeared so thoroughly.

From the tenor of the articles posted, it proved clear that her parents strongly objected to her marrying a 'commoner,' and as a result, sure, the runaway couple might well have told acquaintances that they planned on Canada. To complicate matters and the question of their sudden disappearance, there had been another and more 'suitable' suitor for her hand in marriage, a well-off, older man who'd made his fortune in—bingo!—construction and city projects thrown his way by City Hall. Jude searched for a name and finally her eye settled on Paul Horatio Mannering.

"Mannering, we have to find all we can on this person now."

"I'm way ahead of you," Meriam showed Jude several stories she had duplicated on the Masonic member and friend of the city and City Hall. Mannering was high society enough for Elizabeth's parents, but not at all who they thought he was if he indeed had bricked up this young couple—his final cruelty bricking them up separately, as a symbolic way of keeping them apart through all eternity. None of this story was found in the articles of the day, of course, but as Jude read, she read between the lines.

"Why didn't you show me these articles right away, Meriam."

"I'd hoped for just a little time with you first, my darling workaholic!"

Jude gave her a kiss. "I may be up all night with this, Merr. I need to make a call to Colorado for one thing. You go on to bed and take Squeakums with you. I have to prepare this news just right for Sybil and Dean tomorrow."

"Can't it wait?"

"No, not if I'm going to stand and fight."

"For Elizabeth and Johnathan, how noble."

"I will have to convince Grant to fight off City Hall for these two people who can't speak for themselves, you understand?"

Meriam sighed heavily. "I got some studying to do, and sure, Squeaky here can help, sure. Later then." Meriam kissed her and started away with the cat in her arms.

"You think you'd have time tomorrow to dig around for more information on this man named Mannering?"

"Sure, I guess. No telling what the Chicago Public Library might have on him."

"Thanks. It could help a great deal, as your help already has! I truly appreciate all your digging around the dusty past for me."

"The past is always with us. Our ancestors stand behind and within."

"That's a beautiful sentiment. But again, thanks for this—" Jude held up Meriam's phone with the articles on it. "All this already has amazingly turned things around for us."

"Maybe tonight, you'll sleep soundly, no dreams of being lost in tunnels."

"Good night, sweetheart."

"Good night yourself!"

Jude smiled, breathed deeply, and began to think how to organize all that had transpired this night for a confab and possible confrontation with Dean on his carpet, and for the first time she'd be the one calling the plays. After all, there was now a historical link to two people with names, and there was a DNA link to a modern family clearly identified. Blood relatives.

But then Meriam returned from the bedroom with her slinkiest, sexiest nighty, a see-through one. "So, when are you going to tell me about this Stone person? Is it an old girlfriend or what?"

"Noooo! He's a suspect in the death of Professor Griswald, and he's quite possibly the one who attacked me."

"Damn, no wonder you freaked at the door." Meriam hugged Jude close, and they remained that way for some time. The feel of Meriam's sleep wear against Jude's skin had her wanting to go straight off to bed with her lover, and the warmth turning to heat below the lacey thing only ratcheted Jude's hormones higher. Meriam, quite aware of what she was doing and the effect she had on Jude, quickly kissed her and went off to study in bed. "Gotta lotta medical terms to cover," she shouted as she disappeared into the bedroom.

"Night, love." Jude was determined to not be sidetracked. There was too much to do and too much at stake.

Meriam peaked around the corner and added, "Night, for now, but you know you can wake me later, if you get any ideas…"

19

Alone now, Jude began reading the various and sundry articles that Meriam had wisely copied on Mannering. There were character traits of the man that she immediately thought dire and frightful. His description and drive for money and power was evident, along with his ruthless tactics to get city contracts. He boasted of his father's having founded the family business, how he'd been instrumental in high-rise buildings going up on Michigan Avenue, and how the old man actually helped build the pavillions for the 1893 Chicago World's Fair. He was described as cutthroat in gaining those contracts, and she imagined that his son may well have adopted those same traits. If Mannering senior could not have it, no one could—it read like a family motto.

In total, the man reminded her of a passage in Joseph Conrad's Heart of Darkness, which she went to search for on her bookshelf, opened it and sought the unmarked passage, but no, it was not there. Where the hell'd I see that? Oh, yeah, in another book but one by Joseph Campbell and not Conrad, from a book entitled The Hero with a Thousand Faces. She opened it and saw the dogeared prologue page marking the passage she'd recalled all along and wanted.

In writing the report for Dean's eyes, she knew she must include Campbell's description to lay it over what was known of this man Mannering in the year he contracted with the city to build a portion of the underground subway system, the one leading to and away from City Hall. Campbell's description of a power-mad tyrant, which Jude believed Mannering to be, a man that Griswald himself had once described to her, the madman in Poe's immurement-themed stories, read: The tyrant becomes a curse onto himself as well as the world he lives in, for his life is one of fear and self-loathing

This single line nailed it tight, at least in her mind. Here was a likely suspect, the man jilted by Elizabeth, the Hightower daughter around the time the tunnels had their groundbreaking, 1947. She could well imagine a man of that nature, who might feel more than a sting, but rather an outrage, at the humiliation of being thrown over for a day laborer—possibly one of his own employees, Brawley. Both men would likely be familiar with Edgar Allan Poe's dark and haunting magazine stories such as those involving immurement. Stories of rage, anger, vengeance written by a dark side poet indulging in vengefully walling up a wife, another an acquaintance; in one case a disobedient wife, in another case a rival in life.

Along with Mannering's having grown up playing with bricks rather than blocks, along with his knowledge of masonry, his being not only in the business of building walls, but also contracted to build at exactly the spot where Brawley and Hightower, slated for marriage, wound up, and not together even—separated for eternity. And her with a photo of her parents—no! Given the time period for tintype, the couple in the photo had to be her grandparents, who may well have been cherished above her parents who were forcing Mannering on her.

Jude slowed for a moment, imagining it all, and she wondered if Elizabeth, despite the harm her parents brought on her, still loved them nonetheless. Perhaps so, even as much as she hated Mannering, the last face Elizabeth saw before her death.

The tragedy of it all felt like a great weight on Jude as she finished her report. A report that she would pass by Sybil for commentary, editing, possible objections, but in the end, she meant to place it in Grant's hands tomorrow—their last day before his artificial deadline was up for Elizabeth Saunders Hightower and Johnathan Brawley. Not Grant, nor the city aldermen, nor City Hall lieutenants, nor the mayor could ignore the evidence and the direction all the arrows pointed to after this.

Or could they ignore it? They might deep-six her report and carry on as if none of it mattered as long as Chicago had its newly added, morbid 'attraction,' which by now commuters on the underground rail had visited thousands of times, hundreds by day and night to tease out the spirits of the dead. A spiritualist calling herself Rasputina had blessed the opened graves in the subway. People had made shrines of the sites, covered now with flowers and teddy bears.

No matter, she told her weary self now in the silence of night, for at least she and Sybil could walk away, heads held high, as they had done all in their power to reveal the ugly story in all its salient detail.

I did my job, she told herself, exhausted and asleep now on her living room couch.

◆　◆　◆

With Jude asleep, Meriam slipped quietly into the living room. She'd earlier fallen asleep over her books, but when she'd awakened to find the bed empty save for her and the cat, she opened the flashlight on her cellphone and went looking for Jude, and with her flashlight, she sat near Jude and read her report that Jude meant to hand over to her boss the following day.

She read every word, and she was moved by it, inspired even, and she was angry, knowing that the powers that be might well ignore it and bury it. This fear got her activist mind churning and turning, and she lifted the report and carried it into the kitchen, where, page-by-page, she began copying. She feared Jude was in no position to take on City Hall alone or to break this story alone.

Meriam believed she had the answer to the problem, a workable solution—transparency via the Chicago Tribune. She silently returned Jude's report to Grant to where she'd found it, Jude still snoring. She then returned to bed, hardly disturbing Squeakums, and from the bedroom, she hesitated a moment, asking the cat's advice. "You think I should send out Jude's entire report to a reporter at the Trib?"

Meriam, in her activist role, had had some dealings with this reporter in the past, Louise McGrath. "Give her the story and see it in print, possibly on page one," she said to Squeakums. "Would serve the governor, the mayor, and City Hall right, and Jude may get mad with us, but eventually, she will thank us, Squeaky Wheel, for taking the step that she herself could not do due to her career, you see?"

Meriam had her computer with her, and she had an app that took her photos and digitized them. She then emailed her contact at the Chicago Tribune with the latest news on the mystery of the discovered people walled up in underground Chicago. She hesitated a moment, uncertain how she might explain her actions to Jude, and she knew that going behind Jude's back this way could cost their relationship, but Louise McGrath had supported Meriam's schooling and had a been a great help to her even after their breakup. She took a deep breath and determined that Jude would thank her in the end. After all, no way could Jude put it out there herself—that act would cost Jude dearly. Most likely her job at the coroner's place.

Still, maybe I should at least discuss it with Jude before I send it to Louise, she thought. But what if Jude said no? Then Jude and the others at the coroner's office would bury the story, the real story for those jerks at City Hall, and they win, and the unhappy couple, Jane and John Doe, who now had names, lose! They'd not be given a proper send off, but instead, they'd go to unmarked graves and it'd be walling them up all over again. This time in a pine box paid for by Cook County. With no one in attendance save a couple of grave diggers. That certainly wasn't the Oglala way of doing things. A wild thought invaded her mind—she and some friends rob the Coroner of the subway corpses, take the remains to the Res, and there place them on a pyre and light them up. She immediately decided it was a wild hair notion she liked but would not act on. Going to the press, on the other hand…why not?

Still, reluctant only for fear of how Jude might react, she stayed her hand over the send arrow. She next clasped her hands together in the universal gesture for prayer, took a deep breath, and pressed send. After which, she took another deep breath and shook her head, fearful of what she'd just done; afraid that her just having betrayed Jude would destroy their relationship, afraid that Jude would never forgive her, unless she could convince Jude that it was the right thing to do—here and now, like Spike Lee would say: 'Get on the bus!'. Besides, Meriam felt compelled by her own morality to get ahead of it; to get ahead of Jude's being ordered to stifle the story. Maybe. Perhaps. Seems so…but…

She then felt someone watching her, and in response turned her head. Squeakums, staring, curious, a look of disdain and confusion on his little face. While she knew it was silly to feel this way, Meriam felt as if caught in the act, and that the cat—Jude's best friend—was a metaphor for the end of what was, and could have continued to be, a wonderfully beautiful and imperfect-perfect relationship.

20

Now is the time, Jude thought, to fight, and she left for work with a fire in her eye and her belly, with a bounce in her step, and with a plan of attack and her written report and corroborating evidence, thanks in large measure to Meriam. Meriam, who remained at peaceful slumber. Only Squeakums to send Jude off at the door.

She'd left a hasty note taped to the coffee pot, always Meriam's first destination in the morning. In it, she promised to be home early regardless of what was to transpire today. "I may even be jobless, next time you see me," she had added with an LOL following this.

All the way across the city to downtown Chicago and pulling into the underground lot at the sleek building where she worked, she had tried to put into play her first step in the plan, to have Sybil look the report over and agree to taking it to Grant and insisting it be published in every major market news outlet without passing it by City Hall. As they were sure to balk at it and wish to delay this news, to hold it at least until the carnival atmosphere around the killings dissipated. But for some strange reason, Sybil wasn't answering her calls this morning.

She pulled into her parking space, her classical music droning down for a commercial as she switched off the ignition. When she climbed from her car, she saw some commotion going on at the elevators she routinely took to her floor, when one panel door opened and Sybil began a heated argument with two security guards that Jude only knew as Pamela 'Pam' and Cameron 'Cam.' After a moment, and as Jude started toward the elevators, Sybil's voice rose, and she shouted at the guards, "Let me have a goddamn word with Dr. Avery first, okay? Is that okay? Does that break any rules, shit!"

"What's going on here, Sybil?" asked Jude where they met in the middle of the lot, someone blowing his horn to get past them.

Sybil moved Jude back to her car, taking her arm as she did so. "You might wanna take a day off, Jude."

"What? You know what we've uncovered about the dead wall couple. I need, we need, to take it to Dean, and convince him to immediately call a press conference and—"

"You shouldn't've jumped the gun again, Jude. Dean's fit to be tied with what you've done. He's fired you." She indicated the guards. "Pam and Cam over there are here to escort you to your office with that file box between them, to get your personal belongings out of the lab."

"That's crazy! I don't understand! I've stayed away from the university and the Griswald business!"

"Jude—putting the unhappy couple business in the morning Tribune was just not smart, kiddo. And the whole business of City Hall not wanting the identities found and the mystery solved, oh my God, darling! What were you thinking?"

Jude gasped at this news, and she went limp against the tail end of her car. "Wha...I...I didn't share anything with the Tribune about the case, Sybil. How can you think—"

"The details are the same as you shared with me over the phone last night, Jude. Who else? Who else knew other than me, you, and-and your librarian girlfriend, Marion?"

"Meriam," she corrected the name as the idea hammered through Jude's head. "She wouldn't, she couldn't've. She was with me all night."

"Technology is often a nasty weapon." Sybil held up her cellphone. "Jude, your entire report, paragraph for paragraph, it's all in the paper alongside photos from the past—1947. Hell, yes! Including this suspected murderer who walled them up—Mannering, and they're threatening to sue us all—the Mannering family. Still big in Chicago."

Jude wanted to put her head between her knees, as she felt so nauseated. "I only...I mean..."

"Someone got a copy of your report intended for Dean, I understand, and I was going to back you up, but now, damnit all."

"I need to talk to Dean, explain what happened."

"No, you need to talk to that Indian girlfriend of yours to find out what happened and why she'd want to sabotage you and endanger your career. And damn it all, was she a plant from the get-go?"

"No, I won't believe that, Sybil." Jude seethed for a long moment, and Pam, a heavyset, wide-shouldered young woman with a doughy face said from a distance, "Are we needed here, Dr. Shanley, or can we get back to our posts?"

"Get in your car and leave, Jude. Leave your paperwork with me and go have it out with Meriam, and I'll inform Dean what's happened."

"Jesus, you think you can repair the damage?"

"If anyone can."

"You do have a lot of influence with him."

Sybil laughed at this. "Unfortunately, not enough. She lifted her ringless fingers of her left-hand. "Engaged once, but shit happens…"

"I see."

"Get out of here. Dean'll cool down once he learns you've been betrayed by an intimate friend."

"Can we go, Dr. Shanley," Pam repeated herself.

"Yes, yes! Dr. Avery is leaving until we get this misunderstanding sorted out."

Cam waved Pam onto the elevator, and they disappeared with the empty file box. Jude thanked Sybil and they hugged. "I'm so sorry about all of this, truly I am," Jude said.

"We'll get it right…set it right…one day, promise." Sybil took Jude's briefcase in hand, saying, "I want to see your report for my own eyes, and maybe take it to Dean if…if it passes muster with me."

"I suppose I should say thank you."

"No need to, but yes, you should."

"Spared me embarrassment, except for Pam and Cam."

"Not to worry! They'll spread it throughout the building before day's end."

Jude laughed but tearfully and waved Sybil off. Sybil, even as she returned to the elevator to go up, heard Jude's tires screeching, burning rubber all the way to the underground exit. She imagined Jude might be in no shape to drive, especially on bustling Lower Wacker Drive. She said a soft prayer for Jude's safety.

◆　◆　◆

Jude arrived home to find her door not simply left ajar but broken in, the lock and doorknob dangling. She'd taken to wearing her gun again, having taken Sybil's advice, and all morning, feeling it snug against her left breast and underarm had given her courage. She snatched it out now and held it ahead of her. No sign of Squeakums. An eerie silence filled the place, urging her to call out to Meriam. No response. Jude's fear heightened. What if Meriam was harmed, but a hope rose with the fear: Perhaps she'd gotten out before the intruder had smashed in the door. Perhaps she'd leapt out the bedroom window and onto the top of that dumpster below, or maybe she'd gotten out the back door in the kitchen.

And maybe the bastard who'd dared break into Jude's place was still lurking inside somewhere. In a closet, the walk-in pantry, the shower like in that awful film, Psycho.

Jude inched about the flat. The place seemed suddenly alien, strange. The fact that someone who had no business here having been here, perhaps even here now made the familiar unfamiliar, as she'd never ever considered her home a place of conflict and fear, so that everything now in her mind's eye could be turned into a weapon against her. Her cutlery in the kitchen, her free-standing lamp, the ornamental fireplace tools, purely for show but they could kill a person if wielded like an ax. Candlestick holders, pots and pans, jelly jars, even ice trays and toasters and radios—all possible weapons.

She inched toward her bedroom, still calling Meriam's name. She could hear the wump-wump-wump of the ceiling fan, and she heard her name in the noise of it, Juu-dith, but no response from Meriam. Maybe she'd gotten out and away in time, unharmed.

The last inch that brought Jude into the room placed her in direct line of sight of the clump of bloody bedclothes hiding Meriam beneath. Jude screamed and forgot about shooting anyone or defending herself against an attack by any means. She instead rushed to Meriam to determine the extent of her injuries, and if she were alive or dead. Whoever had kicked in the door had come straight at her here in bed and attacked in a rage.

Jude could not determine how many stab wounds had penetrated Meriam, but she was faintly alive, where she lay entangled in the bedding. It appeared the stabbing had pierced through the blankets and sheets. Jude, crying, terrified for Meriam, pleaded with a 911 operator to send an ambulance and medics, adding, "Competent medics and IV plasma for type-O blood, stat! She's in shock and has lost a great deal of blood."

Jude then surveyed the room. She was alone with Meriam. She sensed it. Whoever had done this, the murderous bastard had earlier fled with his weapon. She wondered if it was someone from Meriam's past, a jilted lover, an angry female with a blade? Maybe even a former boyfriend with a control obsession—the 'If I can't have her, no one can' syndrome. All the scenarios were flitting through her head, even as she began searching for the worst of the knife wounds, aiming to staunch them as best that she could before the blood loss would result in death. Meriam was in hemorrhagic shock as it was.

Jude, so focused on what she could do with the sheets for Meriam's wounds, did not hear the police sirens that'd descended, and she was startled to see several uniformed cops rush in, guns drawn, pointed at her. "I'm medically assisting! I live here, and my girlfriend's been stabbed by an intruder!"

"That's what dispatch told us!" the lead man said.

"Then put your weapons away and do what I tell you! Now!"

"What? Do what?"

"Make room for the medics! Get over here. As I tie off a wound, put pressure on it. Gotta stop the bleeding."

In unison, the cops paused, all staring at the scene, as Jude was hurriedly removing clothing from Meriam and searching for wounds, and one-by-one, she set about staunching each wound and ordering the cops to put pressure on those she'd finish with. The most serious wounds were several—in and around and near the heart.

"Whoever did this was aiming for her heart," said one young cop, blond haired and blue-eyed, and looking as if still a high school grad. "Possibly a crime of passion," he added.

An older cop said to Jude, "The kid's taking the detective's exam in a coupla weeks."

"I'm a Cook County medical examiner," she informed them. "Work under Dr. Grant."

This seemed to impress the cops, all of whom knew of Grant. "Hey, you—are you Dr. Avery?"

"Yah, but how'd—"

"Read your story in the paper this morning!"

Fuck, she thought, my story. Jude could only concentrate on the life and death problem in her arms—Meriam. She worked knotting and tying off another of Meriam's wounds. Used to work for Grant, she thought but did not add.

"That whole Poe angle, that's something, Dr. Avery!"

"Shut up and keep pressing that wound! You too, over there, future detective."

"Yeah, sure."

Jude hadn't heard a siren or the arrival of an ambulance, but two medics rushed in, one immediately testing for a pulse and shouting, "She's breathing!"

"Dr. Avery's kept her with us!" said the closest and more helpful cop, whose name stitched on his uniform shirt read Ames. A tall, black man with hands that Michael Jordan might envy.

Jude fought to maintain her calm, but she pleaded for the others to lift Meriam onto a transfer board to get her to their gurney and out to the ambulance. All the while, she knew that Meriam's blood loss might already have signed her death certificate. The remainder of the bloody bedding that Jude had torn away to use as temporary bandages was balled up and in a corner between the wall and the bed.

"Beautiful woman like that," said the young cop who wanted to be a detective, his hand over one wound. "Who'd do a thing like this?"

"Any immediate thoughts about your girlfriend's enemies?" asked the older cop, Ames, his hand over another wound.

"Stone," she replied. The name dropped like a stone from her sub-conscience mind as her conscience mind was completely focused on saving Meriam's life. She plunged into a full-on cry now, seeing Meriam carried out in her condition and her lacey sleepwear shredded and bloody lying at Jude's feet. She rushed then to keep up with the paramedics, and outside, neighbors looking on, she hoped for a reaction out of Meriam, even the slightest squeeze of her hand or a murmur from her lips, an eyelid slipping open, but it did not come—nothing.

"Has she gone comatose?"

"Good thing, judging," replied the paramedic.

Inside the ambulance, Meriam was quickly hooked up to plasma after Jude assured them that she was type-O blood, so universal plasma could be administered immediately and not two hours later after typing and prepping. "Thank God she's O," said the female medic.

"We talked about it just the other night."

"She's lucky to have you. From all I see, you've kept her alive against all odds."

Two held breaths later, Jude saw a sudden deep breath escape Meriam, and her blue lips began to gain a bit of color along with the pallor of her skin. "She's not comatose. Come on, honey…sweet Jesus, Meriam…Meriam, it's me, Jude. I'm with you."

Meriam was far too weak to respond. Jude squeezed her hand and shouted at the medics, "Get her to Northwestern, stat!"

The male medic who seemed in charge, said to Jude, "You did a great job keeping her in this world, Dr. Avery. Now let us do our job." The female medic attended the IV and the plasma was flowing even before the ambulance took off, sending a tearful Jude against the back door. Had it not been secured, she'd've fallen out the rear.

"Find something to hold onto. Take a seat," ordered the head medic.

Jude found what was needed to hold on, marveling for a moment at how the medics managed to remain standing back here without losing balance. She then had her first moment of clarity regarding what'd happened in her flat, in her bed. If it was Jacob JaCovey Stone, she thought, he thinks he's killed me. This was all meant for me, not Merr.

On the ride to the hospital, she recalled that Grant had spoken of smoking or flushing Stone out of his safe environment, off the university campus for one, out of high society for another. It appeared he'd come down off his perch to slum around in the Humboldt Park area where she lived, and the high-society boy with one mad premeditated plan in mind—to kill Dr. Jude Avery. Just how did Grant intend to smoke the bastard out, and why did he come after her and not anyone else? Had Grant's plan backfired? Of course, when dealing with such a warped personality as that of a JJ Stone, who in his right might could predict the man's actions, plans, goals, or dreams?

Grant surely had to have interviewed the suspect, likely withheld some information even as he laid out a theory of the crime for Stone to sweat over. A man like him would do anything to avoid detection and imprisonment. How very much Stone was like the long dead Mannering, she now thought as the ambulance screeched into the hospital emergency port. When the doors opened and Meriam was whisked away, Jude saw that they were at Northwestern Memorial. That was a bit comforting as was Meriam's condition, as she'd been stabilized. Still, she looked pale and weak, her beautiful raven hair matted with blood.

Still, she did appear far better than she had in that pool of blood and bedding, where she'd obviously put up a fight. Now she must put up another fight—for her life.

Jude was again praised by the medics as having saved Meriam's life, but inside the hospital, Jude felt alone in the busy, crowded waiting room. No one knew her story, she felt, and why should they? In all the faces across the room there were expressions of sadness and hardship. Every wrinkle and bandage told another story. So many shattered eyes, most downturned, some, like hers, searching for meaning. How could this have happened? In so short a period of time; in the time it took Jude to drive to work and turn around for home.

Home. Home no longer. Home defiled. She knew that there was no way she could continue in the flat where she and Squeakums had enjoyed their quiet little world. A world now shattered. She knew she'd never be able to get every drop of Meriam's blood out of that room. She knew from her years as an ME that there'd be blood on the ceiling and on that damned ceiling fan as the attacker, while making successive stabs had surely spread the blood on the back thrust to the walls and above. She pictured this madman straddling Meriam, thinking it was her under the bedding. The ugly image of a demon atop Meriam, driving home the blade, sickened Jude. She could almost feel the pain of each stab.

The blood. Was it all Meriam's? Suppose in the heat of the attack, the beast had cut himself as well? A CSI team needed to get in there. What am I thinking, she silently asked herself, and she found her phone and shakily punched Sybil's phone number. She realized that all this time she'd been in a state of semi-shock herself, unsure how she had handled things as she had till now, but she had not called anyone for help, not even Sybil. Until now.

Shanley came on instantly, first ring. "Jude! Where are you? We got the call and when the police rattled off your address, I raced over."

"You're at my place?"

"Yes, god but there's a shitload of blood in your bedroom. I feared it was you, but a couple of cops told me it was an Indian woman—Meriam, I presume."

"Yes, poor Meriam. She's in surgery now with multiple stab wounds."

"My god! I'm so sorry, Jude. I know how much you care for her. What the hell happened?"

"CSI the place for me, will you, Sybil? The door was kicked in and she was attacked by whomever did the kicking. Blood evidence may indicate who the attacker is. I suspect Jacob J. Stone."

"We never did conclusively find that he was the one who attacked you at Griswald's office. I'll head the investigation into the forensics, kiddo. Bank on it, and if there's any blood other than Meriam's, we'll find it. But…well, how're you doing, emotionally, physically?"

"I feel like a ragdoll, a kicked-around Cabbage Patch doll with broken limbs."

"Do you want me to send a patrol car for you—take you to my place for the night?"

"No, no! I'm here for the duration for Meriam."

"Understood. I'll come by later then—with some burgers or something for you. Maybe sneak in some Jack Daniels in a Pepsi bottle. How's that?"

"That'd be priceless. But tell me, has Dean, Dr. Grant, has he…did he…"

"He's softened up about the whole idea of firing you."

"You mean that?"

"I gave him a talking to, and yes, you still have a job."

"I owe you."

"Dean, like most all of us, understands how it feels to be betrayed by someone you love."

"Aye, yeah, that kind of thing you don't forget." Jude thought of Meriam's betrayal, weighing it now and finding it wanting in terms of priority. "I've got to get her well enough that I can justify yelling at her."

"You think you can ever forgive her? Being unable to forget is one thing, forgive another."

"I think I might…think I can, so much depends on her motives. Why didn't she come to me first?"

"Well for now, let's just all pray for her to pull through. From what the cops guarding the place told me, if you hadn't've been Jude-on-the-spot, she'd be in the morgue instead of the hospital."

"Can you keep me in the loop on what you find as you go?"

"Of course, and by the way, there's a part of Dean that admires you, kiddo, and also a part that got a nasty hearty chuckle out of your doing an end run around the mayor's office. But he paid dearly for it, I can tell you."

"What do you mean?"

"He's out! They fired Dean."

"No!"

"Yes, I'm serious."

"Then, who's in charge downtown?

"Me…lil' ol' me. My turn to be hammered, I guess"

"Sybil, no! I mean, yes! I mean if it has to be someone other than Dean, well now!"

"Thanks. Will take that as a vote of confidence. But honestly, I know Dean's not going to take this lying down."

"Can he fight it?"

"He'll take it to the courts, sure. He's only a few years from retirement, and if fired, he loses his pension, so he had every reason to contest it as an unlawful and unwarranted firing. Used to be the Coroner's Office was independent of politics. That ended with a lousy law pushed through by a Republican governor and the aldermen he controlled some years back. With new blood and an election coming up, the old paradigm could be reinstated along with Dean."

"I know he's a Chicago institution and well-liked and admired by the rank and file."

"He's well known enough he just might run for mayor himself! Ha!"

"Why not. Now I don't feel quite so bad for getting him fired."

Sybil laughed at this and said, "As soon as Lionel, Ralph, and I finish up at the scene here, I'll swing by there, sweetie."

"Thanks again, Sybil. You're a lifesaver, and I'm on the deck of the Titanic."

As soon as they hung up, Jude mentally punished herself for not having remembered to ask Sybil just how Grant had gone about smoking Stone out. Whatever Grant said or did, whether in an interrogation or a surprise visit to Stone's place of business, an investment firm, something had triggered him to target Jude, and to mistakenly attack the wrong person.

Later, when Sybil came by, she'd get to the bottom of what Dean had done to flush out Stone. Meanwhile, she thought of how much her hatred of the attacker had her blood boiling, and had he still been at his bloody attack when she'd gone through the door, she would have shot him in his fevered brain.

She was an excellent shot, practiced at the range every chance she got. She would not miss a shot between the eyes of JJ Stone. She pictured the wealthy man, born into privilege and money, likely a donor father saw to it his entrance into the university. The filthy rich always sailed through, avoiding any real obstacles like low test scores or drunken behavior, sometimes even rape or attempted rape. If Jude had one bias, one prejudice, it was toward such people as Stone. People who daily got away with unlawful behavior and paid no consequence for illegal activity, or sheer meanness and ugliness of heart.

Then another troubling question nagged at Jude where she sat in the silent waiting room, silent except for a few tiny children playing with toys provided by the nurses at the nurse station. How had City Hall reacted to the good news that she and Sybil had tenaciously uncovered the identity of the unfortunate and unhappy subway corpses? Other than firing Dean, that is. How would they spin it? Most likely elated and pleased with the Coroner's Office, regardless of Grant's having to step down. They were likely up all night same as her, but for an entirely different reason—to plan a great send off for the now fortunate, happy couple of corpses, thanks to all that the forensics team had found under the dead lady's corset.

Jude stood and began a concerted pacing of the waiting room. The number of zombie-like waiters in rows of seats had thinned and diminished considerably. All the children were gone, and the overhead TV was showing reruns of Gunsmoke so as to not offend anyone's sensibilities or partisanship. So, Jude paced. That is until a hefty, round-faced nurse blocked her, and in a near whisper, she said, "Miss, there is no pacing here."

"What?"

"If you must pace, you will have to do so outside—on the walk."

"Really?"

"It makes the anxiety of others waiting on word here just so much more, ahh, anxious."

Jude gritted her teeth. "Is there a computer I can use to get on

Google for a search?" Jude asked the nurse, flashing her ME's badge."

"Oh, I…" she read Jude's ID below the badge in her wallet. "This way, Dr. Avery."

Jude follower the nurse into a kind of inner sanctum used by the doctors on staff here. There was a bank of computers, and she found one to work at. She called over her shoulder to the nurse, "Please, if there's any word on Meriam Oglala, you must let me know."

"Yes, of course, doctor."

Jude began a search for Jacob JaCovey Stone. As she did so, she began fantasizing of hunting him down at his doorstep, pulling her gun and frying his brain with a single shot. She was soon seeing him as the successful tycoon, on several boards and not just the university board. He didn't need money, for certain, so why kill Griswald and rob his office of the handwritten manuscript? What motive did he have other than a sick obsession that he and he alone had discovered the answer to the riddle of Poe's death?

Professor Griswald had set off his fanaticism to the point of dispatching the old professor from whom he'd learned so much about Edgar Allan Poe. Such fanaticism and obsession, she well imagined had turned then on her—first at the darkened office, where he had not gotten satisfaction, learning she had survived his attack, and next Grant's possibly flawed investigation into Stone had set him off anew, on a new obsession; one that had as its endgame Jude's corpse on a gurney in her own lab. Thus, the attack on a woman at Jude's home and in Jude's bed.

It all, in a crooked, convoluted way fit. Bingo! She found a home address for one Jacob 'JJ' Stone. It had to be him. She jotted the address on a Post-It note found on the desk. She then went to Google maps and searched the very street where he lived down to the door he'd open when she stood on his doorstep.

Why am I doing this, she then suddenly asked herself. Why am I becoming him? This is not me, not how I operate. Out of anger, uncontrolled vengeance, blood law?

"Ah-ha, they told me I'd find you here!" It was Sybil's lilting voice that had Jude covering the screen as best she could. "Brought you a bite from Wendy's! Your favorite, the spicy chicken, fries, a drink, chili, and a frosty. We can split."

"Oh, you're a godsend, girl. I am famished." Jude shut the screen off."

"Clunker computers back here. You'd think Northwestern would do better by their doctors. What're you working on?"

"Oh, just killing time. Was going nuts in the waiting room out there."

"Checking Yahoo news, eh? Your emails?"

"Yeah, that sorta thing." They'd moved to a small luncheonette table where Jude could partake of the bagged food. Sybil pulled out a small chili and a small frosty for herself. They dined, and over the food and drink, Jude asked her friend and co-worker point blank, "What the devil did Grant do to rile JJ Stone up so badly that he came calling with a damn machete or bowie knife?"

"What do you mean? Grant? Riled Stone?"

"He said he was going to 'smoke' him out, remember?"

"Stone's in lockup."

"Whoa, that was fast."

"No, in jail pending a bail hearing since noon today."

"You've gotta be kidding."

"No, Grant saw to delaying the bail hearing for as long as he can, you know, to hold Stone while we workup more evidence against him."

"For Griswald's staged suicide."

"You were right about the man, Jude, all along."

"But if he's been in jail all this time, then who…"

"Then who attacked Meriam? I wasn't wanting to tell you over the phone, you know, that we'd never find Stone's blood at your place—not for this carnage."

"Why didn't you say so before?"

"You had enough to contend with, and you sounded as if your mind was set, and I didn't want to get into it over the phone, and I had the crime scene to deal with and, and—"

"Understood, but if it wasn't Stone, then who?"

"An old flame maybe? You haven't known Meriam long. How much did she reveal of her past?"

"Not much. I suppose. Jesus."

"What? Why're you invoking Jesus?"

"I could well have done something really stupid if I'd gone after Stone on my own."

"Whataya mean, on your own?"

Jude showed her the crumpled Post-It note with the address scrawled on it."

"Meridian Manor Heights, Suite 1748, Bolingbrook, IL…hmmm, classy neighborhood. Whose is it?"

"Stone, damnitalltobloodyhell, I was going to go after the sonofabitch, armed and dangerous."

"Commm-on, kiddo! That's crazy."

The clock in the room on an overhead wall struck three AM. "We're all a little crazy at three in the morning."

"Thank God I'm here to stop you."

"You've been a great friend, Sybil."

"Ahhh, go on wid-ya. Nothin' to it."

They stood and hugged. The nurse who'd escorted her to the less than luxurious doctors lounge, entered with the message that Meriam was out of surgery and in ICU with a sixty-forty outlook. "She'll remain in the ICU, most likely through a few days. You two may as well go home."

"Come home with me, Jude," suggested Sybil.

"My cat…he was gone, run off."

"Squeakums is down in my car with a box of litter."

"You found him!"

"He was hiding under the living room couch the whole time."

"Poor thing. Okay, I accept your offer."

ybil's place was a high-rise apartment overlooking Lincoln Park, and looking out from on high, Jude stared at the sheet of shimmering, sun-reflecting beautiful Lake Michigan beyond the greenery of the lakefront park. The home was a spacious, sprawling apartment, and it had a guest bedroom, where Jude had earlier fallen into a deep slumber, remaining there until half the next was gone.

Sybil had left behind a note for Jude to find before she had left for work. Jude found the note at the coffee pot, poured a cup and took the note and her coffee to a small table at a window that looked out on north Michigan Avenue, cars and buses busily moving about so far below as to be Tinker Toys. With the sun streaming through the window and bathing Jude in beams, she read Sybil's kind preamble to what she wanted to get to:

> Jude—
>
> I ordered a basket that I'm having delivered to the apartment for the duration—food and succor. My prayers are with you and Meriam. My heart bleeds! This should happen to no one, and I know you care for Meriam so much it hurts. May God shine on your love. I just know Meriam's going to pull through. I just feel it in my bones.

Jude paused to wipe away tears with her napkin and sip at her coffee. She then continued reading from Sybil's note:

> That being said, I'll be working on it! Priority one, and as for you—you stick close by Meriam, and you're staying with me for as long as it takes. No arguments!
>
> Sincerely, your friend and pal,
> Sybil

Jude got on her phone and called the hospital to ask after Meriam's condition. After several minutes, she was connected to the ICU, and a woman, Jude assumed a nurse, came on asking, "Can I help you?"

Jude again asked for an update on Meriam's condition. Then she waited with bated breath. The nurse said, "Just a moment," before then saying, "no change. But of course, she's in an induced coma, and it will be some time before she is to be brought to consciousness, to allow her wounds to heal, Dr. Avery."

It wasn't much info but given HIPPA, Jude had to be happy getting this much out of the ICU. She'd signed a paper saying she was Meriam's wife, and thus far, she had gotten away with it, no doubt because she had the letters MD after her name. Today she would have to ferret around in Miriam's private papers to find contact info for her mother to alert her to her daughter's condition. She was not looking forward to this difficult chore.

"Is she healing? Can you tell me that much?" Jude began crying.

"We think so, we hope so—prayers now. Everyone here is doing everything possible to help her along. She's being monitored very closely."

"I feel so helpless. I'm a doctor, and I cannot stand not being in control."

"Yes, doctor; leastways you understand why her doctors placed her under."

"Can you please contact me when she's to be brought out of coma? I must be there when she opens her eyes."

"I will pass it along to everyone involved in Meriam's care."

"Thank you, thank you."

She hung up and her phone rang. It was Dr. Grant. He opened with his kind words for Meriam and what'd happened at Jude's flat. He then got down to business, adding, "We have separated out blood from Meriam's, and it does appear her attacker left a lot to work with as well!"

"That's good news! But, sir, I thought you'd been, that you were…"

"Fired? You could say I'm using up my accrued vacation time. Not to worry about that. Listen, at some point in the attack, he or she—whomever—was also cut. Likely accidentally during the struggle."

"That's good news," Jude repeated. "All well and good, but suppose we can't find a match for the attacker's blood. What then?" As she said this, the notion that the insomniac who lived overhead had gone mad and had done the deed.

"We fall back on good old-fashioned shoe-leather detection—rely on Chicago's finest detectives."

"Oh, shit."

"Come on, they're not that bad, and right now they're canvassing your neighborhood for anyone who might've seen anything out of the ordinary from newspaper delivery boy to your upstairs neighbor who lies like a rug—claims he heard not a thing."

She privately gasped at this coincidental remark overlaying her previous thoughts on the unseen neighbor. Unsure how to respond, she muttered, "The mystery man. Useless as always."

"Meanwhile, we're searching every data bank possible right now. One of our own is how we're handling your case. It's admittedly a long shot, but so was getting Stone behind bars."

"Could he have hired an assassin to come after me? He's got the money."

"Rather doubt he'd have taken that route, but then cannot be sure. We're vetting his every move, so if there're any shady dealings…"

"If he learned it was me in the office that night I was attacked, he might well think I got a good look at him and could ID him in which case…he'd want me eliminated."

"Well, kiddo—I mean, Dr. Avery, we did a bit of vetting on your friend Meriam Oglala, and she's made a few enemies over the years, so…"

"You think she was targeted instead of me?"

"I am a firm believer that none of us can get through this life without hurting others, and/or being hurt by them in return. Seems part of human nature, the human condition. Even the nicest among us can and do break hearts and anger minds. Sometimes not even realizing it."

"Oh my god!" she replied to Grant, gasping.

"What is it?"

"What you just said, Dr. Grant. It sent an image racing to the forefront of my lame brain! Shit, a picture."

"A picture?"

"A picture of a man who has been a thorn in my side for two years now!"

"Noble? Luther Noble?"

"As late as yesterday, no two days ago, he came up to me and asked for some sort of friendship, even a concert date. He was fingering tickets at his pocket. Talked about getting coffee and repairing out relationship!"

"What relationship?"

"That's what I'm saying! There was never any such thing, other than his hateful pranks!"

"You really think Luther capable of murder—attempted murder?"

"I don't know, but who knows what goes through a man's mind after being fired and turned down by a woman all in the same day."

"His blood is on file here."

"Run it! Whoever's done this, he's still out there."

"Stay inside where you are, and do not open the door for anyone until we have this under control."

"Thanks, Dean, thanks for everything."

"Want you back as soon as all of this is cleared up, and your friend is safely out of harm's way."

Jude took note that he was still talking as her boss. Sybil had indicated that he meant to fight for his job, and it appeared exactly what Dean was about right now.

She thanked him again and asked that he let her know his findings with respect to the blood evidence as soon as he got either a match or a no match. They hung up, and she watched the life on the street ten stories down, and she looked about the apartment and thought one door in and it was the only door out. Although luxurious, although high above the life and activity on the ground so far away, the apartment took on the character of a trap. She thought of what could happen if a fire broke out below this floor, and then she thought what if Meriam's attacker, be it Luther Noble or some other monster, came knocking? A trap.

Obviously, whoever the attacker is, she thought, he or she has been watching me, stalking me, if not Meriam, and suppose he knows I'm here?

Jude went to the rear of the apartment, where she found a fire escape outside a kitchen window. Her escape route if need be. She then returned to the bedroom that Sybil had offered her for the duration.

Squeakums appeared to like this bed better than anything he'd enjoyed before. On the bedpost, she had hung her gun. As she dressed, she replaced the gun on her person, wanting it at the ready should she need it.

By the time she snapped the last blouse button, clothes that Sybil had laid out for her, she was feeling locked away here, even claustrophobic, and she wanted to get out, even if just to wander about the high-end stores along the Miracle Mile only a few blocks away. She was about to pick up the extra key that Sybil had left for her when there came a knock at the door.

She felt her heart leap within her breast. She recalled Sybil's having ordered a basket of food from the bodega somewhere along the avenue. Likely just the delivery boy. Jude went to the door and peered through the viewfinder in the door. No one.

But she heard a raspy male voice calling her name: "Juuu-dithhh, Juuu-dithhh…Judith."

My god, it's him! She recognized the voice—Luther Noble. She flashed on the idea of the apartment now being a deathtrap. This man had kicked in her flat door. Would this door hold against Noble's rage? She pictured him straddling Meriam and repeatedly stabbing her, even after he had to know it wasn't Jude below him. "Juuudithhh, open up! I just want to talk, to explain. Please help me."

She instead got on the phone and called Grant—busy! She called Sybil who answered. "What's up, girl?"

"He's here! Luther, outside your door, and he's Meriam's attacker!"

"I'm sending the cops! Stall him." Sybil hung up, and Jude felt abandoned and alone with a madman.

"Juuu-dith, please, let me innn…"

"Luther, you need to go and go now! I'm on your side. Get out of here! Cops are on the way!"

"Not before I can explain. Please, I need to seeeee you!"

"I'm not going to be alone with you, Luther, ever!"

"We were supposed to go out of this life together, but I fouled it up! I fouled everything up."

"They're looking for you, Luther, for murder! Meriam's dead!" she lied to protect Meriam and to convince him to leave.

"We can only be together then in the next life, Judith!"

Jude finally recalled her knowledge of this kind of obsession that a person could develop over another human being. She knew that the more she engaged, even if screaming and yelling at the person through an impenetrable door, the more he obsesses, and that she needed to disengage with Noble. However, in the same instance that she wanted him to leave, she wanted him to stay—to stay long enough to be caught by the cops. She did not want him to harm anyone else. Neither did she want him to harm her.

Suddenly the calling of her name ended, replaced by the banging of the door with more than his fists or body. Was he working on kicking in the door as he'd done countless times on the job with the Coroner's Office, as many times medics stood back while Luther kicked in a door. He often bragged to people in the lunchroom at the office about his method of unlocking doors. But apparently this older building, with its old oaken doors, proved far stronger than anything he'd kicked in before, but she had no guarantee the door would not give way now that he was pounding with an ax, the blade suddenly slicing through the oak, a blade reflecting light.

She rushed to the kitchen and prepared to escape through the window and down the fire escape when she heard the pounding increase. Gun or fire escape, she questioned her next step. She thought of putting that bullet between his eyes. She slowed and held, and then realized the noise at the door had intensified, still in the maniac's hands. This had her estimating her chances out on the fire escape, and she did not like the odds.

She felt the breeze from the open kitchen window as it teased the curtains in and out, teasing for her to come away as well. Jude instead took a deep breath and returned to the living room, and there she drew close enough to the door to feel the wave of energy brought through the door by the fire ax that he continued to drive through the door, until the gash was large enough to jam his hand and arm through. Luther's hairy, apelike arm, reached through to turn the door lock.

Shoot him in the hand, she thought. The arm. Wound him and maybe the pain'll be so unbearable that he'll either stop or run. But no, she did not want to wound him. She wanted him dead at this point for the pain and fear he'd engendered in both her and Meriam, and for the suffering he'd put Meriam through. Meriam, for all I know may die, may already be dead, thanks to this freak on the attack. Let him come through the door, and sure I'll talk to him—talk to him with my Glock.

Luther tore open the door and came at her like a raging bull, his Bowie knife raised. She fired a single shot that split his brain at the apex of his eyebrows, and Luther went down like a huge bull elephant under tranquilizer, except that Luther was dead. No question of that. She only regretted that he was bleeding all over Sybil's lovely, expensive baby blue Berber rug.

◆　◆　◆

The police who'd first arrived heard the single gunshot as the sound echoed down the corridors, the stairwell, and elevator shaft. The first two to arrive put their guns on Jude and ordered her to drop her gun. She did so without hesitation while a female cop tried for a pulse from Luther Noble. "Wasting your time," Jude said, holding up her badge and ID, her fingers tight about the wallet she carried them in. "He attacked me." She indicated the ax still embedded in the door. "I fired in self-defense."

The second cop stared at the condition of the door and ax. "Looks like he went full *Shining* on you."

The reference to the Stephen King novel was well warranted. Jude's phone was ringing, but she was not hearing it, as she was in a state of shock. "Yeah, he's gone," said the female cop, turning Luther's head to examine the hole between his eyes."

"You're spot on, Kate! No mistaking that much," said cop number two.

Others began to enter the apartment, and the young fellow who'd been studying to be a detective showed up with his partner. "You again," he said to Jude. "Seems trouble follows you, Dr. Avery, right?"

She could tell that his detective's lessons had kicked in. No such thing as coincidence, everybody lies, and alibis only mean that people lie, cheat, and steal for others for countless reasons. Jude read it all in his accusing eyes. Finally, she said to the amassed uniformed Chicago PD, "He put my friend in an IC unit, but the stabbing was meant for me. Bastard came to finish the job. Fixated on me."

"Yeah, that computes," said the female cop first, understanding.

The young wanna-be detective began nodding in agreement.

"The kid cop's partner, shaking his head, simply said, "We gotta stop meeting this way, Dr. Avery. People will talk."

After light laughter among the blue-clad people, the kid cop added, "Just seems every time we see you, there's great globs of blood involved."

The muffled sounds of a siren at street level, followed by another elicited from the female cop, "Meat wagon's here. Firemen as well."

"Gonna go down and guide 'em up," said another.

"Gonna take some doing repairing, that door."

"Ruined that rug."

"Stanley Steemer time."

"Hell no, Budweiser time—a good beer with Super Dawn'll get that out."

"Lot cheaper."

Jude only caught snatches of the police banter over the body and the blood, when the lady cop took her in hand and escorted her to the rear of the apartment, where she sat with her at the kitchen table. "You're going to have to give us a statement. You want to get at it now or later?"

Jude nodded. "Get it over with."

"First, let me say, I'm sorry that this happened to you."

"Thank you."

"You want me to record it, or you want pen and paper?"

"Record."

And, so it went until Sybil rushed in, having raced home, by which time Dean and a crime scene unit—men and women who'd known and worked with Luther Noble, began processing the scene. Given the ax embedded in the shattered door and the fact Noble had wielded the ax, Dean muttered words he would not have spoken at any other crime scene: "Looks like a righteous shooting."

Sybil now sat with Jude after closing the fire escape window. "You were on your way out?" she whispered to Jude.

"I told the lady cop that I opened the window only after stopping him, as I felt faint, needed the air. She asked why I hadn't tried to get out and down the stairs before he could get near me. I lied, and I think she knows it."

"Maybe she'll be a sister first, a cop second."

"I really had no choice. He'd've caught me out there on the fire escape and likely thrown me to my death."

"I get it, but my carpet! I just had that new Berber laid a month ago."

Sybil was holding Jude's hands firmly in hers.

"Am I ever going to stop shaking?" Jude asked.

"You will…in time."

"Sybil, all that business you convinced me of the other day, remember?"

"Business, other day?"

"About my hearing things, voices calling my name in rhythmic noise?"

"Yeah, what of it?"

"Luther before I shot and killed him, outside the door, before, during and after annihilating your door—"

"Yes?"

"Called my name exactly in the voice and manner I'd been hearing in my head for days. It was him all along somehow in my head—all along, and it was him who attacked me at the professor's office, and I was too dense to see it, to understand what was right in front of me."

"No one I know had a clue that he was capable of this kind of maniacal shit, Jude. No one."

"Maybe not, but what about Lisa, his workmate who would never turn on him? How much did she know about his growing insanity?"

"We'll get a CPD detective on her, grill her, see about that."

"Christ, a heads up could have saved Meriam from being attacked, me for that matter, maybe even Luther from himself."

"A danger to himself and others. They'll do a complete vetting of what he's been up to and where he's been, and who he's seen and talked to about you—hell, his entire unit lost their jobs over his last stunt—that phony suicide note left at Griswald's side, mentioning you."

"He must've followed me from Griswald's apartment to his office that night. When they search his lair, if they find Griswald's manuscript, then we'll know for sure."

Jude began to cry, her body shaking with sobs. Sybil leapt to her and hugged her tight. "We'll get past this, and Meriam will get better and come out of coma, needing you to be strong."

"How do I explain this nightmare to her?"

"Just tell her the god's honest truth—be forthright."

"I could lose her that way--truth."

"I suppose that is one possibility, but you could just as well lose her with less than the truth."

"I suppose so."

"Jude, don't give up on her before you know which path to take, and damnit, hold onto hope."

They hugged again, Sybil's tears now joining with Jude's.

Epilogue

hree weeks had passed, and much had been sorted out. JJ Stone made bail, but he was also charged with assault and conspiracy to commit murder in the death of Professor Griswald. Dean Grant and the detectives he had worked with, building on all that Jude had passed along to Sybil regarding the players, found emails and phone calls between Stone and Aaron Fiske Jr., and Fiske had copped to being the one who had attacked Jude in Griswald's office. Fiske had been assured that when the definitive book on Poe's death was to be written, that it would be co-authored by Stone and Fiske. The trial was pending, and the Family Stone had amassed an impressive array of lawyers to plead Stone's case while offering no help to Fiske, who was now fully cooperating with authorities at the attorney general's office.

When all of this had unraveled, it explained why the Griswald manuscript had not been found among Luther Noble's belongings. Luther's iPhone and his computer revealed a great deal of back and forth with his team members, particularly Lisa Anderson, who he'd been going to for advice on wooing Dr. Avery. Lisa had repeatedly tried to dissuade him from the notion that there could ever be anything in the realm of reality that would remotely look like, or be, a relationship between him and Jude. From all of that he'd left behind in his written comments, nothing, nor no one, could have dissuaded him. He had developed some psychological mad notion that he and Jude had been passionately in love with one another in a previous life among the hills and dales of Scotland during an era when the Scots fought the Brits, and at a time when men subjugated women like cattle. As it turned out, he also had a fixation on the Mel Gibson film Braveheart, set in that former time period.

For the past three weeks, the unfortunate and unhappy set of unknown bones found beneath Chicago that had become a rallying point for partying and homage at the same time had worked out well. The Sturgess family now convinced by science of link DNA that Elizabeth Saunders Hightower was indeed an ancestor had collectively fallen in love with Elizabeth and her story of romance and passion. The same story that had led to her and her lover's sad demise at the hand of a man more creature than human—Mannering.

The Sturgess family took Johnathan Brawley's bones as well, and they found a plot for the lovers; so long separated in their 'caves,' they now shared a single plot with a headstone honoring them together. When Jude asked Sybil about this, saying, "I didn't know you could bury two people in a joint plot." Sybil shrugged and said, "Hey, it's Colorado."

Still, not everyone was pleased with how the remains were identified and given identity, not all at City Hall for sure, and certainly not a City Hall-old family contractor group named Mannering and Mannering Incorporated.

In fact, the Mannering Estate was suing everyone involved from Grant to Jude and up the ladder to the mayor. Dr. Grant, a star in his field, had been reinstated to his former position as the CEO of the Coroner's Office. A court opinion had gone in his favor, and the mayor saw to dropping the case against Dr. Grant and returning him to his palatial office. An office that poor Dr. Sybil Shanley was more than anxious to escape, citing way too much crazy stress, piled-on pressure, and political hacks to deal with.

As far as the Mannering suit, Dean called in his entire staff and shouted to the rooftop, "We are entirely in the right, and everyone associated with the subway remains case did a superb job. And let me add that the more I look at it, I am finding it smart to put Dr. Jude Avery and Dr. Sybil Shanley on such challenging cases."

The rest of his speech left everyone under him reassured, as almost all of them, down to Ralph and Lionel had been named in the suit. Mannering's lawyers were working overtime in their search for any minutia that might reflect badly on the collection of evidence, the chain of evidentiary command, the use that evidence was put to and more—the Dean Grant playbook in the end. He okayed Jude and Sybil to write up a science-based article on the case of Elizabeth Hightower and how she was identified, but he wanted editorial control and thusly his name on it as well.

All this while the Mannering Estate lawyers had labeled their efforts as works of fiction. The Mannering lawyers hoped to flip anyone working under Grant down to the janitorial staff, down to security—Cam and Pam—to their side. So far no one had flipped, and there had been no sign whatsoever of disloyalty to Grant or the Cook County Coroner's Office. Nor did anyone expect to see any sort of betrayal whatsoever.

During the past three weeks too, Meriam Oglala had been slowly, cautiously recovering and thus far on her back and healing, but she remained in a mental and even a physical 'turtle shell' of fear and nightmare. Emotionally shattered, she kept insisting and pleading with Jude to "Get me home, back to the Badlands, the Res and my family." She repeatedly called Chicago the 'real Badlands.' Jude had kept close contact with her nurses and doctors, and she had visited every night while Meriam was in coma, and when the doctors thought it safe to bring her out of it, they had contacted her and her family in North Dakota to be on hand. Meriam's mother, an uncle, a brother, and a cousin had all caravanned to Chicago to be here for her when she was finally awakened. It was in many respects a beautiful moment for everyone, but Jude, a stranger to all but Meriam felt like an intruder on the touching scene.

She had given Meriam a kiss on the cheek, a squeeze of the hand, and encouraging words as the Sioux family all spoke in their native tongue to Meriam, calling her by her Indian name, which she'd never shared with Jude, and Jude had made them all laugh in her feeble attempt to say the name, tripping over it badly. At that moment, Jude realized how little she actually knew about Meriam, her childhood, her upbringing, her determination, and her motivation, and she still did not know what'd prompted her to go behind Jude's back to leak all the information amassed the night before the attack by Noble on Meriam.

The family wanted to take Meriam back with them right away, but the doctors prevailed. She would need a long stay and a great deal of rehabilitation for both her physical being as well as her emotional well-being. The doctors insisted on her seeing a psychiatrist as well as a rehab coach. One doctor that Jude had taken aside said that it would take months for her to learn to walk and talk at the level she'd been at before the attack. It was all so disheartening, but Jude held firm to the hope and faith that Meriam would improve day by day.

And she did, but not as rapidly as Meriam or Jude wanted. Jude had to prod her to keep her in-hospital dates with the resident shrink, but she had trouble just finding the motivation to get out of bed, even to take a slow walk down the corridor with her IV on one side and Jude on the other. Then one night after a grueling day at the lab, Jude stepped into Meriam's room only to find her bed empty and made up in military-fashion. She almost pulled out a quarter to bounce it off the sheet, when a nurse she knew as Leona stepped in and said, "She's gone, Dr. Avery."

"Gone? Gone where? A special unit?"

"No, no—she's gone home."

Jude had to stop her lower lip from fluttering, and tears welled up. "Her family?"

"We tried to call you, tried talking her into finishing her rehabilitation, and one of the docs pleaded with the uncle and the mom, but no, they weren't having any of it, and they had a judge's order to release her into their custody."

"A judge's order. Damn him or her, whoever he is."

"You can always visit her in North Dakota. I mean…well, I'm sorry, Dr. Avery. I could tell you that all day, but I know it doesn't help when you love someone so…so deeply."

"I appreciate that, Leona, I do."

"We all of us have been there—broken hearted."

"You sensed it too, that she stopped loving me." It was a statement and not a question.

"We all did, yes, but you shouldn't blame yourself. That girl may never get over the terror that SOB put her through. And while it is a miracle she lived, it's a curse that has been placed on her emotionally, one that is not easily dismissed or overcome. So, you mustn't ah-hem, well, I've said enough."

Jude accepted a hug from the nurse and thanked her for all that she and the entire staff had done for Meriam. Leaving the hospital, knowing it was over between Meriam and her, and after all these heart-wrenching weeks, it felt like a knife twisting in her chest. Like an open, sucking wound, and it did suck entirely. In her car alone now, she sobbed openly and hard, getting it all out. So much pain.

Sybil broke into her grief with a phone call, and Jude assumed she was going to ask if fish, fowl, or steak was okay for dinner, or else she'd want her to pick up paprika, or some other item on her way home. Or it'd be about Squeakums having scratched another leg on another end table, and how Sybil was going to 'drop that cat down the garbage chute' at the end of the hallway. But it was none of that. Instead, Sybil could hardly speak as she was so excited.

"Slow down! I can't understand a word, lady!"

"I've got it in hand—came in the mail today and I tossed all the envelopes aside and only now opened it, and we got our wish, Jude! Kiddo, we're going to Maryland—Baltimore—to meet Edgar face to what's left of his face!"

It finally dawned on Jude what Sybil was saying. Together they had petitioned the City of Baltimore, using the language of public relations to further their cause, to conduct an exhumation and a forensic examination of Edgar Allen Poe's remains to determine the actual cause of death and to put a final end to a nearly one-hundred-seventy-four-year-old mystery. Due in great part to all the publicity Jude and Sybil had engendered for Chicago with the remains of the 'unfortunate' Elizabeth Hightower and Johnathan Brawley—whose marriage certificate had subsequently been unearthed by an investigative reporter for the Tribune named Louise McGrath. For certain, Baltimore wanted some of that PR pie that Chicago had been enjoying with the new mystery surrounding Edgar.

"A new door opens," Jude thought, feeling secure that they would unlock the key to EA Poe's demise at such a young age. "If he was beaten about the head, which could have rocked and rolled a tumor, they'd know it in little time once the grave was upended and they got the remains into a lab in Baltimore. What a challenge, Jude thought now, and she said to Sybil's news, "I love a good challenge!

ROBERT W. WALKER

Robert W. Walker has written and published over 85 novels, 3 short story collections, and the how-to *Dead On Writing*. A graduate of Northwestern University, Rob holds an MA in English Education & teaches at West Virginia State University. While born in Corinth, MS, Rob grew up in Chicago, the setting for many of his novels. Rob's Instinct Series, begun with *Killer Instinct* and his Edge Series are Rob's longest running series, alongside Bloodscreams, a horror series. His first novel, completed in high school, *Daniel Webster Jackson & The Wrongway Railroad*, won Rob a full scholarship to NU. Rob's favorite authors are Twain and Shakespeare. He lives in Nitro, WV with his wife and step-children.

Learn more about Rob and his books at www.RobertWalkerbooks.com